ON WINGS OF THE MORNING

ON WINGS OF THE MORNING

DAN VERNER

eLectio Publishing

Little Elm, TX

www.eLectioPublishing.com

*For Janette,
 with thanks for your interest
and for being a reader.
 I hope you enjoy Otto's adventures.
 Blessings on you and yours,
 Dan June 2014*

On Wings of the Morning

By Dan Verner

Copyright © 2013 by Dan Verner

Cover Copyright © 2013 by eLectio Publishing

ISBN: 0615908667

ISBN-13: 978-0615908663

This is a work of fiction. Any resemblance to any person, living or dead, is purely coincidental.

Chapter 1: Flying—July, 1928	1
Chapter 2: Lessons: October, 1931	13
Chapter 3: A Change Comes to Pioneer Lake—August, 1934	19
Chapter 4: Pioneer Lake Airport—September, 1934	27
Chapter 5: High School Days—November, 1935	31
Chapter 6: Hidden Talent—April, 1936	39
Chapter 7: Flight Lessons—May, 1936	43
Chapter 8: Solo—September, 1936	49
Chapter 9: The End of High School—May, 1938	53
Chapter 10: Good Fences Make Good Neighbors—July, 1938	63
Chapter 11: Nazis and Spies—March, 1939	67
Chapter 12: Adjustments—June, 1939	77
Chapter 13: War—September, 1939	79
Chapter 14: Pitched Battles—1940	83
Chapter 15: Remember Pearl Harbor—December, 1941	91
Chapter 16: Last Days—March, 1942	99
Chapter 17: Basic—Late March, 1942	107
Chapter 18: Advanced Basic—June, 1942	109
Chapter 19: Primary Flight Training—September, 1942	113
Chapter 20: Basic Flight training—December, 1942	117
Chapter 21: Advanced Flight Training—March, 1943	121
Chapter 22: Champaign-Urbana—June, 1943	125
Chapter 23: Intermezzo—July, 1943	131
Chapter 24: Across the Pond—August, 1943	133
Chapter 25: Set to Go—Mid-September, 1943	139
Chapter 26: First Blood—Late September, 1943	147
Chapter 27: Sweet Alice—Early October	153

Chapter 28: Building Time—Early February, 1944   163

Chapter 28: Day In and Day Out—Late February, 1944   167

Chapter 29: Come Live with Me and Be My Love   171

Chapter 30: Mission 23: 0603 hours Zulu, Late March, 1944   177

Chapter 31: Into the Mix—1027 hours Zulu   183

Chapter 32: Falling Fast—1227 hours Zulu   189

Chapter 33: The White Room   193

Chapter 34: The Burn Unit—April, 1944   195

Chapter 35: Conversations—April 8, 1944   201

Chapter 36—May 15, 1944   215

Chapter 37: Going Home—Late July, 1944   227

Chapter 38: Fall and Winter—1944-45   235

Chapter 39: A Letter Arrives—February, 1945   243

Chapter 40: A Chance Encounter—Early March, 1945   245

Chapter 41: Teach Me Tonight—Late March, 1945   251

Chapter 42: Unexpected News—Early April, 1945   263

Chapter 43: Life Goes On—May, 1945   267

Chapter 44: War's End—August, 1945   277

Chapter 45: Northwest Airlines—November, 1945   279

Chapter 46: Serendipity—January, 1946   283

Chapter 47: M & M Airlines—June, 1946   289

Chapter 48: On the Wings of Eagles—December 14, 1946   295

Chapter 49: Flying—December, 1946   299

Dedication   301

Acknowledgements   303

Chapter 1

Flying—July, 1928

Otto was flying. Seated erect in the co-pilot's seat, he rested his left hand loosely on the throttles of the Ryan twin, peering into the darkness of the Pacific night. He caught flashes of lightning among the towering thunderheads, which illuminated the biggest storm cells well enough for him to steer away from them.

In the pilot's seat, Colonel Charles Lindbergh slept, exhausted from preflight preparations and rounds of interviews and picture sessions with the international press eager to get the story of the most famous aviator in the world and his attempt to cross the Pacific. This time Lindbergh was in a twin engine craft, and this time he had a co-pilot. Otto smiled as he remembered the questions about his qualifications.

"Colonel Lindberg, why are you taking along an eight-year-old co-pilot?"

Lindberg fixed the reporter with his eagle eye. "Because Otto Kerchner is the best pilot available to help me make this historic trip."

That silenced all questions. There was only the pop and flare of flash bulbs as the photographers took pictures of the two aviators.

A close cloud-to-cloud lightning flash brought Otto back to the present. He must maintain his alertness. Colonel Lindberg depended on him, and he would not fail.

"Otto! Otto!"

Someone called his name in a heavy German accent. He glanced over his shoulder down the fuselage filled with the giant fuel tanks which kept the twin Wright Cyclone radials running at full bore. There was no one there.

"Otto! Otto Kerchner!"

The voice came from somewhere below him, but that was impossible. There were only thousands of feet of turbulent air and storm down there. No human being could be suspended below their racing aircraft.

"Otto! Answer me! It is your vater!"

The night sky through the windscreen wavered and disappeared, replaced by the dusty dimness of a barn hay loft, illuminated by shafts of late afternoon sunlight. Otto knew where he was. He was on his father's farm, hiding from the chores he detested, reading in the loft about his hero Charles Lindbergh. He must have been dreaming about flying with "Lucky Lindy." He had to answer his father and quickly, or his father would take his books away from him.

"Ja, Papa, I am in the hayloft," he called.

"Vell, come down here, you lazy kinder. There is much for us to do!"

Otto sighed, and with his book in his hand, leaped to his feet and ran the short distance to the edge of the loft. He launched himself into the air. He was flying once again. At least for a while.

Otto had jumped from the hay loft dozens of times before. He had not counted on the floor of the barn, packed by thousands of cattle hooves, being harder than usual because of the drought. It was, in fact, like concrete.

He landed with one leg extended and both heard and felt it break. Something like an electric shock ran up his broken leg and he thought he was going to faint for an instant. The shock was like the one he received when he moistened his fingertips and stuck them on the terminals of the battery that powered their radio, only much, much worse. He lay there, unable to move, almost unable to breathe.

His father ran over from the barnyard where he had been standing, calling to Otto. He knelt by his son, but he knew from his service in the German army during the Great War that the leg was broken. He held Otto down as the shock began to wear off, and the boy started squirming.

"*Gott in Himmel,* Otto, how many times have I told you not to jump out of the hayloft? You've broken your leg. Some help you'll be now! MARIA! MATA!" he screamed at the top of his lungs. "It's Otto! He has broken his leg. Come quick!"

Otto's mother and sister came on a run, his mother dropping to her knees as she started to cradle her boy. Hans shoved her back. "No, don't move him until I immobilize the leg. Mata, go tear a board off the fence!

Maria, go get some strips of cloth and then bring the truck around. This will require a doctor."

Otto lay there, staring up at the sky. His father put a hand on his shoulder. "The only thing we have to give you is whiskey and I can't give that to a child. Doctor Carter will have something for the pain."

Mata returned, holding one of the fence pickets about the same time her mother arrived carrying strips of cloth. Maria dropped them at Hans' feet and tore off for the Model T parked at the side of the garage. She barely knew how to drive, but Hans had showed her how to crank the engine without breaking her arm or thumb. She set the spark and the throttle, ran to the front of the truck, pulled the choke wire and then gave the crank protruding from the radiator a half turn. The engine caught, and she leaped for the driver's seat, retarding the spark and the throttle. She put the truck into gear and slowly pulled it near Otto and Hans. Mata stood there, wringing her hands, almost in tears.

"Mata! Make yourself useful," ordered Hans, "and bind the strips of cloth around the board while I hold it in place next to Otto's leg. Not too tight, now."

Mata made fast work of the bindings, and Hans carried Otto over to the truck and laid him in the bed. "Mata! Go get a blanket to cover your brother!" Mata ran back into the house.

Hans went around to the driver's seat while Maria slid into the back with Otto. Mata handed Maria a blanket which she placed over her boy. Hans made sure he was securely held by his mother and then put the truck into gear, rapidly accelerating down the unpaved road to the main highway, leaving streamers of dust in their wake. Otto was aware enough to see Mata grow smaller and smaller in the distance until he could not make her out at all.

***

Maria hugged Otto, trying to keep him from bouncing around on the hard wooden boards of the truck bed and injured further. The boy's face was gray, like the dirty dishwater she threw out the back door. He wasn't moving and he had lost consciousness. She tried to cradle him without moving his leg, but the violent motion of the truck made that impossible. "Hans!" she screamed over the noise of the engine, "Slow down! You're going to kill us all!" Ordinarily she never shouted at Hans and never questioned his actions or decisions. But this was her boy.

Hans' head whipped around. "Ve must macht schnell!" he thundered back. "Don't worry! I drove an ambulance in the Great War!"

Yes, but your son wasn't on that ambulance, thought Maria as she clung more tightly to Otto's limp frame and buried her head in his chest to escape the spumes of choking dust.

They hit the pavement of the main highway with a hard jounce, and all three occupants bounced in the air. Maria tried to move her body under Otto's but only partially succeeded. His leg came down on the hard boards and he emitted a small groan.

"Hold on, mein liebes kind," she whispered into his ear. She began to sing softly, one of the old German songs, a lullaby she had sung to him when he was a baby. Her voice was lost in the whine of the tires on the asphalt and the roar of the engine.

Guten Abend, gute Nacht,
mit Rosen bedacht,
mit Näglein besteckt,
schlüpf unter die Deck:
Morgen früh, wenn Gott will,
wirst du wieder geweckt,
morgen früh, wenn Gott will,
wirst du wieder geweckt.

It was a long five miles to town, even at Han's demonic pace. He darted partway down the main street, made a sharp left onto a tree-lined lane of larger and finer homes than those in the rest of town. He threw on the brakes, pushed the reverse pedal hard and skidded to a stop in front of Doc Carter's house, which also housed his office in the front parlor room. Hans jumped from the truck and ran up the walk, violently shoving the door open. Maria could hear him shouting, "Doktor! Doktor! Kommen Sie! Es mein kinder!"

Hans ran back through the door with Doctor Carter hard on his heels. They slid to a stop beside the Model T. Doc peered at Otto's leg. The lower part stuck out at an odd angle.

"I tink it is broken," Hans said. "I vas in the Army during the Great War and…"

Doc waved impatiently, "Yeah, we know about your service with the krauts. I was in the war too, and tried to patch up all those kids you goons shot and gassed…"

Maria pleaded through tears, "Stop this! Stop it now! Help mein Otto!"

The two men glared at each other for a brief second. "All right, Hans, you carry the boy; I'll keep his leg still."

Hans took Otto in his arms while Doc gingerly held the leg. Otto groaned and his eyelids fluttered. Maria trotted alongside, smoothing his hair back. The four negotiated the short walk and carried the now-conscious boy into the examination room off the parlor.

Hans carefully laid his son on the examination table with Doc easing the broken leg onto the white covering. Doc pulled open Otto's right eyelid and peered into his pupil. He grunted once and then turned to his wife, who acted as his nurse. "Rose, ether."

She nodded, stepped to a cabinet and pulled out a green bottle and a cotton pad. Doc turned to Hans and Maria. "Hans, you stay here to help hold him. I'm going to set the leg. Maria, if you would wait in the waiting room, please."

Maria backed out of the room. Doc shifted his gaze to Hans. "How did it happen? Farm accident?"

Hans shook his head. "Nein. This foolish kind jumped out of the hayloft. I haf told him a thousand times, you cannot fly, Otto. Do not keep trying. But these kinder, they do not obey."

Doc listened impassively, then nodded to Rose. She stood behind Otto's head and placed the ether-soaked pad over his mouth and nose. Doc looked at Hans, who held Otto by the shoulders. Doc grabbed hold of the leg.

Outside, Maria perched on the large overstuffed sofa. Rose had furnished the waiting room with heavy dark pieces unlike the simple homemade pine furniture at their farmhouse. She began to pray, whispering, "*Gott in Himmel,* please take care of my son. He is only a boy, and sometimes foolish, but please heal him. Amen."

She stared at the pictures of European landscapes on the walls. One was of the ruins of a castle high on a hill above a river. It reminded her of where they had come from in the Rhine Valley. Ach, but that was a lovely place, she thought, shaking her head. It was too bad that the men with their fighting had ruined it all. She was so far from home, and letters from her relatives came only occasionally. She was a little lonely on the farm she and Hans had bought with a loan from the bank. It was not possible to buy such property in the old country. And now that she thought about it, there were her friends at church. *Kochen, kinder, kirche.* Weren't those the essentials? And it was her kinder who was hurt.

She watched the sun move across the carpet just a little ways, filtered by the curtains at the windows. The door swung open and Hans came in, followed by Doc. They looked tired but their expressions told her all she had to know. Otto would be all right.

Doc spoke slowly. "It's a bad break, but it set well and I think his leg will heal just fine. He'll be on crutches for a while." He handed her a piece of paper. "Take this to Fred over at the pharmacy—you'll need it for pain when Otto goes home."

Hans began, "In the war…" but Maria shot him a look that silenced him.

"Thank you, doctor. May I see him?"

"Of course," Doc said. "I'd like to keep him here overnight just to make sure he's all right. We'll take good care of him."

Maria went into the dimly lit examination room. She saw Otto, his blonde hair shining against the white sheet that tucked in at his neck. The bulky form of a cast showed through the covering. His face was still pale, but not ashen as it had been earlier.

She smoothed his hair back from his forehead. His eyes opened briefly and he whispered, "I'm sorry, Mama, I didn't mean to—"

"Hush, Otto, you just rest for now. You'll stay here tonight and we'll come get you in the morning." She kissed him on the forehead as his eyes closed, and then she tiptoed out of the room, closing the door quietly behind her.

***

Otto slept fitfully. Occasionally, Rose came into the room to check on him and ask him softly if he was in pain. "*Nein,*" he said, reverting to the German he had first spoken but which he now refused to speak unless scolded by his father. And he drifted back to sleep.

In one dream, a nightmare really, he thought he had put the twin engine Ryan into a spiral dive. Colonel Lindberg pulled it out by brute force. "Pull, Otto, pull," he yelled, as they both stood on the pedals and pulled the control wheels as hard as they could. The Ryan slowly leveled out, but Lindberg looked at Otto with disappointment. "I'm sorry, Otto, but I can't have an incompetent pilot with me. You come."

They both unbuckled their seat belts and Otto followed Colonel Lindberg to the hatch halfway back along the fuselage. Lindberg's face was stern. He slid open the door. The slipstream howled past the dark opening. The colonel put his hands on Otto's shoulders. "I'm sorry, Otto," he intoned. "I can't risk this mission because of an incompetent pilot." With that, he wrenched Otto to the side, and Otto was thrust out into the cold darkness, falling, falling, falling. After a while the air seemed to buoy him up and he had no sensation of motion, but he knew that the sea lay below. He plunged through layers of cloud and broke through the overcast. The horizon showed as a thin gray line, and the sea was a darker gray than the clouds. The water seemed to rush up to him. It was coming fast, fast, and suddenly he hit.

Otto sat up in the dark examination room. The grandfather clock in the parlor chimed four. He lay back down, feeling the ache of his broken leg. He closed his eyes and tried to sleep.

***

The next morning he was awakened by sunlight streaming through a gap in the heavy curtains. His stomach reminded him he had not eaten since lunch the day before. He sat up again. Rose bustled into the room. "Good morning, Otto, you must have slept well. I didn't hear you all night. How's the leg?"

"It aches, Mrs. Carter," Otto returned.

"Well, that's to be expected. Are you hungry? Would you like to go to the bathroom?"

"Do you mean the privy?" Otto wasn't sure what a bathroom was. He didn't need a bath.

Rose laughed. "A bathroom is an indoor privy," she smiled. "I'll help you to it. You'll find it's much nicer than a smelly old privy." She helped him up and guided him to a door on the other side of the examination room from the parlor. Rose flipped a switch and a light came on. Otto looked up in surprise. He had read about electric lights but had never seen one operate. Rose chuckled and pointed to a white vase. "That's where you do your business, Otto. Pull the chain hanging from the tank when you're done." She closed the door.

Otto gingerly eased himself down on the white vase and "did his business." When he was done, he stood up, pulled up his knickers and pulled down on the chain as instructed. It sounded like water was pouring from the ceiling and he yelped and jumped out of its way as well as he could with his leg. He heard Rose's voice from the other side. "Otto! Are you all right?"

"Yes, Mrs., Carter. I thought I had caused a flood but I'm all right now." She laughed on the other side of the door. "Well, come out when you're finished."

Otto immediately opened the door and started to hobble out. "Wait a minute, young man: you didn't wash your hands."

Otto looked puzzled. "I was going to use the pump in the kitchen if that's all right."

Rose laughed again. "Let me show you," she smiled, and led the way back into the bathroom. She flicked on the light and turned one of the faucets on. "See? Running water with the turn of a knob!"

"Wow, Mrs. Carter, that's pretty keen!"

"Well, wash up and then we'll see about some breakfast. Your folks will be here to pick you up pretty soon."

***

Otto wiped the last of the boiled egg Rose had fixed for him off his mouth, along with some bacon that looked like it was store-bought. It wasn't until he smelled it frying that he realized how hungry he was. Breakfast at home was usually sausage and if there were bacon, it was homemade with a lot of fat. In fact, now that he thought of it, they had sausage about every meal, with potatoes and a few other vegetables his mother grew in the garden. And milk. Lots and lots of milk.

Rose came back into the examining room and took the tray Otto had used for his breakfast. "Doctor Carter will be in to look at you in a few minutes. He was out all night with a difficult birth. Honestly I don't know what would possess anyone to be a doctor. But he loves it."

"I'm glad he could fix my leg," Otto offered.

Rose patted him on the head. He reminded her so of their son Jack at the same age. "He was there when you were born. It'll be up to you to follow orders and the rest is up to the good Lord."

Doctor Carter came into the room looking tired and disheveled. Without a word, he pulled back the sheet and examined the cast on Otto's leg. He grunted and turned to Rose. "Rose, would you excuse us for a moment. I need to talk to Otto here."

Rose looked at him quizzically and then turned and carried the tray out of the room, shutting the door behind her. Doc watched her go and then faced Otto. He looked grave. "I want to talk to you about this airplane foolishness."

Otto's mind went blank for a moment. Foolishness? Why were airplanes foolish? He didn't understand.

Doc continued, "Your remind me of our son Jack when he was your age. The Wright brothers flew when he was ten and he talked and dreamed of airplanes and flying the rest of his life, short as it was. He just had to go into the flying corps when we entered the war, and that's what got him killed."

Otto had seen the memorial to those killed in the Great War. Jack Carter's name was listed near the bottom, one of the last local casualties of the war. "He was a hero," he began.

Doc's face tightened. "He's dead, Otto, and you will be too if you persist. I know you're young, but I'm also telling you to give up this airplane business. Don't put your parents through what we've been through."

Otto couldn't speak. He thought everyone was excited about airplanes, especially after Colonel Lindberg's flight the year before. Everyone but his father, that is. Now he could add Doc to the list. He didn't want to lie and say he would give up airplanes, so he was silent.

Doc looked toward the closed door. "I think your parents are here to pick you up. Remember what we talked about."

Otto nodded, thinking, yes, I will remember but I won't do what you asked.

Mata appeared in the doorway, looking serious and pale. She ran over to Otto and hugged him. "Oh, Otto, I was so afraid when I saw you lying there in the dirt! Mama and Papa said you were all right, but I just had to see for myself." Otto put a hand on the top of her head, noticing as if for the first time how evenly her twin braids came out of her head. Mama braided her hair every morning for her. She said that was how girls wore their hair in Germany.

"I'll be fine, sister. I'll have to use a crutch for a while, but I'll be good as new very soon." Mata raised her head and smiled rapturously at him.

"I'm so glad, Otto. Papa says you can help Mama and me with the chickens and the garden." Otto sighed. There was no escaping work on the farm, even with a broken leg. He had hoped to have extra time to read some of the books he had selected from the bookmobile which came by once a month. The library lady tried to save books on airplanes for him. She knew how much he liked to read about them.

Mama and Papa came in with Dr. Carter. "All right, Otto, you can go home with your parents. Just remember what we talked about," said Carter gravely. "I'll see you back here in a couple of weeks to see how that leg is doing. We should be able to take the cast off in time for school."

Otto struggled to sit up on the side of the bed. Rose came in with a pair of crutches which she gave to him. He put one under each arm. The padded pieces felt funny, but he made one tentative step, then another. Mata held onto him as he traversed the room and slowly went to the door. He turned to look at Doc and Rose. "Thank you, Doctor. Thank you, Mrs. Carter."

Rose waved. "No more jumping from haylofts," she called.

"Good-bye, Mrs. Carter," Otto waved.

He clumped down the path to the Model T. His papa helped him into the truck bed where Mata climbed up beside him. Mama had brought one of the goosedown pillows from the house and put it under his cast. Mata clung to him as if he would float away. Papa started the truck and swung it in a wide half-circle to head out of town. Some of the buildings were decorated with flags and bunting for the upcoming Fourth of July celebration. Otto looked forward to the picnic and fireworks every year. No foot race for me this year, he thought.

Soon they were in the countryside, the fields on either side of them golden beneath the warm sun. Otto felt the breeze from their passage tousling his hair and, tired from lack of sleep the night before, fell into a surprisingly deep slumber and dreamed he was flying above those golden fields.

Chapter 2

Lessons: October, 1931

"Otto! Otto Kerchner!"

Someone was calling his name, it seemed from a long distance away. Otto was thinking hard about the design of a new airplane. He looked down at the paper on his desk where he had sketched a sleek silver monoplane with a huge radial engine. It would be called the Kerchner Model 1 and it would be faster than anything in the skies.

"Otto! Stand and recite!"

Otto snapped out of his reverie. He was in school and being called on to recite by Miss Smith, his fifth grade teacher. She was a small hateful woman. All the kids at school said she hated children, and they wondered why she was a teacher. She had a particular dislike for the children of recent immigrants, and a *special* dislike for Otto. He didn't know why.

He stood beside his desk, hearing snickers from the boys and giggles from the girls in his class from all the girls except for Betty Ross, the banker's daughter. She liked Otto and was kind to him. He looked at her, and she smiled encouragingly.

"Otto!" snapped Miss Smith.

"Yes, ma'am?"

"Now that you have joined us in our class, tell me, please, what town and state you are in. If you can, that is." More snickers and giggles.

"We live in Pioneer Lake, Wisconsin," Otto recited mechanically.

"I'm *so* glad you know where you are, Otto. What are the principal crops of our little community?"

"Local farmers grow wheat, corn, potatoes, and other fruits and vegetables."

"What else do they raise? You should know this!"

"Cows, both dairy and beef."

"What month and year is this?"

"It is October, 1931."

"And who is the President of the United States?"

"Herbert Hoover, ma'am." How long would this go on? Otto knew the answer: far longer than he wanted it to, or until he missed a question.

"And what were you drawing at your desk just now?"

"An airplane."

"Will you show it to us?"

Otto obligingly held up his drawing.

"And what were you supposed to be drawing, young man?"

"A map of Wisconsin."

"I don't recall Wisconsin looking like that. Do pay attention, Otto. I know you're slow, but try to keep up. You may be seated."

Otto took his seat, his cheeks burning. The boy in front of him had turned around when his inquisition began. He sneered at Otto, "Fly boy! Why don't you fly off someplace else?"

Otto started to reply, but the only insults he could think of were in German, and he would be severely punished if Miss Smith heard him speaking German. He had come to first grade speaking only German, and had to repeat the year while he learned English. He wasn't the only one: there were a number of children who spoke only German when they started school.

He pulled out another piece of paper and rapidly sketched an outline of Wisconsin. He penciled in tiny farm houses and barns here and there, drew in a few cows and rounds of cheese and for good measure, larger than any of the other little pictures, several airports complete with hangars, runways and little airplanes taking off and landing. He leaned back and studied his work. It pleased him and he smiled. Just then, a shadow fell across his desk. Miss Smith had sneaked up on and was glaring at him, holding her hand out. "Let me see your work, Otto."

He obediently handed his map to her, hoping she would not tear it up. He wanted to show it to Mata.

"So this is what you think the primary industry of Wisconsin is, Otto? Airplanes?"

Otto couldn't speak. The whole class turned around to stare at him, except for Betty who put her head down on her desk. Miss Smith turned to them.

"You may all go to recess, children—"and looking back at Otto—"You may stay here."

Otto slumped in his seat as the class filed out, some of the boys making faces at him. Betty smiled slightly, and then he was alone with his teacher.

"Otto, how many times have I told you to stop wasting your time with airplanes?"

"But, Miss Smith, airplanes are the future…"

"But we're not in the future, are we, Otto? We're in the present, and in the present the airplane is a dangerous rich man's toy that will never amount to anything. People travel by train. That's the way to go! It's fast, easy and economical."

"Miss Smith, it's faster to fly to the west coast than it is to take the train."

"And do you know that most of that trip is by train?"

"But, Miss Smith…"

"No more from you, Otto. Your work is unacceptable." She ripped his map to tiny shreds. "You may go to recess now." She stood and glared at him as he slumped out of the room.

All the classes were outside in the October sunshine. Some of the girls jumped rope, played hopscotch or stood in little groups talking; the boys played tag or shot marbles in rings drawn in the dirt. Otto went over to one of the benches by the school and sat down and put his head in his hands. He became aware someone had sat beside him. He hoped it wasn't one of the bigger boys who would beat him up. Again. He lifted his head and opened one eye. He saw a nimbus of golden hair and immediately smiled. "Betty!"

She smiled back. "Are you all right, Otto?"

"Yes, I'm fine. Miss Smith didn't like my map. She tore it up."

"I'm sorry." She put a hand on his shoulder. "I don't know why she singles you out."

"I don't either. She just doesn't like me. She thinks I'm dumb. I'm not dumb, am I, Betty?"

Betty smiled at him. "No, you're not dumb, Otto. You're very smart. You know so much about airplanes, and…"

A small boy ran up to them, breathless. "Otto! Otto! Did you bring your airplane?" Otto sometimes brought rubber-powered models that he had built and flew them with some of the smaller boys, who chased them in the field behind the school.

Otto brightened. "Yes, it's right here in my bag. Betty, would you excuse us while we go flying?"

"May I come?"

"Sure, if you want to. I didn't know you were interested in airplanes."

"I think they're so beautiful, like silver birds."

Otto pulled out a silver replica of *The Spirit of St. Louis* about six inches long. He had figured out how to build it from pictures in a German-language magazine that his parents received. He didn't have balsa wood and had no idea how to get any, so he cut thin slices of pine with his knife and assembled the tiny craft, powering it with some pieces of rubber he cut from an old inner tube. He figured out the airfoil from a book he got from the bookmobile about the Wright brothers and painted the model silver with some leftover shed paint. The craft was heavier than he would have liked, but it did fly after a fashion.

Otto and Betty and a cluster of smaller boys made their way to the field beside the recess area. Otto said to the boy who had come up to him, "Merle, you turn the prop while I hold the plane."

Merle studiously turned the propeller with his index finger, his tongue stuck out in concentration.

"Give it a hundred turns," Otto instructed.

"I can't count to a hundred," Merle sighed.

"I'll count for you," Betty offered. "That's nineteen, twenty…"

In a short while Merle had reached the required number of turns. Betty smiled at him. "I'll help you with your numbers!"

"That would be great, Betty!"

Otto reached around and held the prop. "I got it, Merle. Now you guys stand back. We're about to fly!"

He held the tiny aircraft over his head, pushing it forward and letting go of the propeller with one smooth motion. The miniature climbed in a long straight line, rising above the grass of the backfield, making a thin whir against the noise of the school at recess.

It rose to an altitude of perhaps 100 feet, a speck against the blue October sky. The prop stopped and the plane glided down in large lazy circles. The smaller boys took off in a herd toward the airplane, which touched down in the grass and nosed over.

Betty clapped her hands with delight. "Careful, guys!" shouted Otto. "Don't run over it."

One of the smallest boys—Otto thought his name was Johann—reached the plane first. He stooped down and carefully picked it up and then walked slowly back, the other boys grouped around him. He handed it gingerly to Otto.

"Can we do another flight?" Merle asked.

"Sure—" Otto started, but just then the bell rang to end recess.

The smaller boys ran off to join their class lines, shouting, "Thanks, Otto! Thanks!"

Betty laughed lightly and she and Otto started walking toward the school. "You are so kind to those younger boys, Otto. I think that's great."

"They like airplanes, too. I've thought of starting a club, but I need a sponsor. I know Miss Smith wouldn't sponsor us."

"My father might. His bank helps all kinds of people, even since that awful crash a couple of years ago."

Otto shook his head. "It has to be someone from the school. Thanks, though, Betty." The students started moving toward the school door, the boys dusting themselves off, the girls running their fingers through their hair. Betty and Otto stood.

"Otto?"

"Yes?"

"Promise me you'll stay as sweet as you are now."

"I'll try, Betty, I'll try."

And they walked together into the school.

Chapter 3

A Change Comes to Pioneer Lake— August, 1934

Otto knew something was going on at the abandoned farm adjacent to theirs. On early spring mornings he could hear the sound of hammers drifting over the pastures. He wondered if someone was fixing up the old house and barn to start farming again. He wanted to go see what was happening but, as usual, he was tied to the round of chores necessary to keep a dairy herd of a hundred going. He sighed and lifted his bucket of feed, moving along the trough where the cattle stood expectantly. As much as he disliked farming, he had to admit that he liked the big, warm black and white Holsteins with their gentle eyes and huge tongues.

One hot Friday, his parents went to town as they habitually did, leaving him and Mata alone to do as they wished. She took her dolls out and set them up to have a tea party. Otto retrieved his Christmas bicycle from the shed. "I'm going to see what's going on next door," he called to Mata who, concentrating on arranging the tea cups, waved without looking up.

Otto pedaled down the dirt road from their farm to the recently paved main road. It wasn't far to the next farm, and as he came to where the Taverner farm had been, he saw carpenters working on some large wooden frames. Over in the fields a man on a tractor was dragging a huge heavy-looking roller, flattening the grass and compacting the soil. Otto's heart leaped when he realized he was seeing the construction of an airport, right next to where he lived!

He rolled up to a large man holding a large piece of paper. "Excuse me, sir," he ventured, "What are you building?"

The big man looked at him sideways. "It's going to be an airport, son. The Pioneer Lake Airport. We'll be done next month, and then you'll see some planes coming in. Are you from around here?"

"Yessir, I live the next farm over."

The man grunted and unrolled the paper, which Otto saw had the plans for a hangar and an office for the field.

Otto stayed for a couple of hours, sitting in the shade of a tree, watching the four carpenters clamber over the wooden frame, swiftly nailing the boards together with quick circling strokes. With the sun going down, he knew he had to get back. The carpenters gathered their tools and climbed into a pickup which had materialized, taking them off down the road. Otto pedaled quickly home, arriving minutes before his parents did.

He found Mata alone in her bedroom, reading one of those silly mysteries about a girl detective that she liked so much.

"Well, what did you find out?" she asked.

"They're building an airport!"

She put down her book. "How exciting for you! Are there any airplanes there?"

Otto shook his head. "No, not yet. They're constructing the hangar and an office."

"Will big airplanes use it?" Otto had showed her articles about the Ford Trimotor and its use to transport passengers.

"No, just small airplanes. It will be what's called a "Fixed-Base Operation" or an FBO. I wonder if I can get a job there."

"You're only fourteen. What could you do? And you have your chores."

"I'll think of something," Otto muttered, lost in thought.

He went to his room and lay on the bed, looking past the airplane models hanging by threads from the ceiling. What to do…he could think of nothing…

"Otto! Feeding time! Mach schnell! Die Kühe won't wait!"

Otto sighed and sat up. Stupid cows. He called, "Coming, father!"

Hans was halfway to the barn when Otto caught up with him. "Did you have a good trip to town, Father?" Otto asked.

Hans grunted and kept walking.

"Guess what they're building on the Tavener Farm! An airport! Isn't that exciting?"

Hans stopped, a frown on his face. "I suppose that will mean you will be chasing off over there instead of doing your work." Their cows were walking slowly toward the barn.

"I will finish all my work before I go! Please let me! Please!"

Hans looked at the ground for a moment. "Well, only if you finish all your chores. We need everyone to work here or we will not make it. Do you understand?"

"Yes, Papa, I understand! Thank you! Thank you!" And they continued to the barn to feed the herd.

**

The next morning, Otto raced through his chores, finishing them far more quickly than he usually did. He pulled his bike from the shed and pedaled off furiously. He had a sack with a sausage and a boiled potato for his lunch. He was set until the afternoon. He rode up to the airport site to see that the hangar was about half done, as was the office building. He leaned his bike against a tree and sat down to watch the building. He had a small bottle of milk with him and opened that up and sipped on it while he watched. Better drink it before it gets hot, he thought.

He sat there watching the carpenters lift the lumber into place and hammer it in with sure strokes of their hammers. He had driven a few nails himself on the farm and missed as often as he hit. He might take twenty strokes to drive a nail home. These men tapped each nail and then gave it two powerful blows—WHAM! WHAM!—and the nail was in place. Otto supposed that they had special hammers and were driving into soft wood. The wood he had to nail into was old and weathered and about as hard as iron. Yes, that must be it. He would have to ask them about their tools.

The large man he had seen on his previous visit drove up in a green Model A Ford. He got out of the car with difficulty and walked over to the building. One of the carpenters clambered down and spoke to the large man. They smiled and nodded after a while and shook hands. The large man started toward his car and then stopped. He walked toward Otto.

Otto put down his milk bottle and stood up. He wondered if he were in trouble, but the man had a pleasant expression on his face.

"Hey, kid!" he shouted.

"Yessir?"

"You want to make some money?"

"I sure would." The only money Otto could lay his hands on was what his mama gave him from her egg money, a quarter each week. He spent that on airplane magazines when they went to town each Saturday for their shopping trip.

"I'll pay you a quarter a day to pick up nails and get things for the carpenters."

"That would be great, sir. I can only work about four hours a day since I have to do chores on our farm."

"Well, make that fifteen cents a day, then. Fair?" he stuck out his hand.

Otto shook it. "Yessir, very fair." He would be money ahead at that rate.

"Well, get to work—what's your name?"

"Otto, sir, Otto Kerchner."

"Oh, yes. I'm Mr. Wilson. Your father is Hans Kerchner, isn't he?"

Otto nodded.

"I hear he has a fine dairy operation. I guess that's what you help with."

"Yessir."

"Well, Otto Kerchner, get to work for me!" He turned and walked back to his car, crammed himself in, started it up and drove off. Otto was already pacing the perimeter of the barn, looking for dropped nails. He found quite a few.

He had an idea. He had a magnet at home. He would bring it, tie a string around it and drag it through the grass. That would collect the nails better, some of which were hidden in clumps of grass.

The carpenter he had seen talking with Mr. Wilson climbed down, went over to the base of the front wall, took a small paper bag and handed it to Otto. "Here you go, kid. Put the nails in here. When you've picked up as many as you can, go over to the lumber pile—" he pointed to a stack of lumber covered with tar paper—"get a few of the timbers and bring them here and lean them against the wall so we can grab them without coming all the way down the ladder. Watch your head when you're near the ladders. We have been known to drop a hammer or two."

"Yessir, I will!" Otto exclaimed.

"Wilson will be back and pay you about four. What are you getting?"

"Fifteen cents a day."

The carpenter pushed his hat back. "There are men in the city who would love to have that. Do a good job, kid, and we'll see what happens."

Otto circled the building, stopping occasionally to pick up a nail from the grass and dropping it in the bag. He knew there were more he couldn't see. He thought he should bring a rake tomorrow to do a more thorough job. That and the magnet.

He got up all the nails he could see and set the bag at the bottom of one of the ladders. Then he went to the lumber pile and started carrying two by fours over to the building, propping them against the side so the carpenters could reach them. They leaned over and pulled the lumber up to where they nailed it in place, about as fast as Otto could bring it over.

He worked like this until the head carpenter called, "Lunch time!" He had been working so hard he hadn't noticed that the sun was at its zenith. He was used to hard work on the farm, but glad for the chance to sit down. He went over to his bike, took his lunch sack and reached down in it to retrieve the sausage and bread. The rest of the milk wasn't real cold, but it still tasted good. He sat down to eat.

"Hey, kid!" the head carpenter called. "Come eat with us!" The carpenters were sitting in the shade created by the wall of the office.

Otto picked up his lunch and walked over to where the men were pulling out their lunches. He sat at the edge of the small group.

"You got a name, kid?"

"Yessir. It's Otto. Otto Kerchner."

"What you got there for lunch, Otto?"

"I have sausage and black bread and some milk."

"Looks good."

"We eat a lot of sausage. And potatoes. We make the sausage ourselves and grow the potatoes."

"So you live on a farm."

"Yessir. My papa runs about a hundred head of Holsteins. We're a dairy farm."

"So how do you like being a farmer?"

"I don't care for it, but we all have to help. I want to be a pilot."

The men had finished eating. The head carpenter pulled out a small metal flask, took a pull on it, and passed it around the circle of the other carpenters. Otto wondered what was in the flask. They didn't offer him any.

"Well, if you want to become a pilot, an airport is a good place to do it."

"I plan to. Maybe Mr. Wilson will give me a job when the airport is open."

The head carpenter laughed. "Don't expect to be paid if he does, kid. Wilson is one of the cheapest guys around. I'm surprised he's paying you to pick up nails and carry lumber."

I don't care what he's like, Otto thought. I'm just glad there's going to be an airport. He jumped to his feet and started carrying lumber again.

The sun lowered in the sky as Otto carried planks back and forth. One carpenter cut the planks to length and handed them up to the three carpenters on ladders. They nailed the wood into place as siding that went up the wall studs. By late afternoon, they had one side of the wall completely covered. The men on the ladders climbed down.

Wilson's car appeared down the road. He parked and climbed out of the car. Otto watched from a little distance as Wilson conferred with the head carpenter. Wilson came over to him. He reached in his pocket and pulled out a nickel and a dime.

"Here you go, kid. Green here says you worked hard. Can you come back tomorrow?"

Otto nodded enthusiastically. "Yessir! I'll be here right after morning chores!" He mounted his bike and rode off back down the road.

Chapter 4

Pioneer Lake Airport—September, 1934

Otto was glad for once that his family ran a dairy farm. The cows had to be tended every day, but at least he didn't have to help with the harvest that was going on in late September on crop farms. And school didn't start until the harvest was in.

With morning and afternoon chores done quickly, Otto was able to spend a lot of time at the airport. His construction job had changed into what Wilson called a "gofer" job. Otto didn't know what that meant the first time Wilson used the word, but he explained. "It means you 'go fer' things that we need. Get it, kid?"

Otto nodded. As he rode his bike up to the small airport, he remembered the first time he saw an airplane land there. It was a couple of months after he had started working with the carpenters. They finished their work and Green told him that they wouldn't be coming back. They had another job in town.

The day before they finished, a tractor appeared coming down the road, pulling a roller. The driver ran up and down what was to be the landing area, doing a final flattening of the grass and compacting the soil. When he finished, he drove off.

In about an hour, a small silver plane appeared, low on the horizon. It overflew the new hangar and office, circled once, and set down after a long smooth glide to the ground. It taxied up to the hangar and the pilot cut the engine off. Wilson pulled himself out of the small cockpit. He came over to Otto and the carpenters. He handed Green an envelope which held some bills and shook his hand. Green and the others climbed into a truck and drove off. Wilson turned to Otto.

"How'd you like that landing, kid? Here—" He handed Otto the single. "Can you come to work tomorrow?"

Otto gulped. "Thank you, Mr. Wilson. I sure can. Same time?"

"You got it, kid. Now help me push my plane into the hangar."

Otto got on one side of the airplane and Wilson on the other. They each pushed on a wing. Otto was surprised at how easily the plane moved. They moved it into the hangar. Wilson moved around, attaching some lines to various points on the aircraft. Otto followed suit, and soon all the lines were attached.

"Well, that does it," said Wilson, dusting his hands off. "'Bout time for you to go tend to cows, isn't it, kid?" He handed Otto an envelope.

"Yessir. Thank you, sir." Otto hesitated. "Do you suppose I might have a ride in your airplane, Mr. Wilson? She's a beaut!"

Wilson studied him. "Well, you've been a big help here and worked hard. We'll see what we can do. Now scram! See you tomorrow! We have a lot of work to do."

Otto ran over to his bike, which was leaning against a tree. Then he remembered the envelope. He ripped in open and found a five-dollar bill inside. It was more money than he had ever held in his life. He would have to write Mr. Wilson a thank-you note. Wow! Wait until Mata saw this! Maybe he could buy a commercial balsa model to put together, one that would really fly.

He pedaled off toward home, his mind filled with thoughts and expectations for the next day.

***

The next day was rainy and his papa said it had "set in for the day." Otto hurried through his chores. Hans had gone back into the kitchen for a cup of coffee and sat at the table, watching Otto tear back and forth across the barnyard.

"Do you think Otto is sick?" he asked Maria.

"Sick?" answered Maria from the sink where she was washing dishes. Mata stood by with a dish towel to dry.

"Ja. He is running around like there is something wrong with him. I have never seen him move so fast."

"He's excited about the airport," Mata said quietly. "Having one so close is like a dream come true for him."

"Humph," grunted Hans, and went back to his newspaper.

Otto burst into the kitchen. "I'm all done with my chores," he exclaimed. "May I go to the airport now?"

Hans looked up from the paper. "If you are done with your chores. Be back by four."

"I will, Papa, thank you!" Otto grabbed the bag with his lunch in it from the counter, and dashed back through the door. Maria shook her head and Mata smiled as she wiped a plate.

Otto leaped on his bike and pedaled hard for the field. He skidded to a halt in front of the small office building. Wilson came out.

"Hey, there, kid, you ready to work?"

"I'm always ready to work," Otto answered.

Wilson chuckled. "I know that. C'mon, I'll show you what to do."

Wilson explained Otto's duties to him. He was to greet any visiting aviators, fuel their craft if they asked for it and wipe the outside down and be sure the windscreen was clear. When locals brought their aircraft to the field, he would wash them and help move them and tie them down. It didn't seem hard at all to Otto, especially as compared to farming.

"I'll pay you five bucks a week," Wilson offered. "And you can start by washing my plane. It's dusty as hell."

"Yessir!" Otto exclaimed. He ran for the bucket and rags that Wilson showed him and took them over to the water pump at the end of the hangar. He filled the bucket and carried it to Wilson's aircraft. He carefully washed every square inch of the fuselage and used a ladder he found in the hangar to reach the wings. The airplane was covered with a fabric which was tightened by the silver coating. Otto felt as if he were in heaven, touching an airplane, making it shiny and clean.

Wilson came in to inspect his work and grunted with satisfaction. "You do good work, kid. Come on in the office and sit a spell."

"Yessir," Otto said, and thought, Life just can't get any better.

***

Otto was describing his day at the dinner table that evening. The family listened in silence, then his father spoke.

"Vat do you know about this Wilson?"

"He's very nice to me, and he has an expensive car and a beautiful airplane and he gave me a job—"

"I vant you to be careful around him, Otto."

"Careful? Why?"

"Vat I am hearing is that he is involved with bad things in Milwaukee. That he is a gangster into all sorts of crime."

"That's not possible."

"Mit people, everything is possible, Otto. I saw it in Germany before and during the war. It is here, too. You be careful."

Otto sighed. "I will, Papa. I will."

Chapter 5

High School Days—November, 1935

Otto began high school, which in Pioneer Lake sat right beside the elementary school. He had several classes with Betty and sat behind her when he could. Classes where the teacher placed them alphabetically were the exception. He saw her at lunch and they ate together except for days when she wanted to eat with her friends. Otto understood that and sat eating his sausage and bread in the lunch room, thinking that he never wanted to see a pig again. Or a cow, for that matter. He knew his papa said cows fed the family, but being around them every day was a pain. He was glad when the bus showed up to take him to school every morning.

Several large forms blocked the light from the window. Otto sighed. It was Smith and his gang, who continued to harass him. They didn't beat him up any more, but they never missed a chance to bother him, especially when Betty wasn't around.

"Hey, how's the Nazi today?" Smith usually did all the talking while his cronies smirked and punched each other in the arm.

Otto kept eating, saying nothing.

"What's the matter, kraut? Hitler got your tongue?" Smith reached out and knocked Otto's sandwich out of his hands. "Oops. How clumsy of you! Here, let me help you."

Smith bent over and rubbed the half-eaten sandwich on the dirty floor. He dropped it in front of Otto, who stared at it with his head down.

"Too bad you don't eat American food! It's easier to hold on to."

"I'm as much an American as you are, Smith. Your name used to be Schmidt, and someone changed it somewhere along the line. That is, if your father is really your father."

Smith's face turned bright red. "What are you saying, you little punk?"

"Just what I mean, Smith. Maybe your name isn't really Smith after all because your mother is such a whore. Everyone knows it."

Smith reached down and jerked Otto to his feet by the front of his shirt. He drew back one huge fist to smack Otto, but Otto was too fast for him and popped him in the nose. Blood flew and Smith dropped to the floor.

Heads turned toward the fight. Total silence descended on the lunch room. One of the teachers ran over to the little knot of boys. She knelt beside Smith. Someone handed her a handkerchief which she put to his nose to staunch the flow of blood. She stood up. Otto recognized her as Mrs. Miller, a history teacher. He'd heard she was a good teacher. "All right, boys, let's go to the office. What started this?"

Smith lurched to his feet. "He insulted my mom," he spit out, glaring at Otto.

Mrs. Miller turned to Otto. "Did you do that?"

Otto grinned. "I sure did. And for what it's worth, he swung at me first."

"We'll sort that out with Mr. Jackson. Let's go."

Otto walked through the crowd of students that had formed around them. Betty touched him on the sleeve as he went past. "He's needed that for years. Good for you, Otto."

"Thank you, Betty," Otto returned, but he was beginning to think about the trouble he was in, and not just at school. His parents would not be pleased that he was fighting "like a common ruffian," as his mama would say.

Principal Jackson's office was on the front of the school. Mrs. Miller deposited each boy on a separate chair and went into his office. They glared at each other. She came out a minute later, followed by Mr. Jackson. He had a reputation of being stern but fair. Still, no one wanted to end up in his office for the wrong reason. He motioned to Smith and Otto. They rose and followed Jackson into his office.

Jackson indicated two chairs in front of his desk. "Now, what happened? Mr. Smith, you go first."

"This Nazi called my momma a bad name," Smith spat out.

Jackson jumped in. "Mr. Smith, there are no Nazis in this room. We are all Americans here, so I don't want to hear any more of that kind of talk."

"He still called my momma a name."

"What did he call her?"

"It starts with an 'h,'" Smith mumbled.

"I was in the Allied Expeditionary Force," Jackson offered. "There aren't too many names I haven't heard. What did he call her?"

"A whore." Smith said, barely audible.

"A little louder, please."

"He called her a whore! My momma ain't no whore!"

"'Isn't a whore,' please, Mr. Smith. And it starts with a 'w,' not an 'h.'"

"Isn't a whore," Smith muttered, collapsing back into his chair.

"Mr. Smith, sit up straight. Mr. Kerchner, did you call Mr. Smith's mother a whore?"

Otto nodded. "I sure did, Mr. Jackson."

"And why did you do that?"

"Because she is. I said Smith didn't know who his father was because she sleeps around with a bunch of men. So she's a whore."

"Do you know that for certain?"

"That's what everyone says."

"And how do they know?"

"I don't know."

"It would seem to me, Mr. Kerchner, that such a serious accusation would warrant some sort of proof. Do you have any?"

"No, sir, just what I've heard."

"Well, Mr. Kerchner, your turn. Tell me what happened."

"I was eating my sandwich, and Smith and his buddies came up. He called me a Nazi and knocked my sandwich on the floor. He's always bullying someone and it made me mad. That's when I said he didn't know who his father was. I don't think he knows enough to know he is a bas—"

33

"Language, Mr. Kerchner."

"I'm sorry, sir. He doesn't know enough to know that he's illegitimate. You let Smith say 'whore.' Sir."

"Because I had to know what you called his mother. All right, gentlemen, who threw the first punch?"

"He did," the two boys said in unison, pointing at each other.

Mr. Jackson suppressed a smile. "You both can't have thrown the first punch unless you did so at the same time, which I doubt. Mr. Smith, is it possible that Mr. Kerchner's calling your mother a name made you mad enough to punch him?"

"I didn't actually hit him, sir."

"Oh? Why?"

Smith put his head down. "I missed."

Jackson turned to Otto. "And you didn't miss, Mr. Kerchner?"

"No, sir, I popped him right in the nose. It was a big target."

Smith glared at Otto.

"That's enough with the fight night description, Mr. Kerchner. I think I understand enough of the situation to give you your punishment. Each of you will stay after school for a month and work together to clean the school. I will have a letter for your parents for you to take home before you leave school today."

"I ain't workin' with him," Smith exclaimed.

"'I'm not working with him," Jackson said smoothly.

"That's right, I ain't!"

"Mr. Smith, either you accept this punishment or you will spend the month at home. Judging from your grades, that would mean you would repeat ninth grade. I'm sure you don't want that."

"My dad will be in to see about this. He doesn't like the krauts any better than I do."

"Let him come, Mr. Smith. We will have a good talk about how you behave in school. Mr. Kerchner, you may go to class. Mrs. Hall will write you a pass. Mr. Smith, you stay here."

Otto couldn't help smirking at Smith as he left. Smith curled his upper lip in a silent snarl.

Mrs. Hall, the school secretary, was already reaching for the pad of hall pass forms as Otto came toward her desk. He liked Mrs. Hall. She went to his church and sang in the choir. "I'm surprised to see you in the office for getting in trouble, Otto. Whatever happened?"

Otto blushed. "Not much, Mrs. Hall. I just had to take care of a bully."

"Well, Otto, remember to love your enemies."

"Yes, ma'am, I'll try," Otto offered as he took the pass and went to his math class. As he walked the silent halls, he wondered how his father would take the news of his fight and punishment. And he wondered if he would still have a job after he told Wilson he couldn't come after school for a month.

***

Otto walked in the kitchen with the letter. He handed it to his mama. She scanned it quickly and said, "My English is not so good for this kind of letter. You tell me what it says."

"It says I have to stay after school for a month as a punishment for fighting."

"Why were you fighting? Who were you fighting?"

Otto went over to the basket on the table, picked up an apple and started eating it. "It was the Smith kid. He called me a Nazi and ruined my sandwich."

"So you fought with him. His family is our neighbors. We have to get along."

"I'm sorry, Mama. He made me mad."

"Fighting is not a way to solve problems."

"Yes, ma'am."

"Your father will not be pleased with this."

"I know, Mama. He fought in the war."

"That was for the Vaterland. And it did not turn out well. You men and your fighting. It only causes grief and pain."

Hans indeed was not pleased that Otto would be delayed getting home to help with chores. He told Otto as his punishment that he could not go to the airport for the month he was being punished at school. Otto was to ride over and tell Wilson. He would probably lose his job, but hoped he would be able to continue working at the airport. It was a busy time for them, with pilots coming in from Madison and Milwaukee. They liked to come to the airport as a destination to build some time and to get away from the bigger cities.

Otto pedaled over slowly. Wilson was outside talking to a man in a dark pinstripe suit. He peeled some bills and handed them to the man who climbed into a big black Cadillac and roared off. Otto knew better than to ask who the man was or what his business was.

"All right, Kiddo! You ready to work?"

"Mr. Wilson, after today, I won't be able to work for a month after school."

Wilson looked at him hard. "Why? What happened?"

"I got in trouble at school. I got into a fight."

"What were you fighting about? A dame?"

"Nosir, I punched a bully. He called me a Nazi and ruined my sandwich."

"So you fought with him."

"Yessir, I popped him in the nose and made it bleed."

Wilson threw his head back and roared with laughter. "I never took you for a fighter, kid. Maybe I should get you a bout in Minneapolis."

"I don't think so, sir."

Wilson tousled Otto's hair. "Just kidding. So, who's the palooka who gave you a hard time?"

"It's the Smith kid from the farm next to ours. He never has liked me."

"He's a jerk, then," Wilson spat out. "Do you want me to take care of him?"

"'Take care of him,' Mr. Wilson? I don't understand. "

"You know, arrange for him to have a little accident and hurt himself some. Just a warning to leave you alone. I have some friends…"

"Oh, no, Mr. Wilson! I appreciate the offer, but my mama would be really mad if I asked you to do that."

"Well, all right, kid, but if you change your mind, the offer still stands."

"Thanks, Mr. Wilson," Otto said, and wondered if his father was right.

Chapter 6

Hidden Talent—April, 1936

Otto pounded his glove. "Make him hit it to me," he called to the pitcher. It was barely fifty degrees, but the third period boys' PE class stood in their positions on the diamond behind the school. They played as if they were in the World Series. Otto had never played baseball until they had a unit in class. He discovered he was quite good at it. He had skipped countless rocks across the stock pond, which helped his throwing speed and accuracy. He had worked up his stamina and speed by chasing cows that got through the fence. He had good hand-eye coordination which seemed to come naturally to him. He poised himself on his toes, his gloved hand on one knee and the bare hand on the other. They didn't keep score, but played for sheer enjoyment. There was a man on first and one out. No one knew which inning it was in this continuous game played each weekday the weather permitted.

"Crack!" The batter drove a hard grounder right at Otto. He fielded it cleanly and flipped it to the second baseman, who pivoted and threw to first. "Whoo! Double play!" Coach Gregory shouted. "Nice play, boys! Now hit the showers."

As Otto trotted toward the school, the coach held out an arm to stop him. "Hold on there, Kerchner. Where'd you learn to play ball like that?"

"I never played before this, Coach."

Gregory was coach of the Pioneer Lake Superiors, the school's baseball team. "I want you to come for tryouts next week."

"Gee, Coach, I don't know it I have the time. I work at the airport and have my chores to do on the farm."

"Well, talk to your boss and I'll talk to your father when I see him in town. Now get going!"

"Yessir," said Otto and took off for the school. He had never imagined himself a baseball player, but it might be fun.

After his shower, he had math class. Betty sat in front of him. "Hi, Betty," he whispered to her as the teacher droned on in front of the class.

"Hi, Otto," she returned without moving her lips. "How are you?"

"I'm good. Coach Gregory asked me to try out for the team."

"That's great! Are you going to do it?"

"I might."

"I'll come see you play."

Just then the teacher spoke, "Miss Ross, what is the answer to number 7?"

Betty looked down at her homework. "The answer to number 7 is 42, Miss Cannon."

"That is correct. Thank you. Mr. Kerchner, do you have the answer to number 8?

"Yes, ma'am, I have 107 for number 8."

"Very good, Mr. Kerchner." Her voice faded off into a distant buzz as she continued around the room, asking for answers to the previous night's homework. Otto was soon lost in thought.

He saw himself standing in the batter's box at the country championships. The bases were loaded, there were two outs in the bottom of the ninth, and the Superiors trailed by three runs. The pitcher was a tall kid from Madison who had a wicked fast ball.

Otto was not a power hitter. He hit hard line drives that tended to fall in front of outfielders and had good speed on the bases, so his average hovered somewhere around .420. Coach batted him third.

He stood in against the pitcher, who unleashed a fastball that tailed off at the last second. Otto swung and missed. This guy had the best arm the Superiors had seen. Otto tapped the plate with his bat and awaited the next pitch. The kid from Madison wound up and delivered, this time a curve that broke over the plate. Otto swung high. Oh and two. One more strike and they would have a long bus ride back to Pioneer Lake. The crowd had to be making noise, but Otto felt like they were behind a glass wall.

The pitcher wound up and grooved a fast ball right down the middle of the plate. Otto was ready for him and brought the bat around in a smooth level swing. *Crack!* He could tell he had gotten all of this one. He watched the ball soar high above the field, high above the outfielders. It kept going, clearing not only the fence but the grandstands beyond. Home run! They had won the state championship! Otto trotted the bases, stepping emphatically on home plate. His teammates mobbed him, beating him on the head and shoulders. He smiled.

He felt a light tap on his shoulder. "Otto? Otto? Are you all right?"

It was Betty, standing there with a concerned look on her face. He looked around to see an empty classroom. "Yes, I'm fine. I was just thinking."

"You'd better get to geography. See you after school?"

"You betcha, Betty. See you!"

He watched her walk away, meeting up with a girl from her sixth period class. Otto shook his head and quickly made his way to his next class.

***

The next week at tryouts, Coach Gregory stood at home plate with his bat. "Here it comes, Jones!" A boy Otto did not know crouched in his ready position at short. Otto was next in line at the tryouts.

Coach's bat came around, and the ball hissed along the grass. Jones ran awkwardly toward the ball, sticking his glove to one side. The ball skidded beneath his glove into the outfield. Gregory shook his head.

"Get in *front* of the ball, Jones!" he yelled. "All right, Kerchner! You're next!"

Otto pounded his glove and took his stance. Coach hit him a bouncing grounder. Otto charged it, smoothly gloved it on the big hop and threw across his body falling away. His throw popped home in the first baseman's mitt. "Attaway, Kerchner! Now try this!" He whipped his bat around and a hard liner tore through the air to Otto's left. He dived toward the ball, laying out parallel to the ground, feeling the ball pull his glove toward the outfield as it made contact. He hit the ground full length, bouncing once, holding his glove up with the ball firmly in the pocket.

"Way to hustle, Kerchner!" coach called out, and then, "All right boys, gather around me."

When all the players had run in from their positions, Coach Gregory looked around at them. "I will make my choices for the team this evening. Some of you were on the team last year. That does not mean you will be on the team this year. I will post the roster outside my door before school tomorrow. Now hit the showers! Good efforts today!" The boys scattered and the coach tucked his clipboard under his arm. Otto found himself conflicted as he took a shower. He loved working at the airport, but he also enjoyed baseball. He had talked to Wilson about just working Saturdays during the season, which was only twelve games. Now, he wasn't so sure he wanted to make the team after all. Ah, well, he sighed to himself, he hadn't made it yet.

***

Otto was glad the bus was early to school the next morning so he could see if he made the team. He went down the long hall that led to the coaches' offices, his stomach in a knot, not knowing what he was wishing for. There taped to the wall beside the coach's office door was the yellow sheet titled, "TEAM ROSTER: PIONEER LAKE SUPERIORS," and there, number six on the list was his name: "Kerchner, Otto, SS." He had made the team!

As Otto made his way back to his first period science class, he saw Betty at her locker. They had science together, so he went over to her. "Betty! I made the team!"

She smiled her radiant smile. "I'm so happy for you, Otto! When is the first game?"

"It's in a couple of weeks. We have to practice every school day until then."

Betty closed her locker, holding her books to her chest. "I'm glad you made it, Otto. I'll come see you play."

"That would be swell, Betty," Otto murmured, and they walked together to science class.

Chapter 7

Flight Lessons—May, 1936

As it turned out, the baseball season was a disappointment. Otto did well, making a number of good plays and hitting .411, but the rest of the players weren't that good. They lost all their games but one, which was a forfeit because the other team didn't have enough players. Away games meant long bus rides, and while Otto enjoyed playing, he determined that he would rather be at the airport. Maybe he would play again in the future, but not any time soon. He fulfilled his obligation to the coach, cleaned out his locker and shook hands with Coach Gregory, who looked sad and discouraged. "Will we see you next year, Kerchner?" he asked.

"I don't know, sir, I'm awfully busy at the airport." And so, late in May, with school out, Otto worked every hour he could at the airport.

Wilson had hired a flight instructor, a World War I vet named "Sparky" Duncan. He was fond of the bottle, and often as not, Otto would find him asleep in a back room when one of his lessons showed up. Otto roused him, got him a wet towel to run over his face and guided him in the general direction of the plane.

Wilson never said anything about Duncan's drinking; he even drank with him on occasion. The thing was, Sparky could be unsteady on his feet, but once he climbed into the cockpit, he was as steady as a rock. Otto didn't get it, but then he didn't have to. He propped the engine for Sparky and watched him taxi out lesson after lesson.

Wilson had bought a Fleet Model 1 twin cockpit biplane as a trainer, and Sparky stayed busy with lessons. One day, as Otto watched Sparky line up on the runway with another student in the front seat, Wilson came up.

"Say, Otto, would you like to learn to fly?"

Otto couldn't believe his ears. "Would I! You betcha, Mr. Wilson! But I can't afford it."

Wilson chuckled. "Tell you what. I'll give you one lesson a week instead of paying you until you get your license. Then you can rent the Fleet if you want to fly. Deal?"

Otto reached out and shook his hand. "It's a deal, Mr. Wilson!"

His first lesson was the next day. Sparky was asleep in the back room, as usual. Otto went in and shook his shoulder. Duncan stirred and opened one eye. "Wha' is it, kid?"

"Time for my lesson, Mr. Duncan."

"Lesson? I don't know nothin' about no lesson."

"Mr. Wilson said you would give me flight lessons."

"OK, then kid, give me a minute." He raised himself to a seated position and sat there for a long moment with this head down. Finally he stood up, unsteadily. Otto reached out a hand to keep him from falling.

Duncan waved him off. "I'm OK. Just a little sleepy. Lessee, where's my helmet? Oh, here it is." He plucked a dirty cloth flying helmet from the bed and pulled it on. He went to a small cabinet hanging on the wall and took out a cleaner twin. "Here—you'll need this. Some goggles, too. I think they're in the airplane."

Otto followed him as he walked unsteadily toward the hangar. The Fleet stood there in the darkness. "C'mon, boy, help me push it out." He got on one side and Otto the other and together they pushed on the lower wing until the airplane was outside in the sunlight.

Suddenly Sparky was all business. "OK, first thing is to check your fuel." He unscrewed a cap in front of the forward cockpit, went back into the hangar and returned with a stick about two feet long. He stuck it in the opening and pulled it out. It was wet nearly its entire length. "See, plenty of fuel." Otto nodded.

"Next, we walk around the aircraft and make sure everything is still attached." He and Otto made a circuit of the Fleet. Duncan pulled cables and manipulated control surfaces. When they returned to where they had started, he nodded and said, "Put your helmet on." Otto complied and Sparky handed him a pair of goggles he had taken from the front cockpit. "Put these on when you get in. Now you prop the engine after I get in." He climbed up the lower wing and threw one leg over the rear cockpit wall.

Otto knew exactly what to do. He went to the front of the aircraft. "Switch on!" Duncan called.

"Switch on," Otto returned.

"Contact!"

"Contact!" With that, Otto put both hands on the upper portion of the wooden blade and pulled down hard, backing away as the prop swung through its arc. The engine caught, and Duncan revved it a couple of times. Otto went around and climbed in the front cockpit, putting his helmet and goggles on.

Sparky advanced the throttles, and they moved out to the takeoff zone.

"All right," he called over the engine. "First, test your control surfaces. Make sure they're all working like they should. Look around with me." Otto twisted his neck first to the right and then to the left. He saw the ailerons move on the right wing, and then on the left as the stick beneath his legs moved.

"Put your feet on the rudder pedals but don't press down. Just rest them lightly." Otto did so and swiveled his head to the rear of the aircraft. He saw Duncan looking very serious, and, beyond him, the rudder moving left and right as the pedal deflected under his feet.

"Got it, kid?" Duncan shouted, and Otto nodded his head. "OK, here we go. Just put your hands and feet lightly on the controls."

Otto did as he was instructed and Sparky advanced the throttle. The Fleet bumped out to the end of the runway area. Otto rolled and compacted the landing area regularly, so he was surprised at the unevenness of the field. The airplane thumped and shook as it made its way down the grass.

They reached the place where they would start their takeoff roll.

"Always look at the wind sock and take off *into* the wind," Duncan instructed. Otto dutifully looked at the long white tube hanging from a pole by the hangar. No wind at all.

"There's no wind so we'll just take off from here. When we land, I'll look at the sock again and land into the wind, if there is any."

Otto nodded and looked forward. Duncan advanced the throttle and the Fleet bumped over the ground, slowly at first but more and more rapidly.

They were moving along pretty fast and it seemed to Otto that the airplane was growing lighter as if it wanted to lift off the ground.

He felt the stick move back and the aircraft smoothly lifted from the ground, all vibration gone, and they climbed into the sky. Otto wanted to shout for joy as they gained altitude. He looked back and saw the hangar and office growing smaller and smaller. Wilson came out of the office and waved at them. Otto waved back.

The silver aircraft banked to the right. Farmland lay all around them, different shades of green in the slanting afternoon sun. Otto saw their farm and the cattle calmly grazing. He remembered when the noise disturbed the herd, but they had made the adjustment and didn't even look up as they flew over.

So this was real flying, Otto thought. He had dreamed about what it would be like for so long, and now he was doing it and it was even better than he imagined. It was like he was floating and free, up there with the clouds and birds. It was a wonder that anyone ever wanted to land.

The wings seemed to reach out for the horizon and Otto felt as if he could hold his arms out and touch the horizon on either side. There was nothing between him and that distant line, and he reveled in the sense of freedom and release.

Sparky straightened them out and shouted to Otto, "You take the controls. Just try to keep her straight and level and right-side-up."

Otto grasped the stick more firmly. He felt the airplane nudge over to the right and brought the stick back to the left. The craft lurched to the left and he corrected to the right, this time skewing in that direction. He could hear Duncan laughing behind him.

"Just a gentle touch, kid. This ain't no cow you have to push on to get her to move."

After a few minutes Otto was able to hold the airplane in a reasonably straight line.

"Look down, kid," exclaimed Sparky. Otto did, and gasped. The ground was a lot closer than it had been. "You've got to watch your altimeter or you'll fly right into the ground. I have the controls." Otto felt his stick move with authority as Duncan pushed the throttle forward and they climbed for altitude. He wracked the Fleet around in a hard turn that had them practically standing sideways on their wings. Otto looked down at the ground sliding by. His stomach heaved.

Sparky straightened the ship out and lined up on the field. He cut the throttle and they glided in on a smooth line for the landing area as if they were on a rail.

Otto watched the ground tilt toward their craft, and Duncan pulled back on the stick just before they would have flown into the ground. The ship stalled just above the ground and settled with a single bounce on the grass. Then they were rolling, slowing until they were moving along at a walking pace. Sparky pressed part of the right rudder pedal that controlled the brake on that side and the airplane turned toward the hangar. He advanced the throttle and soon they were parked in front of the hangar. Otto climbed out of the cockpit.

"Now, that last little bit right before we landed is called a flare," Sparky told him. "You stall the aircraft right above the ground; it quits flying and if you do it right, you settle to the runway nice and easy. I bounced it once, not too bad, but a good landing don't have no bounces."

Otto nodded, speechless from what he experienced.

"Normally you don't want to stall, but landing's a special occasion. I'll show you how to recover from stalls next week. Now help me push this thing into the hangar."

Duncan took one wing and Otto the other. Together they moved the silver craft back into the darkness of the hangar.

"OK, kid, more next week. I need a drink," Sparky said, and wandered off to his room beside the office. Wilson came out of the door.

"How was it, kid?"

"It was great, Mr. Wilson," Otto smiled.

"Well, old' Duncan ain't much to look at, but he's a fine pilot. You'll learn a lot from him."

"Yessir," Otto murmured, thinking that he could hardly wait for next week.

The lessons proceeded, week after week. Sometimes Sparky kept them up for a couple of hours. Otto learned about altimeter settings, carb heat, mixtures, coordinated turns, slipping, stall recovery, and point-to-point navigation. One day they flew down to Madison, had a sandwich at the counter there, refueled, and flew back to Pioneer Lake. Duncan let Otto handle the takeoff and landing, grunting with satisfaction as Otto managed his first landing with only one bounce. They taxied to the hangar.

"All right, kid, why don't we go up again tomorrow and shoot some takeoffs and landings?"

"Sounds great to me, Mr. Duncan. Won't that be more than one lesson this week, though?"

Sparky clapped him on the back. "This one's on me, kid. You've been a good student. Wish everyone had your natural talent."

"Thanks, Mr. Duncan! I appreciate that!" Otto hopped on his bicycle and pedaled for home. He pretended he was flying.

Chapter 8

Solo—September, 1936

The next day dawned clear and bright with just a touch of chill in the air. Otto rushed through his chores, picked up his lunch pail from his mama and biked over to the airport. Dew still stood on the aircraft tied down at the field. He went into the office to check his task list for the day. In Wilson's florid script was a single notation: "Go flying!"

Otto sat impatiently in the chair in the office, waiting for Sparky to make an appearance. After a while, he came out of the back room, yawning, with his hair disheveled. "Hey, kid, you're here early," he said to Otto.

"It's nearly ten o'clock, sir," Otto ventured.

Duncan cocked an eye toward the clock above Wilson's desk. "So it is. Wanna go flying?"

"You bet!" Otto exclaimed.

"Wal, help me find my helmet, then." Otto reached over to the desk and handed Duncan the filthy scrap of cloth. "What's that doing there?" Sparky pulled the helmet on and started out the door to the Fleet. Otto trotted along behind him.

They preflighted the airplane and Duncan climbed into the rear cockpit while Otto propped the engine. The prop swung through one arc and then the engine caught. Sparky blipped the throttle as Otto clambered over the side into the front cockpit, pulled on his helmet and adjusted his goggles over his eyes.

"Take 'er out and take 'er up!" Sparky shouted. Otto taxied to the end of the field, "S" turning as Duncan had taught him. He lined up in the center of the grassy expanse, pushed the throttle forward and began his takeoff roll.

The Fleet moved slowly at first, and then accelerated as the tail came up. Otto made small inputs to the rudder once they were underway to keep the nose straight. He felt the ship lighten, and as the airspeed reached 100, pulled back lightly on the stick. The wheels ceased vibrating and they were in the air. Otto thought that he would never tire of that sensation, of breaking free of Earth and soaring with the birds. He grinned widely, pulling the airplane into a right hand bank to exit the traffic pattern. Behind him, Duncan looked first to one side and then the other.

They flew on for about five minutes and then Sparky called back, "Go ahead and land."

Otto was puzzled; usually they stayed up longer. Maybe something was wrong with Sparky. He made a 180 degree turn and was soon on final to land.

Otto cut the throttle and drifted down, flaring perfectly onto the grass. He taxied to the hangar. Sparky climbed out of his cockpit and Otto was pulling off his helmet when Duncan put a hand on his shoulder. "Keep that on. Take 'er up."

Sparky jumped off the wing onto the ground. Otto couldn't speak. Sparky wanted him to solo! Was he ready? Would he forget anything?

He nodded to Sparky, who stood watching him. He advanced the throttle and was soon lined up on the runway. He ran through the familiar pre-takeoff routine, pushed the throttle forward and was off, rolling along the grass, feeling the Fleet lift its tail up and then ease into the air. He was flying again, but this time by himself. He felt such a sense of freedom. He could go anywhere and do anything, he thought, but then reminded himself that it wasn't his aircraft and that he was limited by the amount of fuel on board. But the whole world was out there and he could go and do what he pleased—within limits. He did some banks and turns for sheer joy for about half an hour and then recalled that his lesson time was about up. He brought the ship around on a heading for the airport, knowing that he would remember these moments as long as he lived.

Too soon the field came in sight and he lined up into the wind. The Fleet slid smoothly down its descent path, flared and touched down smoothly. Otto taxied to the terminal, thinking he should get one of those white silk scarves so he would *look* like an aviator. He turned in front of the hangar and chopped the throttle.

Sparky and Wilson came toward him. Sparky carried a pair of scissors; Wilson had a bottle of scotch in one hand and three glasses in the other. Otto wasn't sure what would happen next.

He climbed out of the cockpit. Wilson put the bottle and glasses down and took Otto's hand in both of his. "Way to go, kid! You did it! This calls for a celebration." He took the bottle and unscrewed the top.

"Hold on there, Wilson," Sparky exclaimed. "First things first!" Wilson put the top back on the bottle and watched intently. Duncan pulled Otto's shirttail out and cut it off with the scissors. "There you go, kid. A souvenir of your solo! We'll all autograph it when we get back in the office." He handed Otto the scrap of material as Otto wondered how he was going to explain to his mama why his shirttail had been cut off. He decided to tell the truth.

Wilson poured a glass half full of scotch and handed it to Otto. "Here you go, kid. Drink up! Here's to you and to many good flights!"

"Mr. Wilson, I don't drink. I'm underage," Otto protested.

"This isn't drinking, this is celebration," Wilson laughed, pouring a glass for Duncan and one for himself. Sparky eyed the drink as if he had never seen good whiskey, which he probably hadn't. Otto sighed and took a small sip from his glass. It tasted like the turpentine smelled that they used on the farm. He let it slip down his throat and started coughing. Wilson and Duncan had already pounded theirs down. Duncan smacked Otto on the back. "You learned how to fly, now you gotta learn how to drink!" he exclaimed, and he and Wilson laughed uproariously. Then they went into the office and took turns signing the tail of Otto's shirt. He placed it in the basket of his bicycle and rode home.

Mama immediately noticed what had happened to his shirt when he came in the door. She didn't miss much. "Otto, where is the rest of your shirt?" The look on her face meant it was unlikely that she would not believe any story he could make up, so Otto's resolve to tell the truth was affirmed.

"They cut it off after I soloed today, Mama! I soloed!"

Maria looked puzzled. "You do this and they cut off your shirt? I do not understand…"

"It's a custom—a tradition among pilots. When you solo, they cut off the bottom of your shirt and then everyone signs it. See?" He held up the autographed shirttail for her to see.

"Yes, I see, but I think it a very strange custom to cut up a perfectly good shirt that I worked for hours to sew for you."

"I'm sorry, Mama. I didn't mean to spoil the shirt."

Maria sighed. "Well, I suppose you didn't do it. But the next time you solo, wear an old shirt."

Otto thought of explaining that this only happened the first time you soloed but decided not to say any more and went to his room. There he laid the shirttail out on his bed and admired it. He could fly by himself now. He could hardly wait for Saturday to come when it would be time for him to fly again. Life was good.

Chapter 9

The End of High School—May, 1938

Otto knocked nervously on the door of the biggest house in town. It belonged to Betty's family, and he was here to practice dancing with her. He and Mata had practiced at home to the radio, but dancing with a pretty girl, even if she was your best friend, was different from dancing with your sister.

Mata was a very good dancer. Otto didn't know how she had learned—it just seemed to be something that girls knew how to do. He hadn't paid much attention to what she was doing in her room, but gathered that she had taught herself how to dance. In fact, she seemed pleased when he asked her to teach him. "Of course, Otto! I'll be glad to," she had exclaimed. That was a month ago, and they had practiced almost every night. Their mother looked on smiling while Papa hid himself behind his German-language newspaper.

So they practiced, although Mata had allowed that Otto would never be very good, but at least he wouldn't cripple his partner by stepping all over her toes. He and Betty were going to the school prom at the end of May, and they had agreed to meet several times to practice dancing so they would be used to each other when the time came.

A uniformed maid answered the door. "Yes?" she queried.

"Hi, 'mam, I'm Otto Kerchner, and I'm here to see Betty." He hadn't expected a maid to open the door. This was really uptown.

"Please come in, sir. Miss Ross is expecting you." The maid turned and walked away in such a way that Otto knew he was expected to follow.

Otto followed her past a large staircase, down a long hall and into a large room with floor-to-ceiling windows along one wall. The maid indicated with a gesture that he should sit on a sofa covered in a rich floral fabric. He took his seat as she glided silently out of the room.

After a minute or so, Betty came into the room. She was wearing a yellow dress Otto had never seen before. Otto stood up, and she took both his hands in hers. "Otto! Thank you so much for coming! This is going to be fun!" She let go of his hands and twirled around once. "How do you like my dress? It's for the prom! I'm so glad we're going together!"

Otto couldn't speak for a few seconds. Finally he said, "It's lovely, Betty. I'm glad we can practice before. That way we'll dance better at the prom."

Betty smiled. "Well, let's get going, then, shall we?" She took him by the hand and led him to an open area. She went over to a small record player and started a record. The strains of a big band orchestra filled the room. Otto recognized the song, "Smoke Gets in Your Eyes."

Otto put his right hand on Betty's waist and held her right hand in his left. They stood for a moment to sense the beat and then Otto pushed lightly on Betty's waist. They moved around the room, a bit awkwardly at first, but then more smoothly as they became accustomed to each other. Betty pulled him closer. "It's easier when you hold me close," she said. Otto felt faint for a moment as they continued to glide around the room. The music continued,

> *They said someday you'll find*
> *All who love are blind*
> *Oh, when your heart's on fire*
> *You must realize*
> *Smoke gets in your eyes.*

"You've done this before," Betty smiled.

"I've been practicing," Otto admitted.

They practiced for about half an hour. Betty said, "Let's take a break and have something to eat."

"All right," Otto said. She led him by the hand over to the sofa. A small bell was sitting on the coffee table. Betty picked it up and rang it. The maid Otto had seen earlier appeared at the door.

"Sarah, we'll have our refreshments now."

The maid nodded. "Yes, Miss Betty." She left the room and came back in a few minutes with a tray laden with cookies and a carafe of coffee.

"You like coffee, don't you?"

"I sure do," said Otto. Sarah set the tray on the table and backed up.

"Will there be anything else?"

"No, Sarah, that's all we need for this evening. Thank you."

Sarah curtsied and walked smoothly out of the room.

"So, Otto, what do you plan to do after graduation?"

"Continue to work on the farm, I suppose. Mata thinks I should take some courses at the Ag school, but I don't want that to interfere with my work at the airport."

"Will you take me up some time?"

"I'd be glad to, Betty. I'll have more time to do that after we graduate."

"Sure. It's a date, then."

"What are you going to do, Betty?"

"Well, my father says I can work as a teller in his bank. But I have to be twice as good as anyone else since I'm the boss's daughter." She laughed. "There's something I need to ask you."

"Sure. Go ahead."

"Would you mind if we drove my car to the prom? You're planning to drive your father's pickup, right?"

"Yes, I was."

"Well, that's fine, but I think my convertible would allow us to make a grander entrance. My father said you could drive it."

"Gee, that'd be swell, Betty, but I wouldn't want to take a chance of wrecking your car. It's OK if you drive."

"If you'd like."

"I would like."

They finished their snack and practiced dancing some more. About eleven, Otto said, "I'm going to have to be going, Betty. I have to be at the airport early on Saturdays."

"Certainly. Thank you for a nice evening. You're a good dancer."

"So are you. Thank you for having me over."

She walked him to the door. He stuck out his hand. "Well, good night, Betty."

She looked startled for a moment, then took his hand and shook it. "Good night, Otto."

***

They practiced their dancing a couple more times before the prom, and then the big night arrived. Otto dressed up in his Sunday suit. Mata was practically dancing with delight, waving her Brownie camera around. Otto posed for pictures in the living room. Maria looked at him with tears in her eyes. "You are so handsome, Otto."

Hans held his paper in front of his face. He had told Otto that he regarded dances as frivolities that he would have no part of.

Mata took picture after picture. Finally Otto waved her off. "I've got spots in front of my eyes, Mata. I won't be able to see to drive."

"It's just so exciting!" she exclaimed. "You must tell me all about it!"

"I'd better be going."

"Have a wonderful time," Maria told him.

"I'll be late," he said as he went out the door.

He set the throttle and spark on the old pickup and pulled the choke wire, turning the crank through a full revolution. The engine caught, and he jumped into the seat.

He drove quickly to Betty's house, nervously thinking ahead to the dance. Would he be able to think of anything to talk about? Would he say the right things? The wrong things? C'mon, Kerchner, you've known Betty as long as you've been in school. Just act normal.

He pulled into the circular driveway and parked off to the side as Betty had told him to. He went to the front door and was greeted by the same maid. "Come in, Mr. Kerchner," she told him. "Miss Ross is expecting you."

She ushered Otto in to the living room and indicated he should take a seat. Otto sat expectantly on the edge of the couch, waiting for Betty to come into the room.

After a few minutes, she came down the stairs, wearing a green dress that matched the color of her car. Otto felt as if he couldn't breathe as he stood up. Betty twirled around. "Do you like my dress, Otto? I decided not to wear the yellow one. I had it specially made to match the color of my car."

Otto gulped once. Betty was transformed. She had her hair piled on her head in the latest style worn by movie stars and she smiled radiantly. "You look swell, Betty. Everyone will be looking at you at the dance."

Betty laughed and took his hand. "We're going to take some pictures first. I hope you don't mind." She led him into another large room which had floor-to-ceiling windows. Betty's mother and father were waiting there. Her father shook Otto's hand. He was holding a large complicated-looking camera like the ones the press used. "Good evening, Otto. It's time for pictures!"

Betty's mother smiled at him and Otto bowed to her slightly. "Good evening Mrs. Ross, Mr. Ross." Her mother looked like an older version of Betty, which only made sense, Otto thought.

They stood in front of a fireplace on a back wall. "Move in closer," Mr. Ross directed. "I don't think you'll bite each other." They moved in closer; Otto put his arm around Betty's shoulder and Betty put her arm around his waist. He felt faint.

The flash on the camera went off what seemed like dozens of times. Otto had blue patches in his vision from the bright light. Finally Mr. Ross waved at them. "I got some good shots. Now you two kids run along and have a good time."

Betty went over and kissed her father and mother on the cheek. She came back to Otto and said, "Let's go, shall we?" and offered him her arm.

Otto took it and they went out the main hall. The maid he had seen earlier stood along with a man who was evidently a butler. They wished them well as they walked by. "Good night, Sarah; good night, James; don't wait up for us!" Betty laughed again.

They went over to Betty's convertible. "I've left the top up so it won't mess up my hair, but I'll stop when we get close to the school and you can put it down. That way we can make a grand entrance."

"That would be great, Betty," Otto said. He opened the driver's door and Betty slid into place. She started the car as Otto went around and climbed in the passenger seat. They pulled down the long driveway and turned onto the main road which led to the school. It wasn't far, and as the moon hung low on the horizon, Otto looked over at Betty and thought how pretty she was. Soon school would be over and they wouldn't see each other every day. He would have to think of a way to see her as much as he could. Maybe he could visit the bank where she would be working as much as he could.

They drove through town and Betty started to turn in at the high school. She had told Otto she had been at the school all day, decorating the gym for the dance. The theme was "Once Upon a Dream," and the decorations featured white clouds and ideal landscapes. Betty pulled over before she got to the parking lot. "We can put the top down here. Would you get out and do that? Just undo these two latches and pull up and back. It folds into the little compartment you see and then the cover snaps over it."

Otto jumped out and folded the top back and secured it. He climbed back into his seat and looked at Betty. "Ready?" she smiled at him.

"I'm ready," he said.

"Let's do it, then," and she moved the car toward the parking lot.

A number of couples were gathered around the entrance to the gym to watch others come in. Betty caused quite a stir when she swept up to the curb in the green Packard with her gold hair shining. Otto felt proud to be sitting beside her.

She stopped the car and Otto jumped out to come around and open her door. She eased out gracefully, curtseying to him. "Thank you, kind sir," she murmured.

"Think nothing of it, ma'am," Otto returned, and they both laughed. He offered his arm and they went in to the prom.

The dance was well underway, awash with couples. Betty took Otto by the hand and led him to the dance floor. The small orchestra the senior class had hired from Madison swung into "In the Mood," and Betty and Otto were soon moving to the rhythms of the song. The band next moved into "Smoke Gets in Your Eyes." They moved close together and glided around the floor. Otto was glad they had practiced. He sang along with the lyrics,

> *They said some day you'll find*
> *All who love are blind*
> *When your heart's on fire, you must realize*
> *Smoke gets in your eyes.*

Betty laughed quietly at the end of the verse. Otto looked at her. "What's so funny?"

"You!"

"Me?" He smiled at her and she smiled back.

"Yes, dear Otto, I have to say that you dance better than you sing."

Otto knew it was true so he didn't object. "All right, then, no more singing."

They danced on through the evening until it came time for the last tune. The band played "The Party's Over," which the female vocalist sang, and then the chaperones turned up the lights. The prom was over. Couples made their way to the doors and spilled in the parking lot. They got into their cars and most drove off. Otto and Betty sat in the Packard for a moment.

"I don't want to go home, Otto," she said. "Let's go someplace."

"That's a swell idea, Betty. Where would you like to go?"

She chewed her lip for an instant. "How about Spencer's?" That was the all-night diner that the kids liked to frequent. They knew they would know plenty of people there.

"Good idea," Otto said. "Let's go."

Betty started the engine, put the car into gear and they were off. Spencer's was at the other end of the main street through town and they followed what seemed to be a parade of cars headed in the same direction.

Spencer's lot was filled with cars and young people from the prom standing and talking with each other. Some of them were making their way into the diner, which seemed to be almost filled to capacity. Betty seemed to greet everyone in the parking lot. They finally pushed through the door to the diner and found a couple of places at a corner table. It looked like Spencer's had put on extra waitresses in anticipation of the after-prom crush.

One came over to them. "Hi, Betty; hi, Otto. What can I get you to drink?"

"I'd like a Coke," Betty said. Otto echoed her.

When the waitress had turned to go, Betty looked right at Otto. "So, we're going to have some changes in our lives. I'll be working at the bank and you'll be farming and flying."

"I really don't want to be a farmer, but until something better comes along, I need to help out."

"It's the same way with me, but I'll have fun getting to see people I know all day. I hope we can see each other."

"I come into the bank from time to time—"

"No, I meant outside the bank. Like this. You know."

"Gee, I'd like that, Betty." The waitress brought their Cokes.

"What would you like to eat?"

"I'll have the tuna salad on rye," Betty told her, closing her menu.

"And I'd like a cheeseburger," Otto said.

"You got it," said the waitress, taking their menus.

Remember, I want you to take me flying. Could you do that?"

"Well, sure. I don't have that many hours…"

"I just know you're a good pilot and I'd love to see what it's like to soar like the birds."

"It's pretty amazing. Let's do that. I'll let you know a good time."

"That would be great, Otto. Thank you."

They ate their food in silence and then climbed into Betty's car and rolled back through town to her house. The lights were still on. "Mom and Dad are still up. Would you like to come in?"

"I'd better get going. Cows don't go to prom so they'll be up at the usual time. Thanks for going with me this evening."

"It was wonderful," Betty told him as they got out of the Packard. Otto walked with her to her door. He stuck out his hand.

"Well, good night," he said.

"Oh, Otto," Betty exclaimed, stood on tiptoe and kissed him on the lips. Otto stood there for a moment.

"Thank you, Betty." She laughed, squeezed his arm and slipped in the door. Otto stood there for a moment, remembering the touch of her lips on his. What did that mean? Probably nothing. Just gratitude. He went over to the pickup, started it and drove back through town. The moon shone on newly planted fields, and Otto found himself singing over the noise of the engine.

Blue moon, you left me standing alone
Without a dream in my heart
Without a love of my own…

This was going to be a good summer indeed.

Chapter 10

Good Fences Make Good Neighbors—July, 1938

"Otto! Kommen Sie! Ve are going to inspect the fence."

Otto sighed and turned over in his bed from the book he was reading about a new bomber the Army had developed. It had four engines and was made by Boeing. The article called it the Flying Fortress because it was so heavily armed. Wouldn't he love to fly one of those one day? But he would probably never have the chance. He rose heavily from his bed and went into the kitchen. Papa was drinking the last of his coffee.

There was much that Otto hated about farming, but probably he hated "inspecting" and fixing the fence around their property the most. It meant trailing behind Papa looking for breaks or sags and then mending them. He had to carry the roll of barbed wire, the stretcher bar, a hammer and some staples. He went to the barn and got the equipment, grabbed one of the empty feed bags lying around, put the tools and material into the bag and slung it over his shoulder. The bag was heavy and the day was hot already. They would be out all day with a break for lunch.

They started with the section next to the house. One part had a staple pulled out of the locust fence post. That was easy to fix. Otto rummaged around in the bag and took out the hammer and a staple. He hammered it home, placing the staple so it secured the length of wire. He dropped the hammer back into the bag, shouldered it again, and followed Hans down the line. Once Papa saw what was wrong with the fence, he kept walking, leaving Otto to run to catch up.

"Papa, can't you stop and wait while I do the repair? That way I won't have to run to catch up with you."

"Nein," Papa said. "Ve must keep moving or ve will not finish. Then the cows will be in the corn and Herr Smith will not be happy with us." The Smiths had the farm next door and they were not very good neighbors, always complaining about the condition of the fence and any cows that got over. It happened from time to time, and Hans always paid for damages, but it was always an unpleasant situation.

Otto's nemesis from high school was the youngest son of the family. He had dropped out his sophomore year and spent his time hanging around the pool hall in town. He had committed a few small burglaries, but the sheriff always released him to his family. He said he would put him in jail the next time. Talk around town was that would be a good idea. Steve was a foul-tempered troublemaker and most people avoided him except for his pool hall cronies. Otto had not seen him since their run-in freshman year. It was just as well.

Otto and Hans followed the fence line all day, stopping only for lunch when they came around to the back acres where they could walk across the field to the house. Mata and Maria had lunch ready for them, and then they were off again, picking up where they had left off.

They found a couple of breaks and repaired them and replaced a post that had rotted and broken off. As the sun lowered toward the horizon they finished their survey and repair and walked wearily back to the house. The women had supper ready, and they ate quietly. Otto went to his bedroom and picked up his Fortress book. He soon fell asleep, dreaming of being at the controls of the big bomber.

***

A week later, Otto and Hans were painting the barn. A large black Ford sedan turned into the driveway. Otto recognized the occupants of the car first. It was the Smiths, the male relatives, all eight of them, and Otto didn't think they had come to pay a social visit. He touched Hans on the arm, who straightened up from where he had been painting some of the lower boards.

The Ford braked to a stop and the Smiths climbed out. John Smith, the patriarch of the family, strode over to Hans and Otto. He grew corn, and a couple of times in the past, Hans' cows had gotten through the fence and eaten some of Smith's corn.

Smith stopped five feet short of where Hans stood. His sons crowded around behind him. They all had serious looks. Steve glared at Otto. Otto looked back at him, expressionless.

"Listen, Kerchner, your damn cows have gotten into my corn again and eaten a bunch of it up! Here's the bill! I expect you to pay—now!" He thrust a piece of paper at Hans.

Hans walked over and took the piece of paper. "Otto," he said quietly, "please go get my glasses from the table beside my chair."

Otto hesitated. "But, Papa, I don't think—"

Hans turned his head to him. "Please go get my glasses now."

Otto reluctantly went inside and ran back with Hans' glasses. Hans put them on. He studied the hand-written figures on the paper and then started to chuckle.

"What's so funny, you Hun bastard?" Smith growled, taking another step forward.

"I vas chust thinking," Hans began, "that I want to know where you sell your corn. Because from these figures you're getting about ten times the market value for it."

"Well, that's what it's worth." He stuck out his chin.

Hans reached into his pocket and pulled out a twenty and handed it to Smith. "Here you go. You know, it's funny that we inspected that fence last week and it was fine."

Smith folded the bill and put it in his front pocket. "Well, it's broken now. You'd better keep your cows out of my corn or I *will* call the sheriff." He stalked back to the car and waited for his brood to pile in. He jerked the car backward in a turn and then flew down the driveway.

"Papa, why did you give in to them?" Otto said when they were gone. "You know they were making that up. They want to buy our farm and are trying to force us out."

"It is easy just to go along with them, especially when there are eight of them and only two of us. In the Army, if we were faced with a superior force, it was the better part of valor to retreat."

"This isn't the Great War, Papa."

"It very well could be, Otto. Ve shall see." He picked up the paint brush and continued applying the thick liquid to the boards.

After lunch Otto and Hans went over to look at the fence line between their farm and the Smiths'. Halfway down, Hans picked up the ends of broken strands which created the gap where the cattle had gotten through. He looked at the ends carefully and grunted. "What is it, Papa?" Otto asked.

"These ends have been cut," observed Hans. "And I would suspect by our neighbors."

"What are you going to do about it?"

"Nothing."

"Nothing?"

"Nothing at all. For now, anyhow. Let's go home. Tomorrow is another day."

They walked back through the deepening twilight. Otto saw the moon rising, looking large and orange as it sat near the horizon. It was beautiful.

Chapter 11

Nazis and Spies—March, 1939

Otto took some of the money he earned at the airport and bought a shortwave radio. He ordered it from a catalogue and waited impatiently until the mailman brought it in late January. He asked Hans if he could run an antenna wire from the barn to the house. Hans reluctantly agreed. "I do not want this radio taking you away from your responsibilities with the farm."

"It won't, Papa. I'll have more energy from listening to aircraft as they call each other." Sometimes Otto saw silver transports, including the new DC-3, as they flew high over the farm. He knew that the pilots were in radio contact with the ground, and he wanted to listen in. That would be so swell.

And so Otto put the radio in his room, ran the antenna and ground wires out the window and turned it on the same evening it came in the mail. He put on his headphones and heard the hiss of static and then a burst of German. With a shock he realized he was listening to Radio Berlin, which was no doubt spouting some sort of Nazi nonsense. In fact, he thought it was Hitler himself ranting. Otto quickly dialed past that, searching for aircraft transmissions. He finally found a channel for American Airlines and listened late into the night, lost in a new world.

Listening soon became a nightly habit, and he heard not only aircraft transmissions but also the BBC World Service. He felt like he had a front-row seat on what was happening abroad. With what the Nazis and Italians were doing in Europe and the Japanese in Asia, war was inevitable. The powers that were could try to avoid it as much as they could, but Otto didn't see how Britain and even the United States could stay out of the conflict. He knew there was plenty of sentiment in the U.S. to stay out of any war; even his hero Colonel Lindbergh was an isolationist. Well, time would tell.

Otto had been listening for about two months and was in the barnyard one afternoon raking up material that gathered there. It was a tedious and smelly task. He saw a line of cars coming up the drive and felt instinctively that they had not come for a friendly visit.

"Papa! Papa!" he shouted, running toward the barn. Hans appeared at the entrance, pitchfork in hand. Otto pointed to the cars. Hans tossed the pitchfork to Otto and then went into the house, emerging with his Mauser from the war. He apparently had the same feeling as Otto. Mata and Maria came out. "Get back in the house, Mata, Maria," Hans ordered. "There's going to be trouble."

Mata and Maria obeyed instantly although Otto could see them peering out the window. "Get away from the window!" Hans shouted. Then the cars were upon them and there was no time to look around.

The cars slid to a stop and twenty men got out of them. Otto recognized some of them. Smith was the apparent leader, with his sons close behind him.

"Get off my land!" shouted Hans, raising the rifle. "You are up to no good and I order you off my property."

Smith just grinned and kept walking toward them. Otto lowered his pitchfork so that it stuck out like a lance.

"Nazis can't own property in this country," Smith snarled.

"Well, then I am not a Nazi, so you must leave."

"You ARE a Nazi," Smith shouted in a sudden fury. "And a spy! There's the antenna to your Nazi spy radio." He pointed to the wire running between the barn and house.

Hans looked up quickly. "Nein. That is the antenna for Otto's shortwave that he listens to airplanes with."

"Or you broadcast secrets to your Nazi handlers. Let's just have a look at this spy radio." He turned toward the house.

"NEIN!" shouted Hans and shot at Smith's feet. The dirt kicked up and the bullet ricocheted away into the pasture.

Smith stopped short and turned, his face contorted by fury. "Now you've committed assault, you stinkin' Hun."

"I am defending my home," Hans said, standing his ground.

Steve ran around the little group with something in his hand. Otto ran toward him. Steve lit the match he was holding and, diving into the barn, threw it on the nearest pile of hay. The dry material exploded into a fireball. In seconds the barn was engulfed in flames. Otto heard the cattle lowing in fear.

Smith stumbled out of the barn. Otto was waiting for him and decked him with one hard blow to the jaw. The group of men cheered the fire. Hans shouted, "Mein kinen! Mein kinen!" and dropped his rifle, running into the barn.

"Papa, no! Don't!" Otto started after him. A couple of cows came wandering out. He could hear Papa shouting at the cows to get them out, and then there was a tremendous crash as part of the loft collapsed. Otto put his head down and drove toward the location of the crash. Through the smoke he saw his father pinned by the huge beam which lay across his back. He was unconscious. Otto pulled on the beam with a strength born of desperation and lifted it from his father. He pulled Hans out into the barnyard.

Mata and Maria were there, holding on to each other. When Otto appeared dragging Hans, Mata ran over and helped him. Hans' eyes flickered. "Mein legs…" he gasped. "I cannot feel mein legs." Maria knelt down and held him. "Shush, Hans, you will be all right," she whispered.

They sat there as the barn continued to burn. The vigilantes had left while Otto was in the barn.

In a few minutes, a different line of cars appeared in the driveway. Neighbors had seen smoke from the fire and came as quickly as they could to help put it out. As they pulled up in the barnyard, it was obvious there was little they could do. They stood and watched as the barn burned completely down. Ed Lawrence, from two farms over, knelt down beside Hans. "Hans, can you hear me?"

"Ja, I can hear you. I cannot move my legs."

Ed looked at Hans' bent legs. "We'd better get you to Doc Carter," he said. "Otto, can you get a large board, large enough to put your dad on?"

Otto ran off to the woodpile where they kept scraps of lumber and picked out a piece that would serve as a backboard. He and Ed and several other men carefully slid Hans onto the board and put the board onto Ed's pickup. Otto climbed into the passenger seat.

Ed started the truck and drove off toward town, leaving the silent group of neighbors and Mata and Maria standing in the barnyard. There was only the roar of the flames from what was left of the barn and a huge plume of smoke rising high into the clear sky.

***

Doc Carter examined Hans carefully. He looked up at Otto and Ed and shook his head. Doc put a hand on Hans' shoulder. "We're going to have to send you to the hospital in Eau Claire, Hans. There's not much I can do here."

Hans sighed. "I understand."

"You are not having any pain?"

"Nein. I just cannot feel or move my legs."

"OK I'll get Rose to call an ambulance." He indicated with his eyes that Otto and Ed should go out with him. They followed him into the waiting room.

Mata and Maria came through the door. "How is he—?" Maria started. She saw the look on their faces.

"Everyone please sit down while I go speak to Rose." Doc went out of the room. They all took seats in the overstuffed furniture. Otto put his arm around Maria. She was holding a handkerchief to her mouth. Mata sat on the other side. Ed sat across from them.

Doc came back quickly. "I have to tell you," he said, "that I think the paralysis is permanent. Probably severed his spinal cord. I'm sending him to the hospital in Eau Claire for further tests, but I saw too many injuries of this sort in the war. I'm sorry."

Maria stood. "May I see him?" she asked.

"Certainly," Doc answered. "Rose will go in with you. Stay as long as you like."

Maria went out of the room. Doc turned to Otto, his face flushed. "So the Smiths are responsible for this."

Otto nodded, his mouth tight.

"They're a no-good bunch we would do well to be rid of. I'll call Sheriff Draper. He's been looking for an excuse to put Steve in jail, and I think this will do it."

Rose came out. "She wants to go to the hospital with him."

"That's fine," Doc said. "Mata, you and Otto go on home. He doesn't need a lot of company until he gets settled. You can see him tomorrow."

The three stood. Otto shook Doc's hand. "Thank you, Doctor Carter."

Carter sighed. "I wish I could do more, but I can't. Go on home."

Ed drove them back in silence. He dropped them off, saying "Anything you need, let us know. I'll come back tomorrow to see about the barn."

"Thank you, Ed," Mata and Otto said in unison. They stood and watched him go. They turned to the pile of charred lumber which had been the barn. It was still smoldering.

***

Otto was out a couple of hours later poking in the debris when he saw the sheriff's car coming down the drive. He stood still as Joe Draper climbed out of his car. He walked over and surveyed the damage, pushed his cap back on his head and whistled.

"I'm sorry, Otto," he finally said. "The Smiths did this?"

Otto nodded. "Steve started the fire, but he was with the whole bunch."

"Well," said Draper, "I suppose my next stop is the Smith farm. Steve has been heading for something like this for a long time." He clapped Otto on the shoulders. "We'll take care of this, son, don't you worry."

Otto hung his head. "Thank you, Sheriff."

Draper climbed back into his car and drove off. Somehow, Otto didn't feel any better. He went into the house.

He supposed he was in charge of the farm now, although he didn't want to be. Maria couldn't run it by herself. Mata could, so maybe she could be in charge. They could hire a man to help, and that would give him more time to work at the airport. Business was up sharply, and Wilson needed him practically full time. He would have to think about his options. As soon as he saw to his father.

***

Ed Lawrence came by early the next morning. "I have a message from your mom," he told them after Mata had invited him in for a cup of coffee. "Maria called last night and said that your father might be in the hospital for a few weeks, so she has found a nice German woman near the hospital to stay with. She asked that you bring her some clothes and some money."

"I can fly over there this afternoon," Otto told him. "I need to start cleaning up the barn site."

"I wouldn't worry too much about that," Ed said. "Look out the window."

Otto and Mata went over to the kitchen window and saw a caravan of cars and trucks bearing building materials. They recognized their neighbors, and friends from church, even Doc Carter, Betty Ross and her father from the bank, and old Mr. Rice who ran the hardware store. Ed pulled out some work gloves. "We're going to build another barn for you. You go work at the airport and take the stuff to your mom. Don't worry about it—we'll take care of it."

Mata began weeping. Otto shook Ed's hand. "Thank you, Mr. Lawrence. I have a feeling you had a lot to do with this."

"I'm not doing anything one neighbor wouldn't do for another," Ed told him, and he and Otto went outside to greet the workers.

***

Otto drove out to the airport with the barn well under way. Some of the men had built more than one barn, so, with their supervision, the structure went up quickly.

He parked in the lot and pulled the bag with Mama's clothing and cash out of the back seat. He went into the office to check with Wilson.

"Otto! Good to see you!"

"I need to take the Cub and fly this bag to my mom at the hospital in Eau Claire," he returned.

"Fine. Take it. I heard you had a fire at your place yesterday."

"Yes, we did."

"I heard it wasn't accidental."

"No. Steve Smith set it. My dad was badly hurt trying to save his cows."

"So I hear," mumbled Wilson around an unlit cigar. "I hear this Smith is a punk."

"That's one of the nicer terms I would use. His family is bad news."

"You want something should happen to Smith? A little accident with injury, perhaps?"

"No, Mr. Wilson, the sheriff is investigating. He'll do the right thing."

"Well, my associates and I have been known to help the local police from time to time. And they help us. Let me see what I can do. I don't like no punk messin' with one of my boys."

"Really, Mr. Wilson, I appreciate it, but please don't make the situation worse. We'll be all right."

Wilson grunted and turned back to his tip sheet.

Otto went out and prepped and pre-flighted the Cub. He was soon flying northeast through cloudless skies.

***

The airport at Eau Claire was familiar to Otto as he climbed out of the Cub with his bag. He went over and got into a waiting cab, giving the driver the address of the hospital that Rose Carter had given him. It was a short trip, and Otto got out of the cab, thinking that most hospitals looked alike. And smelled alike. He went in, and the receptionist directed him to Hans' room.

The room was on the second floor and down a long hall. As Otto neared the door, Maria came out. She recognized him from a distance and embraced him in a huge hug. "Mein kinder, it is so good to see you! Thank you! Thank you!"

Otto thought she looked tired. He had no doubt she was spending most of her waking hours at the hospital. "How is Papa?"

She cast down her eyes. "He is about the same. The doctors here say he will never walk again. He will have to live in a wheelchair." Otto embraced her again.

"We will all take care of him," he told her. "May I go in and see him?"

Maria took his hand. "Come," she said.

Hans was lying in a hospital bed. He looked pale and his eyes were closed. "Hans," Maria whispered gently, "There's someone here to see you."

Hans' eyelids flickered and then he opened his eyes. "Otto," he whispered.

"Yes, Papa, I am here." He took his father's hand. "How are you feeling?"

Hans groaned. "Not good. I cannot move my legs. I am useless."

"No, Papa, you will never be useless. You will get better and we will raise even more cows."

"It is because of cattle that I am here."

"No, it is my fault, Papa. If I hadn't had the radio, the Smiths would not have accused us."

Hans waved a hand. "They would have found something else. Listening to a radio is an innocent thing compared to being a hoodlum like young Smith."

"The neighbors rebuilt your barn, Papa."

Hans waved a hand. "They are good people. We help each other. And now, Otto, I am very tired and wish to take a nap."

"All right, Papa. I have to get back to the airport, but I'll visit you when I can." Hans' eyes closed, and Maria and Otto slipped out of the room.

"Will you be all right, Mama? I worry that you are here alone."

"I have been through worse," she replied. "The people here are very nice and Mrs. Schmidt, who I am renting the room from, comes from the same area of Germany that we did. We have had several good talks already. And she is a wonderful cook, so I will have a little vacation from cooking."

She walked with Otto to the entrance where they embraced again. "You and Mata take good care of each other."

"We will, Mama. I'll be back Saturday."

"Be careful, mein kinder. Remember your old mama."

Otto took a taxi back to the airport and was home before dark. As he drove up the drive, he could see the new barn was finished. He had had so many conflicting emotions in the last 24 hours. Good things can come out of bad, he thought.

***

Otto was up early, looking around the barn. It was beautifully constructed, and their three surviving cows were lying peacefully in their stalls. He heard a car pull up and walked out to see Sheriff Draper getting out of his patrol car. He came over and shook Otto's hand. "I arrested Steve Smith last night and charged him with arson. He'll be in jail for a while, I promise you. I couldn't charge him with more since your father went into the barn of his own volition."

"Well, isn't there something else you can get them on? Destruction of property? Something like that?"

"That's part of the arson charge. And the judge knows Steve very well so I think he'll be spending some time in Green Bay. "

"That doesn't give my father the use of his legs."

Draper put his hand on Otto's shoulder. "No, but it does give him justice. And that's better than an endless vendetta. It stops here."

Otto looked at the ground.

"Well, I gotta go," said Draper. "You take care and—how's your father's getting along?"

"The doctors say he will never walk again. He'll be in the hospital for a while."

Draper shook his head. "I'm sorry. It's all so unnecessary."

Otto nodded and stood there watching as Draper drove off.

Chapter 12

Adjustments—June, 1939

Otto walked into the house, wiping his hands. He found his father in the living room, in his wheelchair, looking through his newspaper. Otto knelt down. "Papa, I have something to show you."

"Vat is it? A new pair of legs?" Hans had not gone out since he came home from the hospital a month before. He had not recovered any use of his legs. The doctors discharged him, telling the family that there might be a treatment for Hans in the future, but they foresaw nothing in the next few years. It had been a quiet, long drive home.

Otto wheeled Hans through the kitchen and into the barnyard. The Model T was sitting there. Otto stopped a few feet from it. "Here it is!"

"Vat? This old truck? I have seen this many times."

"But look—" Otto wheeled him closer. "—look at the steering wheel."

"I see some levers where there weren't any before," Hans offered. He looked interested.

"I rigged up some hand levers so you can drive without using your feet. This one---controls the brakes. This one—the clutch."

"I see. How clever of you!"

"So you can drive around and see what's going on. You can even drive to town."

"Help me up into the seat."

Otto lifted Hans into the seat, noticing how much weight he had lost during his time in the hospital. Hans sat behind the wheel. Otto ran around and cranked the car. Hans advanced the throttle and pulled down on the clutch lever. The T lurched forward, and as it gained speed, Otto could hear Hans whooping all the way down the driveway. He stood there with a huge grin on his face.

77

Mata came out of the house. "What is Papa doing in the truck?" she asked.

"He's driving it, Mata," Otto said quietly as Hans turned in a wide circle and came speeding back to them. When he got close, he pulled on the brake lever and slid to a stop. Mata ran over and hugged him, and Otto joined them. "Thank you, mein son! Now I don't have to be useless!" As they embraced Otto saw, for the first time in his life, that his father was crying.

Chapter 13

War—September, 1939

The day was bright and clear as Otto went into the hardware store to buy some nails to build a better chicken house. He had just taken the paper bag from old Mr. Rice when he heard a commotion in the street. It was a newsboy, holding a local paper high above his head while he screamed "EXTRA! EXTRA! It's war! Germans invade Poland! Read all about it!"

Otto went over to the kid and gave him a nickel and sat on one of the benches in front of the newspaper office to read the paper. It looked like the Germans had done it this time. He didn't see how England could stay out of war now. Or France. The U.S. he wasn't sure about. He would have to see what happened.

He got back into the old pickup. The whole family practiced traditional German thrift, so they had not gotten anything newer. He would have to talk to Mata about updating to a newer model, even though it would be a used one, maybe a '36 or a '37.

He drove home thoughtfully, the newspaper open to the front page on the seat beside him. When he pulled into the barnyard, Mata was hanging clothes. At least she had bought a gas-powered washer at his insistence. Doing laundry by hand was such a chore for her and Maria, and Maria helped less and less. It seemed as if she had lost all her spirit since Hans' injury.

He went over to Mata, who was pinning the last of his shirts to the line. He showed her the headline. She took the paper and looked at it carefully and sighed. "Let's not tell Mama," she cautioned. "It would only upset her and do no good. She has such bad memories of being in Germany during the last war."

She gathered up her laundry basket and clothespin bag and followed Otto into the house. Maria was sitting at the kitchen table, idly cutting up some potatoes. Most of them still had some peel on them. Mata would have to re-do them. She went over and took the bowl from Maria and picked up a knife from beside the kitchen sink. She sat down and started re-peeling the potatoes. Otto sat down across from her.

"Hans, where have you been?" Maria asked Otto.

"Mama, I'm Otto. Hans is—" He stopped short of saying that Hans was in the other room when Mata shot him a look. "Papa is out working."

This explanation seemed to satisfy Maria. She arose from the table and went into the living room and sat in her chair. "I'll bring Papa out in a few minutes. She thinks you're Papa and she doesn't recognize him at all. She'll sit in there for a while, waiting for Papa to come home. I'll tell Papa about the attack. I'll also tell him not to say anything around Mama," Mata whispered.

"How long has she been doing this?" Otto asked.

"For a couple of weeks, on and off. I hope it doesn't go any further. Most of the time she's all right."

"How did I miss this?"

"You've been working on the farm and at the airport. I spend all day with her. I wasn't certain what I was seeing and I didn't want to bother you with it."

"Anyhow, what do you think of the news of the day? Will we be involved in the war if it comes?"

"I think it will come," said Mata. "It's inevitable. What do you think?"

"I don't know. The British are our friends, and we go back a long way together. At the same time, there's a lot of sentiment for isolationism in this country. Even Charles Lindbergh is for that position."

"But how do *you* feel, Otto? You stand to lose a great deal if there is war and you have to serve."

"Maybe it would be a chance to demonstrate to Smith and his like that I am as American as he is."

"You don't have to demonstrate anything to anyone, brother. You are a fine man. I know your heart. It is loyal and true."

"Spoken like a true sister. Well, as Mama says, we'll cross that bridge when we come to it."

Mata smiled slightly. "She would also say, 'The Lord will provide.'"

"So she would, Mata. So she would. You have a serious look. Is it the news?"

"Well, that's some of it, but I've been thinking about changing something and I wanted your opinion since I can't ask Mama."

"Of course. I'm always glad to share my opinion."

"It's kind of trivial, but do you think I should stop wearing my hair in braids?" Mata wore her hair in traditional German style in two long braids that she pinned to her head. Otto didn't know for sure, but he imagined it took some time to fix the braids. They had to be heavy as well.

"You're a modern young woman, Mata. Do anything with your hair you like."

"It's an old-fashioned style. I think Mama kept it because Papa insisted on it. But maybe it's time for a change. I wouldn't do anything outrageous like a bob. I'm thinking of shoulder length, if that's all right with you."

Otto laughed and stood up. "You do as you wish, Mata. I'm your brother, not your master. And anyone who basically runs a good-sized farm certainly can decide how to wear her hair."

"Thank you, Otto. I knew you would understand."

"Not much to understand, Mata. Nothing like international politics anyhow."

"That's the truth, brother. Now let me get Papa up and we can have lunch."

Chapter 14

Pitched Battles—1940

The situation in Europe grew worse. The Germans rolled over France and were sitting at the Channel, looking across at England. There was news of plans for a German invasion, but Hitler wanted to soften up the British by bombing them before such an invasion.

In Pioneer Lake, residents were very much aware of the war in Europe from newspapers, radio and newsreels. On the other hand, little had changed about day-to-day life. President Roosevelt pushed through Lend-Lease legislation. It was controversial, as was the case with much of the legislation that Roosevelt proposed. Lend-Lease made sense to Otto. It was a way to be involved in helping the Brits by lending or leasing equipment to them without actually going to war. For the time being, it seemed the right thing to do.

Otto spent as much time as he could at the airport. Wilson seemed to be spending more and more time there, away from his business in Minneapolis, whatever that was. He and Sparky spent a great deal of each day in the office when Wilson was there. They kept a bottle of scotch on the desk between them, tossing back shot after shot.

Sparky still taught a lesson or two. One day, he landed with a new student, climbed unsteadily down from the Fleet and wandered past Otto. "You ought to get your instructor's license, kid. That way I won't have to teach everyone who shows up. In fact, you can teach them all. I don't care. Talk to Wilson about it." He wandered off to his room. Otto saw him lie down and promptly fall asleep.

No time like the present, Otto thought. He went into the office where Wilson was staring moodily out the window.

"Mr. Wilson?"

"Yeah, Otto. What's going on?"

Otto gulped. "I just talked to Sparky—I mean Mr. Duncan. He thinks I should get my instructor license and take some of the load off him. In fact, he suggested I do all the instructing. He told me to talk to you."

Wilson glanced up at him. "Yeah, that's fine with me. I'll pay for it. Ol' Sparky is getting a little ragged around the edges so I suppose we could give him some help. Say, Otto, speaking of finances, didn't you say that your sister managed the books for your farm?"

"She does. She's quite good at it."

"Ask her if she would keep our books. I had a guy doing it for me and he was dipping into the till. He won't be doing that no more. He won't be doing nothin' no more, if you catch my drift."

Otto nodded and thought that he didn't want to know what had happened to Wilson's financial guy.

"I'll ask her, Mr. Wilson. I'm sure she'll be able to help you out."

Wilson rose from his desk and clapped Otto on the shoulder. "That's my boy! Tell her I'll pay her good. She won't regret it. You've been such a good worker; I'm sure she is as well."

"She is that, Mr. Wilson."

"Well, why don't you practice some flying? I'll call about the paperwork and see if you'll need to go to Madison or wherever for the exam. I'll let you know."

While Sparky didn't have that many students those days, the little airport was busy. Some of the wealthier men in town, including Betty's father, had bought aircraft and kept them there. Mr. Ross hired a pilot who came in when he needed to go to Minneapolis on business. They flew a beautiful silver twin-engine Beechcraft. Otto was itching to get his hands on it, but he wasn't certified for twin engine aircraft. Maybe one day, he thought.

He saw the Beech on final and thought that Mr. Ross would be showing up soon. The sliver craft touched down smoothly and taxied up to the hangar. The pilot swung it around smartly and chopped the throttles. Otto rushed over to the door as it opened. Ross's pilot, Don Libeau, had gotten to know Otto in the past few weeks.

He reached up and took Libeau's flight case from him. "Hi, Mr. Libeau! How are you! Come into the office and I'll get you a sandwich and something to drink. Would you like the usual?"

"Hey, Otto! How are you, kid? I'd love a ham sandwich and some coffee if you have some made fresh."

"I just made a fresh pot and made the sandwiches this morning. Is Mr. Ross coming soon?"

Libeau looked at his watch. "I meet him in half an hour," he said. "Let's get that food, OK? I didn't have time to get something to eat before I left. Top off the tank and sweep out the carpet before Mr. Ross gets here, will you?"

"Sure will, Mr. Libeau. How are things in Minneapolis?" Libeau lived in the city and kept the aircraft there. It was easier to have maintenance done at the larger airport.

"About the same, Otto. Thanks for asking."

Otto got Libeau his sandwich and coffee, and the pilot sat down at a table in the outer room that stood outside Wilson's office. Otto didn't see Wilson and supposed he was over having a drink with Sparky.

He got the fuel cart from the side of the building, rolled it over to the Beechcraft and filled the tank, taking care not to overfill it. He grabbed a broom from the hangar wall and swept down the red carpeted aisle. Since he had a few minutes, he went into the cockpit and sat in the pilot's seat for a moment, running his hands over the throttles and looking at the instruments. Everything looked familiar but also different. Otto was building his time in a two-person Piper Cub, painted "Piper Yellow." It wasn't the fastest thing in the sky, but it was good for putting around in. Still, it would be so great to fly something like the plane he was sitting in. In time, Otto, he told himself. Get your instructor's license and then see about a multi-engine ticket.

"How do you like it, kid?" Libeau had finished his sandwich and coffee and stuck his head into the cockpit.

Otto started and jumped up from the seat. "I'm sorry, I just wanted to see what it was like to sit here."

"It's OK, kid. I was the same way once. In fact, you remind me of myself when I was starting out."

"Mr. Libeau, it must be so swell to fly an airplane like this one. She's a beaut."

"Well, it's a job, I suppose, but I understand what you're saying. And I have a feeling that some day you'll be flying something even bigger than this."

"Gosh, I hope so," Otto said, threading past Libeau and down the aisle. He walked over to the Piper sitting by the hangar and began his preflight. The journey of a thousand miles starts with a single step, he thought. Or a single flight. He completed his inspection, climbed into the cockpit, pulled the choke, set the throttle, got out, pulled the prop through one revolution and then gave it a sharp swing. He backed away from the spinning blade as the engine caught. He jumped in the cockpit and taxied out to the runway.

Otto checked the few instruments on the Cub's panel and then advanced the throttle. The little yellow plane bounced and vibrated along the grassy surface for a bit and then lifted its tail When he could feel the controls lighten, Otto pulled back on the stick and the Cub was airborne, headed on a slow climb to some white clouds drifting along in the bright blue sky. Otto turned toward Pioneer Lake, not too far away, and was soon moving along above the streets of well-kept businesses and houses. He could see the mansion—for that was what it was—Betty lived in, the high school, the lumber yard, and all the rest of Main Street. Cars creeping along the road looked like insects.

Flying was pure freedom for Otto. It always had been, and every flight brought something new. A bird, perhaps a falcon, paced him for a while as he flew over the town limits. The bird suddenly dove and was gone, evidently spotting some prey far below. He kept going for a while, enjoying a feeling of freedom from his concerns—Hans, Maria, the farm, his relationship with Betty—they all fell away in the sky. After a while, he reluctantly turned 180 degrees back toward the airport. He entered the traffic pattern, upwind, crosswind, downwind, base, final approach and landed smoothly taxiing to the hangar. He cut the engine and sat there a while, enjoying the feeling he always had when he finished a flight. He pulled his log book out of his pocket and put in the date, the time he was aloft and, under comments, "Nice flight." Most of the comments said something similar. He noticed that the Lockheed was gone. He wasn't sure what Mr. Ross did in Minneapolis, but thought it was something related to banking. He would be back later that evening. Otto made a mental note to talk to Wilson about lights for the field. That would be a big improvement. He walked toward the office.

***

A week later, as Otto was washing some of the aircraft tied down outside the hangar, he heard the unmistakable sound of a large rotary engine which meant it belonged to a large airplane. He moved to one side of the hangar so he could see what produced such a noise.

A silver aircraft of a type he hadn't seen before turned on base leg. It looked to be the sleekest aircraft he had ever seen. As he watched, it turned smoothly onto final and made about the best landing he had ever witnessed. Whoever was flying it was one fine pilot. Otto knew of only one pilot who could fly like that--Charles Lindbergh, but what would Charles Lindbergh be doing at little Pioneer Lake? It wasn't possible. Well, he would find out who it was soon enough.

The big plane taxied in and pulled to a stop by the hangar. The pilot threw back the canopy and climbed out. He removed his helmet, goggles and gloves and slid down the wing to the ground. Otto went over to him and just about fainted. It was Charles Lindbergh! He would have recognized that famous face and piercing blue eyes anywhere! He felt as if he couldn't speak.

"Hello, young man," Lindbergh said. "Can I get something to eat? And can you refuel my plane?"

"Yessir, Colonel," Otto returned. "We have some ham sandwiches I just made up and some coffee that's not too old. I'll go get the refueling wagon."

"And could you point the way to the bathroom?" The famous aviator smiled.

Otto pointed. "It's through that door in the ready room. You can't miss it!"

Lindbergh walked somewhat stiffly in the direction of the office. Otto followed him, pulling out the ham sandwich from the refrigerator. He poured some coffee from the urn into one of the white china cups they used. He set both on a tray and had it ready when Lindbergh came out.

"If you wouldn't mind—what's your name, young fellow?"

"It's Otto, sir, Otto Kerchner."

"Well, if it's all right with you, I'd like to take my sandwich and coffee and eat over by the airplane. I don't want a lot of people knowing I'm here, although you're the only one I see at this point."

"Yessir, I'll take your tray, and the only people here are my boss and the chief pilot and they're both, uh, asleep. I'll keep anyone else that shows up away."

"Thank you, Otto. I appreciate it. You seem like a sensible young fellow."

Otto and Lindbergh walked back over to his aircraft. Lindberg sat on the wing and tore into the sandwich, taking occasional sips of coffee.

Otto ran over and got the refueling cart and ran the hose to the filler hole in the Lockheed. He turned the crank and quickly transferred the fuel to the aircraft's tank. He pulled the hose out when he was done and coiled it neatly on the cart.

Lindbergh was finishing his sandwich. "Well, I'd better get on to Minneapolis. It has been nice to stop here. Is this a good place to live?"

"I think so, sir. It's quiet and there's a lot to do if you like the outdoors."

"Do you like airplanes, Otto?"

"Do I ever, Colonel Lindbergh! And I've been a big fan of yours since I was a kid. I got my private pilot's license four years ago and I want to be a flight instructor."

"Very impressive," said Lindbergh. "I hope it works out well for you. I'd better be on my way." He reached out and shook Otto's hand. "It has been a pleasure meeting you. Happy flying to you."

Otto took his hand, feeling the firm grip. "The pleasure is all mine, sir. I can't believe you flew into our airport."

"Oh—one thing more, Otto. If you would, please don't say anything about my presence here to anyone. The reason I'm on this trip is very secret and it would be better if no one knew I was in the area."

That meant he couldn't tell anyone he had met Lindbergh. Well, he would know it and that was what counted. "I won't tell a soul, Colonel."

Lindbergh put one foot on the wing of the fighter. He took the gloves he had pulled off in the cockpit and tossed them to Otto. "Here you go. A present from one pilot to another. I have a spare set in here."

Otto examined the well-worn gloves. What a treasure, he thought. He would keep them forever. He held them tightly as Lindbergh closed the cockpit cover. The engine fired up on the big aircraft. Lindberg looked over and snapped a salute to Otto, who returned it.

The silver airplane taxied out to the end of the grassy field. Lindbergh held it there for a few seconds, testing the controls and then advanced the throttle. The big radial ran up to takeoff power. It was about the smoothest and most resonant engine Otto had ever heard.

Lindbergh ran the airplane down the field, rotating it smoothly into the air. He climbed rapidly for altitude and waggled his wings as he disappeared to the west. Otto felt as if he hadn't breathed the entire time the great aviator had been there. All he could think was oh wow oh wow oh wow.

***

Shortly after Otto's encounter with Lindbergh, he began training for his instructor certification in Eau Claire. Once a week, on Friday, he flew the Cub to the airport and spent the morning training in a Piper J-5, a more powerful and roomier version of Otto's J-2 Cub. He quickly caught on to what his instructor showed him, and after minimal instruction time, he was certified. He returned to Pioneer Lake Airport and took up the bulk of flight instruction. He didn't see much of Sparky, who continued to live at the airport, or Wilson either, but they were both there.

Otto had a string of undistinguished students. Most of them would take far more than the average instructional time, but Otto didn't mind. Wilson certainly didn't mind, as long as the money kept rolling in.

***

The war in Europe escalated, as Germany sent waves of bombers night after night in attacks that came to be known as the Battle of Britain. Otto listened to the BBC, which continued to broadcast even as the raids turned their targets from airfields to cities and towns in early September. He was mesmerized by an entire nation under attack. Mata left when he tuned in the big radio in the living room, saying she couldn't bear to hear about more death and destruction.

She also refused to sit through the newsreels when they went to a rare movie, preferring instead to visit in the lobby with some women she knew until the feature had begun. She went to movies for escape, not for information, she told Otto.

Otto tried to sign up for the Army Air Corps in September when he was in Eau Claire on some airpost business. The sergeant told him there was no need for more pilots at present funding levels. If war came, they would need his piloting skills and those of many more men. That promise had to be good enough for Otto for the moment.

Chapter 15

Remember Pearl Harbor—December, 1941

Otto and Mata sat in the living room as was their custom on Sunday afternoons, listening to the radio. Otto nodded over the paper and Mata busied herself with some mending. Maria remained sitting at the dining room table, expectantly watching the door to the outside. Hans had gone to sleep in the bedroom after lunch.

Their customary program was interrupted by an announcement:

From the NBC Newsroom in New York: President Roosevelt said in a statement today that the Japanese have attacked (the) Pearl Harbor, Hawaii, from the air. I'll repeat that, President Roosevelt says that the Japanese have attacked Pearl Harbor from the air. This bulletin came to you from the NBC Newsroom in New York.

There was a moment of silence. Than Mata said, "Otto, did you hear that?"

"Yes, the bulletin woke me up when it came on."

"What do you think will happen?"

"I think there will be war."

"Oh, no..."

"We have to fight now. They've attacked us." He stood up. "I need to get out to the airfield. It should be secured and there's no one there on Sundays.

"I thought Mr. Duncan lived there."

"Just as I said, there's no one there on Sundays."

Otto went over to the closet and took out Hans' Mauser. "No, Otto, not a gun!"

"I don't know what I'll run into, Mata. Don't worry; I'll be careful!" He ran out the door, climbed into the pickup and roared off.

Mata went into the kitchen to be with Maria. She decided not to tell her about the attack. "Where was Hans going?" she asked Mata.

"He just had an errand, Mama," Mata told her, patting her hands. "He'll be back soon."

***

Otto drove the familiar road to the airport, not sure of what he would find. The office looked secured and the hangar and aircraft untouched, but when he opened the locked office, a familiar rough voice greeted him. "Otto? That you?"

He went over to Wilson's office whose door was open with the light on. Wilson was in his customary pose with a bottle on the desk and a drink in his hand. He uncustomarily had a Minneapolis extra edition open to the front page on his lap. Duncan lay asleep on the sofa across from him.

"Siddown. In the chair, kid. Unless you want to sit on Duncan. I don't think he'd care too much."

Otto sat in the chair. "So what do you think, Mr. Wilson?"

"What do I think? I think we're as good as at war. And I think there's a lot of money to be made in the years ahead. Oh, not by young guys like you, poor guys. It'll be made by guys like me who stay home and own the 'means of production' as someone once said. Yep, we'll stay home and produce the things you need to beat the Jap and the Hun and Uncle Sam will pay us handsomely because that's what your mommies and daddies want for you—only the best."

Wilson stopped, out of breath. It was a long speech for him, but he seemed to be habitually out of breath.

"You sound like you think the war is a good thing, Mr. Wilson."

"I ain't sayin' it's good or bad, kid. It just is, and because it is and because it had to be, there's money to be made. So it might as well be made by the likes of yours truly."

"What will you make it in?"

"Oh, various things. Businesses I have interests in. This and that."

Otto knew better than to push him for specifics. Wilson was always vague about the nature of his "businesses." All Otto knew was that they were profitable—Wilson always dressed in tailored clothes and wore flashy watches and rings—and that they were probably illegal. He suspected the airport was a cover for some of his criminal activities. Not that the airport was one bit out of step with the law. Mata made sure of that. All the books were above board and accurate and reflected a growing—and honest—business. The others, no one knew but Wilson, and he wasn't telling.

"So, what are you planning to do, Otto?"

"I'm going to sign up for the Army Air Corps first thing in the morning. I know there'll be a line and I want to be at the head of it.'

"Well, good luck to you, kid." Wilson raised his glass. "Good luck to us all."

***

Otto didn't have a problem getting up early since it was his habit to do so to tend the cows anyhow. The frozen mud of the barnyard crunched underfoot as he made his way to the barn, fed and watered the stock and attached the milking machines one by one. He was glad they no longer had to milk by hand. Mata had made a good investment, and their production had gone up. He wondered what would happen to demand with the coming of war.

His morning chores done, Otto left the cows to the hired man and ducked back into the house. Mata was sitting at the table nursing a cup of coffee.

"Guten morgen, Bruder."

"Guten morgen, Schwester."

He sat down across from her. "I'm off to join up."

Her eyes looked troubled. "I wish you wouldn't."

"If I don't they'll draft me. This is something I have to do."

"Let me see if we can get you an agricultural deferment. Those are available for certain types of farmers."

"I don't want to dodge this, Mata. I want to get over there, defeat these monsters and get back as soon as I can. You'll see. I'll be back in a year, tops."

He stood up, went over and kissed her on the top of her head. "I'll be fine. You'll see." Mata put her left hand up and he took it. "I'll be back as soon as I can."

"Be careful, dear brother."

Otto went out to the truck, got in, started it and soon was driving through familiar fields, glowing golden this morning with the low sunlight illuminating the frost. Traffic grew as he neared the recruiting station located down from the high school. There were so many cars and trucks parked nearby he had to park two blocks away and walk over.

Inside the small office, organized chaos reigned. Four Army sergeants formed up the men who had come into four lines. The would-be recruits stood talking with each other, each grasping a sheaf of paper, waiting to be called back into the medical office.

Sergeant Johnston, the head recruiter, recognized Otto from his prior visits and rushed over to him. "Hey, Otto, no need for you to wait in line. I have your paperwork we filled out the last time you were here, so we can use that."

"Thanks, Sergeant. Looks like you've got your hands full."

Johnston surveyed the room. "Yep, we're pretty busy. But they sent me a telegram last night telling me what to expect and sent along some help from Minneapolis. Those are the four handsome gentlemen you see out here. We'll get it done but it'll be a long haul. You can go right through that door and Doc Carter will examine you.'

"Thank you," Otto said as Johnston turned to the next man in line.

Otto opened the door to the examining room where the fellow before him was pulling up his pants. Doc handed him a sheaf of papers and pointed to a door on the other wall. Otto handed him his paperwork and as Doc glanced at the name and then up at Otto's face, and frowned. "So you finally will have a chance to kill yourself in the air, huh, Otto?"

Otto sighed. Here it came again. "I just want to serve my country and win the war."

"Couldn't you do it from the ground? Or the sea?"

"I suppose I could, but I want to do it from the air. I want to *fly*."

Doc motioned for him to take off his shirt and then moved a stethoscope around his back as Otto breathed in and out four times. "Well, I suppose I could fail you on the physical…"

"Have you found something?" Otto asked sharply.

"Oh no, just doing a little theoretical thinking. But I suppose I still do have some integrity left… look left…look right…OK, cough…that's it. You have a pulse and you're breathing, so you're qualified."

"Thanks, Doc."

"Don't thank me. Now you'll learn the most basic part of military life."

"What's that?"

"'Hurry up and wait.' Take your papers, go through that door, collect some stamps from the happy fellows at the table and then wait until you're called."

"Wait? How long?"

"Until you're in service? No one knows. We're new to this. Weeks. Months. Maybe years . . . ."

"Years? But the war is going on *now*!"

"Yeah, and don't get too anxious about getting into it. There are people who are seriously dead as a result of war."

"That's not funny."

"No, it's not." Carter studied Otto for a long moment. "I've known you since before there was a 'you.' Took care of your mom when she was carrying you. Tried to take care of that hard-headed German father of yours, God bless him." He shook his head.

"So listen to an old man who knows you and who knows what he is talking about. Please be careful no matter where you are, no matter what you end up doing. There are plenty of dead heroes. I'd rather welcome back a live ordinary guy who had the smarts to survive." He stuck out his hand. "Promise me you'll do that much."

Otto took his hand and shook it. "I'll try, Doc. I'll do my best to, anyhow." Doc patted him on the back and Otto stepped through the door into the next room where, as Doc predicted, his papers were stamped by four bored-looking corporals. He was then sent home to wait.

***

Doc was also right about the waiting. It simply took time to gather the men necessary to run the biggest war machine ever built, to design the aircraft, ships, tanks, trucks and weapons, to mine the ores and resources necessary to build them, to manufacture these Articles of War and then to ship them to the people who would use them. And it took time to put into place the training systems where the people would be taught to operate the machines and systems designed to bring death and defeat to the enemy and his people.

And so Otto, along with millions of his fellow Americans, waited. They didn't necessarily wait patiently, but they waited. Through long days, longer weeks, long months as they listened to their radios and to news of the war, which was mostly bad. They built camps and training facilities, and they began to train the young men and women who would carry the war to the far corners of the world.

Otto continued to operate the farm and to run the airport. Wilson was largely absent, in Minneapolis, he guessed, and Duncan spent most of his days in a drunken stupor. How he was still alive was beyond him. He seemed to subsist on sleep, stale ham sandwiches and whiskey. Otto wasn't sure he knew there was a war on.

There was in truth little business at the airfield. The military had slapped heavy restrictions on civilian air traffic, and with fuel chiefly reserved for the military uses, no one else was flying, or driving much for that matter. Otto spent his days keeping the field clean and listening to the floating discussion group of pilots who sat in the ready room and exchanged opinions. There seemed to be little else to do.

"Well, I think this is Roosevelt's war—one he started to make himself and his rich friends richer…"

"Ah, you're full of it! How could Roosevelt control events thousands of miles away?"

"These rich people have their ways. They're not like you and me!"

"Hey, Kerchner! You haven't said anything. What do you think?"

Otto turned from where he was making another urn of coffee. "I don't know. It is what it is, I suppose, and the sooner we get into it, the sooner it's over."

"Well, listen to the philosopher, will you?" This was followed by a round of laughter.

"You asked," Otto said quietly, and went into the office. It was going to be a long war indeed, particularly if nothing happened.

Chapter 16

Last Days—March, 1942

Except for rationing and a few young men going off to war from Pioneer Lake, things did not seem to change much. There were still cows to be milked and fed every day, and forms to fill out and discussions to overhear at the airfield. Life went on.

One Saturday morning in February, Mata came back from the mailbox at the end of the drive bearing several letters. She waved a rather thick official-looking envelope at Otto. "This one's for you," she cried. "I think it's from the Army!"

Otto tore it open and sat down at the kitchen table where he had been having coffee after finishing morning chores. He read rapidly:

February 16, 1942
Cadet Otto Kerchner
R.R. 6, Box 803
Pioneer Lake, Wisconsin
Cadet Kerchner:

You are directed forthwith to set your affairs in order and report to Camp Atterbury, Edinburg, Indiana, by 0800 hours on Monday, March 16 for basic training leading eventually to flight training.

Travel letters are enclosed for passage from your location to Camp Atterbury and meal chits are provided.

You will receive further direction upon completion of basic training at this facility.

There was more, but Otto didn't read it right then. He put the sheaves of paper on the table and stared at them. Mata came into the kitchen. She had checked on Maria, who was in bed, and on Hans, who sat with his head down in the living room.

"Otto, what is it? Good news or bad news?"

Otto raised the sheets from the table. "Both, Mata. It's my orders to report for training. I'm actually going to get to fly and fight." He stood up and she walked over and embraced him. She was smiling at the same time tears ran down her cheeks. "I'm so proud of you," she told him, "but also very frightened for you. Promise me you'll come back."

"I promise, Mata," he murmured, but he was wondering, Will I come back at all?

They stayed that way for a moment, then broke apart. Otto stuffed the envelope and letters into the desk by the door. "So, what's for lunch?" he asked, rubbing his hands. "I'll need as much home cooking as I can get since I won't have any for a long while."

"I've fixed dumplings and sausage, your favorite," Mata exclaimed, moving into the kitchen. "It'll be ready in about ten minutes. Go ahead and wash up. I'll get Mama and Papa going and would appreciate some help bringing the food out."

"You got it, Sis." Otto washed his hands from the kitchen taps Mata had installed the year before. He smiled as he remembered the first time he had seen indoor plumbing at Dr. Carter's, such a long time ago. He dried his hands on a towel and lit the burner under the frying pan where Mata had placed the sausages and then did the same with the one under the pot containing the dumplings. He monitored both to make sure they wouldn't burn. Mata came in as both were heating nicely.

"Whew!" she exclaimed, pushing her hair back from her face. "I must look a fright. Mama is harder and harder to get out of bed and dressed, but I got her to the parlor. Papa is not so bad to get him into his wheelchair. Give me just a minute." She leaned on the kitchen counter, fanning herself with one hand.

Otto got the plates out, measured out some of each part of the meal, and walked the plates to the kitchen two at a time. He came back where Mata was still standing. "And what, dear sister, would you like to have to drink with your lunch?"

She leaned her head to one side. "If you have any, sir, I would like some milk."

Otto bowed in her direction. "You are very lucky, Fraulein, because today we are featuring—" Here he opened the ice box with a flourish "—milk!" The interior of the chest was packed with bottle after bottle of milk, which, as Mata was fond of saying, was only to be expected on a dairy farm.

Otto poured four big glasses of milk and set them on the table. Hans and Maria were sitting there. Mata began cutting up Maria's sausage.

"Good morning, Mama," Otto said. "How are you? Did you sleep well?"

Maria looked at him with some confusion in her eyes. "Hans? Is that you?"

Mata raised her eyebrows and nodded slightly at Otto as she fed Maria a piece of sausage which she chewed slowly.

"Ja, it's me. I've been out tending the cows."

Maria smiled. "You are so good with cows, Hans. It's like you can talk to them." She faded off as Mata continued to feed her.

Hans spoke up. "So you are going off to war, Otto."

Otto and Mata looked at each other. "How did you know that, Papa?"

"Well, I might be crippled, but I'm not deaf. And you're just the age I was when I joined up. Have you thought about how you will feel possibly fighting people who might be your relatives?"

"I won't think of them as relatives. I am an American and they are the enemy."

Hans nodded slowly and turned to his food. He didn't say much after his injury.

"So, Otto, I think all the girls will think you are very handsome in your uniform when you come home on leave," Mata teased.

"I think they will think I look like every other soldier in an Army uniform," returned Otto.

"Oh, but I know Betty Ross will be very impressed with your appearance."

"Betty and I are friends," said Otto, blushing.

"That's not what I hear," Mata teased. "I hear that you two are sweet on each other."

"We've been out a few times."

"I hear you've been out a lot of times to Spenser's and to the airport. You take her flying."

"I'm glad everyone is so interested in what I'm doing."

"I think it's adorable. My brother, going to marry the banker's daughter."

"I'm not going to marry anyone! And what about you?"

"What about me?"

"Where are all your beaux? I'd think there'd be a different one here every night."

"If you've noticed, dear brother, the pickings are pretty slim around here."

"There're are the guys at school. Some of them are nice."

"Yeah, nice and stupid."

"What about the boys at church?"

"Honestly, Otto, for heaven's sake!"

"Are there any men in this county who meet your high standards?"

Mata's expression turned serious. "Probably not. I'm OK with my girlfriends. We have a good time when we go out. I'm sure I'll meet someone nice one day."

"I'm sure you will, sister." Otto stood up from the table. "Thanks for preparing lunch."

Mata smiled. "It's more like you prepared it."

"I just fixed what *you* had prepared."

"Get to work, M. le Chef. I know you have plenty to do before you go off to save the world."

Otto stood with his hand on the doorknob. "So I do. I'd better get to it."

***

The two weeks until Otto reported for basic passed rapidly. He worked hard on both the airport and farm to make sure they were prepared for his absence, although he had no idea how long that would be. It could be years or he might be back very quickly if he washed out of flying school. He hoped not, but that was a distinct possibility.

He was cleaning up the aircraft on his last day at home when he saw Wilson's plane in the landing pattern. The big man landed, heaved himself out of the cockpit, and walked over to Otto. "Can you come to the office?"

"Sure," Otto replied. He noticed that Wilson was carrying a package wrapped up in brown paper. They went into the office and Wilson sat at his desk.

"So today's your last day?"

"That's right. I ship out tomorrow."

"Have a seat." Otto sat. "I got a little something for you. Here—" Wilson handed the package to Otto. It was heavy.

"You didn't have to get me anything. You've been so good to me."

"Yeah, well, I take care of my boys. And you're one of them. Open the package."

Otto tore open the paper, and there was a beautiful pearl-handled Colt .45. He gasped. "Mr. Wilson, I can't accept this. It's too expensive."

Wilson waved his hand. "I want you to have it. You'll need protection against the Nazis. Hell, you need protection from the yahoos around here."

"Well, I'll take it and wear it proudly. Thank you and thank you for all you've done for me."

He and Wilson stood at the same time and shook hands. "Good luck, kid. Knock 'em dead."

"I plan to, Mr. Wilson. I plan to."

***

That afternoon Otto went to town to pick up some things for Mata. There he ran across Betty in front of the town hall.

"Otto! How have you been?"

"Busy, like everyone else. I'm sorry I haven't gotten back to you. I suppose you heard I enlisted in the Army Air Corps."

"Yes, I did." She studied his face, and, for once, he could not read her expression.

"Could we go somewhere and talk for a few minutes? I'd like to catch up."

"Sure. We can go in my car. Not to be rude, but are you ever going to get a new truck?"

"Some day," Otto told her as he climbed into the Packard. "Is Spencer's okay?"

"It's fine," she said as she started the car, put it in gear and backed in a semi-circle into the street.

Five minutes later they were seated in a booth by the window at Spencer's. Betty ordered a Coke; Otto, a coffee, and they looked around as they waited for their order.

"So, when…" they both said at the same time. They laughed and Otto started again. "Ladies first," indicating that Betty should go ahead.

"So, when do you leave?" she continued. "It has to be soon."

"Tomorrow on the 2 PM. I'm about ready. Mata keeps packing and repacking my bag although I've told her I'll get all the clothes I need in the service."

"Mata is such a sweetie. Grownup for her age, too."

"Yes, she has pretty much run the farm since Papa's injury."

"I still feel so bad about your Papa. I know he was always so active."

Otto peered into his coffee cup. "He gets around. He's just not too happy. That's understandable, considering."

"You're so philosophical and understanding, Otto. I really admire both qualities in you."

"I guess I'm just resigned to what happened. Don't think I haven't laid awake nights thinking of ways to hurt the whole Smith tribe—preferably by crippling every last one of them. I'm not proud of those thoughts, but I have them."

She reached over and took his hand. "Those are perfectly natural thoughts, I'd say."

He smiled at her and then grew serious. "I want to talk about us, Betty."

"Us?"

"Yes, as in what kind of relationship we're going to have while I'm gone."

"What kind of relationship do we have now, Otto?"

He spoke carefully. "A friendship, I'd say." Again, he couldn't read her expression. She looked sad and serious at the same time.

"All right, we have a friendship, then. So what does that mean for us in the future?"

"I think it means that we'll continue to be friends."

"All right, we can do that." She definitely looked angry now and her tone was sharp. Betty stood up and stuck out her hand. "Good-bye and good luck, Otto. I wish you well."

Otto took her hand and shook it. He was puzzled. Had he said something wrong? "Will you write me if I write you, Betty?"

"Oh, sure," she said with a sarcastic tone he had never heard her use with him before. "We can be little pen pals and write each other little letters. I hope you'll enjoy doing that." She turned on her heel, slammed the door to the diner, got in her car and spewed gravel all over as she tore out of the parking lot and onto the street. By the time Otto paid the bill and got to his truck, she was gone.

Smoothly played, Kerchner, he thought. Smoothly played.

Chapter 17

Basic—late March, 1942

March 27, 1942
Dear Mata,

I'm writing to you from Camp Atterbury. It has been raining ever since we got here. I am with a group of 200 other cadets for what is called basic training. It's the Army part of the Army Air Corps. Some of the fellows from the city are having a rough time of it. I don't think they had to get up before dawn to tend cattle or do much physical work.

We get up, "police" (clean up) the barracks, march to breakfast, try to recognize what they're feeding us (I miss your cooking!), do some more marching, have some sort of training, eat lunch, march some more, attend classes on military law and protocol, do some shooting on the rifle range (not that I expect to ever carry a rifle—pilots carry sidearms), have supper and then some free time to read or write or play cards or whatever.

Some of the fellows got passes to go into town this past Friday. I stayed here and read. I have little interest in "painting the town red." Maybe it's because I have painted too many barns red, ha ha.

The other cadets are from all over the Midwest and we all have one thing in common. We want to be pilots. As far as I know, no one else is a pilot already, but I'm not telling anyone that I am. I have a feeling that the Army wants to train us in their own way, not in the civilian method.

In any case, it's comfortable here, the food is edible, and I'm eager to get this step behind me and go on to some actual flying.

One funny thing—whoever hooked up the toilets goofed up and ran hot water to them. There's a sign that warns users to beware a hot water spray when they flush! I'm glad someone put up a sign or there would be a lot of surprised soldiers!

I hope you and Mama and Papa are well.

I am your brother,

Otto

Otto finished the letter, folded it, placed it in the envelope and put on a stamp. He was glad that Sundays were quiet. Most of the fellows slept or played cards or talked quietly. He liked to write letters and read. Just then he was about halfway through Joseph Conrad's *Heart of Darkness*. He thought Conrad was a master of English prose, which was incredible considering that his first language was Polish. He had taken the book out of the small base library which seemed to have castoffs of trashy novels with a few classics like Conrad mixed in. In truth, most of his fellow soldiers seemed to prefer activity to sitting and reading. Otto just needed a period of calm in the midst of all that was going on. He figured they would have about six weeks of learning to be soldiers and then about the same amount of time on "advanced basic" training where they would probably learn to be even better soldiers. He wouldn't get near an airplane for another six months. He hoped he didn't forget how to fly.

Chapter 18

Advanced Basic—June, 1942

June 16, 1942
Dear Mata,

Now I'm in the South and I do mean the South. Everyone here except the cadets has a strong Southern accent, y'all. They use "y'all" a lot, like "y'all need to come over here." It's a funny expression. Most of the instructors have accents but we don't say anything about it since we don't want to have to do pushups.

I thought basic training was disciplined but not too hard. Now I'm in advanced basic and it is like military school. We have to eat in "brace position" which means we sit stiff and erect at the table with our chins down against chests. Our instructors circulate to make sure we're maintaining a "good military posture," and if we don't, we have to do pushups. I've avoided having to do too many, although some fellows are going to have the world's most developed biceps from doing hundreds of them.

It's hot here. And it's humid. In Wisconsin, I imagine it's pleasant now. I am really getting to see a lot of the country, although it has been from trains, not from airplanes. We spend days on troop trains getting from place to place. A lot of times we pull onto a siding and let trains carrying tanks and jeeps pass. I suppose they're vital to the war effort, but then so are we. We've all become very good at "hurry up and wait," which is a favorite expression in the Army.

I've "hurried up and waited" so long I've probably forgotten how to fly. It's been four months since I've been in an airplane. They seem determined to keep us away from them until they're good and ready. Supposedly that comes with the next phase of training.

Your letters caught up with me from a while back. Thank you for the news. I'm sorry Mama is not doing well. You are one of those who "only stand and wait" for your service, only I don't see you standing and waiting at all! You do far too much!

I have become quite good at cleaning my part of the barracks. Maybe we could have a house cleaning contest when I get back. I think I would lose.

It's about time for dinner. Sundays they give us steak, so I don't want to miss that. My love to you and to Mama and to Papa.

Your brother,

Otto

Otto re-read what he had written and then folded the letter carefully and put it in the envelope. He stamped it and slipped it into his pocket and went out to drop it in the letter drop. Other cadets were making their way to the mess hall. He dropped the letter off and caught sight of Bob Donovan, a fellow from Eau Claire he had befriended. One of the first things troops did when they met up for the first time was try to find someone from near their home town. Donovan was in a different barracks, and he and Otto had hit it off the first time they met.

"Otto! What's going on?" Donovan exclaimed.

"Not much, Bob, what's new with you?"

"Oh, New York, New Jersey, New Brunswick…you know." They both laughed although Donovan had used the line hundreds of times.

"You ready to eat, OK?"

"Yeah, I'm starved. Let's go!"

They made their way in a crowd of jostling, joking cadets to the mess hall. Sundays were good, Otto reflected. Time to think, time to write home and time to have a steak dinner. He went into the dining hall in a state of high expectation, intensified by the smell of freshly cooked steaks.

Chapter 19

Primary Flight Training—September, 1942

Dear Mata,

Finally! They let us near an airplane! We do basic flight training on what is called a Stearman, a biplane like the Fleet I learned to fly on, but much more powerful. Tomorrow we start our instruction with ground school in the morning and orientation to the aircraft in the afternoon. I haven't told anyone I have my pilot's license, although I suspect that the brass knows it. I've found out there's the way I do things and the way the Army wants me to do things and it will go a lot better for me if I do it their way.

We're in South Carolina and it's still very warm. I thought I might try to organize a couple of baseball teams while we're here. I haven't played since high school, but the rec officer has a supply of balls, bats and gloves. Some of the guys here are pretty good players—or at least they say they are. One guy was called up to the minors with the Yankees until the war broke out. He's in the Army now, like the rest of us.

It's very flat here, semi-tropical and supposed to stay warm until September. I'll write more after they teach me to fly, ha ha.

My love to you and Mama and Papa. I hope I get some leave and visit around Christmas. That will depend on where I am since I'd have a four-day pass at the most to come home.

Your brother,

Otto

Lieutenant Ralston, the head instructor for ten cadets including Otto and their ten instructors, addressed the group gathered around the Stearman with yellow wings and a blue fuselage.

"Gentlemen," Ralston began, "This is a PT-17 Stearman, a primary trainer. It has yellow wings so real pilots can spot it and get the hell out of your way. We will teach you to fly in the aircraft, but you must pay attention and do as you're told. Otherwise you can end up seriously dead or injured and that's your business, but you might kill or injure someone else or damage government property, in which case the cost of the aircraft will be taken out of your check. You won't pay it off until 1954.

"We need all the pilots we can get, so rule number one is stay safe. If in doubt, follow your training, do as your instructor says and we'll try to get you through this."

"Cadet Kerchner, front and center!"

What the—Otto thought as he stepped forward. "Yes, Lieutenant Ralston!" he shouted, snapping off a salute.

"At ease, Kerchner." Otto stood at ease. "I understand that you have your pilot's license."

"That is correct, sir!"

"So you don't need flight instruction, is that correct?"

"Begging your pardon, sir, I need plenty of flight instruction."

"Why is that Cadet Kerchner? How did you learn to fly?"

"I learned to fly the wrong way, sir!"

"The wrong way? What is the wrong way?"

"The civilian way, sir!"

"And what is the right way?"

"The Army way, sir!

Ralston laughed. "Good answer, Kerchner! You're OK In fact, since your initials are OK, I'm going to call you Second Lieutenant OK in military situations and 'The OK Kid' the rest of the time. Is that all right with you, Lieutenant OK?"

"That's fine with me, sir!"

"Well, all right. Let's get started, then. Beginning at the front of the aircraft is the engine. This is a very powerful engine, gentlemen, and it can get you into a pile of trouble if you don't keep up with it…"

Otto, half listening, was chewing over his new nickname. It wasn't a bad one, he thought. Better than a lot of others.

"Kerchner! What is this part of the aircraft called?"

"That's the windscreen, sir!"

"Very good, Kerchner, very good."

Chapter 20

Basic Flight training—December, 1942

Dear Mata,

Your letter from a month ago finally caught up with me. That's not too bad, considering how much I've moved around. At least I'm still in the same state.

They have us flying a larger monoplane (one wing) aircraft called a BT-13. It has a huge single engine, but the wings aren't long enough, and it's prone to spins. You have to pay attention to it every second or it will get away from you. And vibrate…man, does it vibrate. In fact, that's what everyone calls it—the Vultee Vibrator. That term has a second meaning, but it's not fit to share with a lady.

This camp is much like the others. I think the military had one plan for their camps and they used it over and over. Saves time and money, I suppose.

I forgot to tell you about my G.I. insurance. We each sign up for a life insurance policy and I named you as beneficiary. There's an interesting expression pilots use when someone crashes and dies. We say he "bought the farm," because the payout for the insurance will pay the mortgage on the farm. I can tell from what you write about the farm that it is doing well. I'm proud of you, sis, and the work you and all the other women are doing. Some of the fellas say their sisters and mothers and wives are working in factories, building aircraft and jeeps and tanks. They're doing their part, as are you, and that will help bring this war to an end and let us get back to our lives.

I miss your cooking and I miss you and Mama and Papa. I hope you are well.

Time to get dressed for my baseball game. I'm playing shortstop like I did in high school, but there are some pitchers here who are really good. The first time I saw a curve ball I couldn't believe my eyes. The ball really curved! And I didn't hit it, I was so surprised! I'm a little more used to it now.

Take care and write when you can. I'll let you know when I get my wings and hope you can come see me then. I should also have a leave home, depending on where I am.

Your brother,

Otto

Otto looked back over his shoulder at the line of aircraft in chevron formation. He was number two left, off the lead Vultee. Number 5 seemed to be having trouble staying in formation and there wasn't much room for error.

He heard a huge thud back to his left and whipped his head around to see that the number 5 and 6 aircraft had collided. The left wing sheared off number 6 and it fell off, trailing smoke. Number 5 nosed up, its left tailplane gone, stalled and then went into a spin. Otto hoped the men would be able to bail out, but as he watched the two aircraft spiral to earth, no chutes appeared.

"Concentrate on what you're doing, airmen." It was the lead instructor in the number 1 airplane on the com. He called in the crashes. "Sumter field, this is flight 43, reporting two aircraft down, 13 miles northwest of the field. Repeat, two aircraft down, 13 miles northwest of the field. "

"Roger that," came back the field. "Any survivors?"

"None that I can see."

"Roger."

There was a long silence on the radio as the flight droned on. They made a pass over the field and, one by one, peeled off and landed. Otto brought the big aircraft in and set it down gently. Poor fellows, he thought. They never knew what hit them. He shoved the canopy back and breathed in the humid air. Life really did rest on a knife's edge, he thought.

Chapter 21

Advanced Flight Training—March, 1943

Dear Mata,

I'm in Indiana! Finally close to home, so I can come see you and you can see me get my wings! It will be great to be with you again.

We start twin-engine instruction tomorrow, using something called an AT-9. I'll have a co-pilot, and mine is Bob Donovan. Sometimes you keep the same co-pilot the rest of the time, so I hope it will be Bob. He's a fine fellow, from Eau Claire, and flies very well. I feel like I can trust him.

It's a little cold for baseball here so that will have to wait. My team did very well at the last base, going 13 and 5. We led the league, although I think I will never learn to hit a curve ball. I had a .445 batting average because most of the pitchers couldn't throw a curve. I also hit twelve home runs, although I'm not much of a power hitter. Maybe it's the weight I've gained from Army food.

I'm one step away from flying one of the big bombers. That will entail another change in location, and then it will likely be overseas to my assignment. I don't know where I will be stationed. I have no say in it.

The AT-9 doesn't have the same difficult handling characteristics as the BT-13. We have lost eight pilots out of three hundred from accidents. I'm told that is about average for a class our size, but I don't think it's an average experience for those who lost their sons and brothers and friends. I suppose sacrifices must be made to win this war, and these are some of the ultimate sacrifices.

Thinking of you and Mama and Papa and hoping you are well.

I am your brother,

Otto

Otto sat up with a jerk. He looked around the cockpit of the AT-9 and realized with horror that he had fallen asleep on a practice navigational flight back from Indianapolis. He looked at Donovan and saw he, too, had fallen asleep. It was a night flight and they were exhausted, but that was no excuse.

"Bob! Bob! Wake up!"

Donovan snapped awake. It took him a second to realize where he was.

"Wha'?" He blurted.

"We both fell asleep, Bob. Now where the hell are we?" They were at 10,000 feet, supposedly on their way back from a night cross-country practice mission. That much of the flight had gone well, but they had drifted off on the way back.

Donovan struggled with some charts. "Let's see…" He dialed in some settings on the ADF. "OK, the field is twenty degrees to starboard, about ten miles away. We should see the lights in a minute."

Otto steered the aircraft to the right, and in a couple of minutes, the lights of the field came into view. As they neared, Otto called the tower. "Freeman Control, this is Dark Side 442 requesting permission to land."

The answer came back. "Roger, 442, you are cleared straight in to land on Runway 32."

"Roger that, tower. Straight in on 32. Over and out."

The controller clicked his mike button twice to acknowledge Otto's transmission.

As the plane lowered toward the runway, Otto glanced over at Bob. "Not a word about this to anyone, Bob."

"My lips are sealed, my friend."

"I knew I could count on you."

The AT-9 flared and touched the tarmac smoothly. Otto taxied over to the flight line, swung the plane around and cut the engine. The ground crew hurried to put wheel chocks on place. Otto and Donovan gathered up their paperwork and made their way to the briefing room where they signed off on their flight plan.

As they walked over to their barracks, Otto clapped Donovan on the back. "That was a close one, Lieutenant Donovan."

"It was, Lieutenant OK. I suspect there will be quite a few of those before we're through with this."

"I think you're right," said Otto. "I think you're right."

Chapter 22

Champaign-Urbana—June, 1943

Dear Mata,

Finally!!!!! I'm at a base where we learn to fly the big bombers—the B-17's, which I've wanted to fly ever since I read about it going into production years ago. We'll be flying some older models, not the latest "F" variant. Those are used on the front lines. Still, the one we'll be flying is pretty impressive. Just to give you an idea of its power, it has four Wright Cyclone engines rated at 1200 horsepower each (total of 4800 hp if you've completely forgotten how to multiply). By comparison, your Ford has eighty-five horsepower. And you really see why it's called the "Flying Fortress" when all of the guns open up at once! The sound is loud, even with headphones on.

We also joined up with our full crew that will stay together throughout our deployment. I was with Bob Donovan at the last camp—I've told you about him. Ed Detwiler from Bridgeport, Connecticut, is our bombardier and Steve King from Omaha, the navigator. Berle Robinson is the flight engineer and radio operator. He's from Collins, Iowa. Sam Adams of Boston and Juan Espinosa of Santa Clara are our waist gunners; Frank Stone, the tail gunner. Frank's from Tacoma. Norman Cousins is the ball gunner. He's from Reno, Nevada. And then Arthur Marx from Richmond, Virginia, is the top gunner. They all trained at different bases for their specialty and from what I see, they're a good crew. Everyone gets along, although they like to joke a bit much for my taste. I suppose I'm more serious because I'm responsible for the lives of nine other men.

We've been up on a few orientation flights, nothing fancy, just getting used to the aircraft and to each other. Talk about a powerful machine! When I advance the throttles to "full" for takeoff, the vibration shakes the whole plane. Then we speed along the runway and practically leap into the air. I know that will be different when we have a full load of fuel and bombs, but for now it's such an awe-inspiring experience.

We've got a lot to learn, both in the classroom and by flying—the nature of German fighter tactics, formation flying, using a parachute, escape and evasion if we're shot down, the Articles of War. We'll get it all in, though, because I've never been so motivated in all my life, and everyone else seems the same way.

It's not all work, though. There's a baseball league, and my crew makes up a team. We're pretty good. We call ourselves "The OK Corral," since as I told you my nickname is "Lieutenant OK" or "The OK Kid." There's a funny story about that—we went out to inspect our bomber when we first got here and every crew gets to name their aircraft. I pulled rank on the crew because they wanted to call the airplane "The OK Corral," but I said I wanted to name it after you and Mama, so it's the "Mata Maria." I told them they could use the "Corral" name for the baseball team as a kind of consolation prize. There's a sergeant in the motor pool who's very good at painting pictures on the noses of the aircraft. I want him to paint a kind of Santa Maria ship (but with wings) that's dropping bombs. Then you and Mama's name will be in a nice script at the bottom of the painting. I'll send you a picture when it's finished. I hope you'll like it.

Well, it's about time to eat again. Maybe I'll eat a little less so I'll still fit into the pilot's seat of the "Mata Maria." I just like writing that name.

I miss you and Mama and Papa. My love to you all.

Your brother,

Otto

***

Otto was playing cards with some of his crew when a corporal assigned to HQ appeared through the doorway. A low overcast and heavy rain had cancelled their formation training flight, so the crews had a rare day off. Some stayed in barracks and slept or read; some, like Otto, gathered in the mess hall between meals and wrote letters or played cards or just talked. There was always talk, Otto thought. An inexhaustible supply of talk.

The corporal walked up to Otto and saluted. Otto gave him a quick salute. Someone from HQ was never good news. "Lieutenant OK," the corporal said. "Colonel Meachum has asked that you report to the ready room ASAP."

"All right, corporal," Otto said. "I'm out," he said to the other players, tossing down his cards. He followed the corporal through the rain to the ready room about 200 yards away.

I look like a drowned rat, he thought. So much for a military appearance. He and the corporal walked into the ready room. Meachum was there, standing by the large table where four chairs had been drawn up. Otto saluted and the colonel returned the salute.

"Kerchner, you speak German, correct?"

"Yes, sir, it was my first language, although I didn't use it much after first grade."

"But you can still speak and comprehend it, right?"

"Yes, sir."

"We need your help. We have a captured Luftwaffe ace who will only speak to an officer of German background. We can't do too much to force him to talk, but I had him brought here so you could interrogate him about tactics and strategy. Are you game?"

"I'll try, sir."

Meachum nodded to the corporal, who went out of the room and returned quickly, followed by a man in a P.O.W. uniform. He was over six feet tall with blond hair and blue eyes. Well, he looks the part of the Master Race, Otto thought. Two M.P.'s came in on either side of him. The group stopped before Otto.

"Lieutenant Kerchner, this is Major Hans Krieger; Major, Lieutenant Kerchner."

Otto reflexively started to put out his hand but caught himself. Krieger bowed from the waist and said in German, "I was hoping for a Colonel, more my equal."

"I'm about as good as you'll get, Major. May we all sit down?" He quickly repeated his comments in English and continued to do so the rest of the conversation.

"So, you are of German background, Lieutenant. My wife has Kerchners in her background. Perhaps you are related."

"Maybe," Otto returned. "That's not what we're here to talk about."

"What *are* we here to talk about, then?"

"We want to know your tactics for taking on our bombers."

"I just bet you would."

"I can promise better treatment if you cooperate." Otto quickly looked at Meachum, who nodded.

"I am treated well now. You Americans are soft. You do not even know how to discipline P.O.W.'s."

"Again, we're not here to talk about that. We want to know your tactics."

"Our tactic is to strike hard and often until you are swept from the skies."

"Specifically, which quadrant do you use for attacks? Do you come in high or low? Singly or in groups?"

"My dear lad, we use whatever tactics work. We have superior machines and superior pilots. We *are* a superior people."

This guy really believes that crap, Otto thought.

"And frankly, Lieutenant, I am surprised that someone like you would fight against the Fatherland. There are ways you can join us."

"No thanks, Major. I'm an American and soon I'll be in a bomber and I hope it will be to rain down destruction on the likes of you."

"We will see about that, Lieutenant. We will see. I have nothing more to say."

Otto translated this last bit and then shook his head at Meachum. The colonel sighed and nodded to the M.P.'s who escorted Krieger out of the room.

"Arrogant s-o-b., ain't he, Kerchner? Thanks for trying."

"Yes, sir. I'm not trained in interrogation. I don't think my translations of what he said conveyed the coldness and self-assurance of the man. Here he is, in prison for the duration, and he's making threats about destroying us. That takes arrogance, all right."

"Thank you for your help, Kerchner. I'll note it in your record."

"Thank you sir," Otto said, saluted and walked back to the mess hall and his card game. The rain continued to pour down.

Chapter 23

Intermezzo—July, 1943

Dear Mata,

We've had a spell of rain here so that gives me time to write you an "extra" letter. There's not much to do outside in this weather so we read and talk or sleep. And eat. Eating is very popular.

I wanted to tell you about an ugly episode recently that turned out well from my point of view. We were having lunch in the mess hall and this jerk pilot named Rogers came by. I don't know what his problem is, but he said that we had misnamed our aircraft. I ignored him because he wants to stir things up, but Bob Donovan can't stand the guy so he answered. He said Rogers could have named his a/c the Jerk Express. Rogers told him that we should call our ship the Kraut Wagon since so many of us on the crew are of German background. Donovan stood up at that, called Rogers a name that's not fit for ladies to read and was about to smash Rogers in the face. The major came over and broke it up before it started. The C.O. has a rule that any fight goes to the ring in the rec center. Boxing with gloves settles the matter. It provides a break from the routine.

Well, the match was set up for a couple of days later. I told Donovan he didn't have to fight, to just ignore the guy, but he was determined to see it through. He said he couldn't stand a bully. We found out why he was so confident.

The day of the match came, and I think everyone in camp had placed bets on the outcome. Rogers came out swinging; Bob ducked his wild punches, stood up, and floored Rogers with a right to the jaw. It lasted maybe ten seconds. There was a stunned silence and then cheering from all those who had put money on Donovan.

I asked him afterward why he was so good. "I was a Golden Glove champ three years running in Eau Claire," he said. That would explain it.

I know you don't like fights or violence but I thought this was an interesting story.

All my love to you and Mama and Papa. You won't hear from me for a while until the mail catches up, but I will write.

Your brother,

Otto

Chapter 24

Across the Pond—August, 1943

Dear Mata,

The practice missions have continued and become more complicated. We've had missions for gunnery practice—our guys are really good! Watch out, Jerry! Then there's formation flying—it's the best way to protect each other. A formation of a hundred Forts brings 1300 machine guns to bear on attacking aircraft. I would hate to fly into a hail of bullets, but the Germans do it, and sometimes damage or shoot down our aircraft. But not if we shoot them down first.

We also have long-distance navigation exercises. Our navigator, John King, is the best. He was lead navigator on our long-range practice bombing mission. I can't tell you exactly where we flew to "drop" our practice bombs, but it's an island 90 miles south of Florida. We did very well, but I still worry about running into another aircraft in formation or having to ditch over water or put down in an emergency. I feel a lot of guys are depending on me.

Some fellows drink a lot. I might have a few beers at the officers' club, but I unwind by studying our manuals so I know all I can about what I'm doing or playing baseball (the "OK Corral" is 12 and 2 for the season! Hooray for us!) or reading or writing a letter like this.

These days I'm reading the Bible and Shakespeare's plays, mostly. I notice how many wars are recounted in the Bible. The chaplain here talked to us about a just war. We're fighting this for not only our own freedoms and dignity but also for people all over the world. These brutal totalitarian regimes have to be stopped! And we're the ones to do it.

I just finished re-reading Shakespeare's Henry V. That's about war as well, but it's so inspired and inspiring. I love the St. Crispin's Day speech that Henry gives to the troops right before the battle and particularly the lines:

We few, we happy few, we band of brothers.

I feel my crew and I are a band of brothers, and those bands are all over the Allied forces. We are sharing something that is stronger and deeper than most blood relationships.

But not deeper than the bond we share, dear Mata. I am so proud of you, taking care of Mama and Papa and running the farm so well!

I was glad to see you and Mama and Papa when I finally made it home a couple of weeks ago. I'm sorry the train was so late and also sorry that I couldn't stay longer. Duty called, as the saying goes.

We don't know when we ship out or where we're going, except that we will fly the bomber there. Well, I guess it will either be the Atlantic or the Pacific, unless we're posted to the Aleutians. We should be able to tell by the clothes we draw. Although even with that you can never tell with the Army. One group recently drew cold weather gear and they were posted to India! Bet they were plenty warm!

I will send a quick note when I find out our departure date.

Take care. My love to you and Mama and Papa.

Your brother,

Otto

Otto looked around the airfield. It was seasonably hot and humid, but where they were headed it wouldn't be. They would take off as soon as the *Mata Maria* was refueled and then they were bound for the air base at Goose Bay, Labrador, where they would spend the night, then over Greenland to Iceland where they would have another layover, rest, refuel and then press on for Wales. From what he had heard about this northern passage, he was glad that King was their navigator. He'd hate to have to put down on an ice floe.

Otto saw the crew coming back from the ops shack across the tarmac. He had done a walkaround although the crew chief at the base had signed off on the aircraft. He wanted to see with his own eyes that everything looked all right.

He saw that Stone was carrying a large bag and Detwiler had a metal carafe, probably full of coffee. Stone raised the bag. "Hey, Lieutenant OK! I got sandwiches!"

"Good thing," Otto called "There are no restaurants for about 1500 miles."

He went over to the *Mata Maria* and hoisted himself through the nose hatch. The rest of the crew followed suit. He and Donovan climbed into their seats and buckled in. The engines were still warm from a runup by the crew chief, so they should start easily, Otto thought. He stuck his head through the side window.

A ground crew corporal gave him the "start engine" sign. Donovan punched the start button for each of the four Wright Cyclones in succession and soon all were running at idle. Otto got on the intercom.

"Prepare for taxi and takeoff, gentlemen!"

"OK, Lieutenant OK" That was Stone's voice. Otto sighed and keyed the intercom.

"Don't call me that on a mission," he said to the whole crew. "It's 'pilot.' And identify yourself by position when you call."

"OK, Lieutenant—uh, pilot. This is tail over and out."

Donovan advanced the throttles and they rolled to the end of the runway. Otto keyed the microphone. "Ground control, this is Ferry Flight 301, requesting permission to take off."

"Roger," came the reply through his headphones. You are cleared for takeoff. Good luck and good flight, *Mata Maria*."

"Thank you, ground. This is *Mata Maria* starting our takeoff roll. Over and out."

***

Otto and Donovan took two-hour turns flying the long featureless stretches of ocean and then of ice. The desolate landscape stretched as far as the eye could see. You'd never know there was a war on, Otto thought.

"Man, I'd hate to have to land on a glacier," Bob said, echoing Otto's thoughts.

"Yeah, if you managed to land in one piece, you'd have to survive the deep freeze."

"Glad we had arctic survival classes. Although I don't know what we'd do in a blizzard."

"Huddle inside the plane and hope someone comes to get us, I suppose."

"If there's enough of the a/c left to huddle in."

"Do you have less than full confidence in my ability to crash land this beast, co-pilot?"

They both laughed.

The 1550-mile leg to Reykjavik took seven hours, and it was with relief that Otto put the *Mata Maria* down on the runway there. The crew piled out of the bomber. Otto turned it over to the crew chief. "Number four seems to be running a little rough."

"I'll check it out, Lieutenant," the sergeant answered.

The crew stumbled into the reception room, where they dispersed to their quarters overnight. "Breakfast is at 0700 hours," the officer on duty told them.

"Is that Icelandic Frozen Time?" Cousins piped up. No one paid him any attention.

With his officers settled in the transient officers' quarters, Otto prepared for bed and lay under the blankets with the light on. He didn't feel like reading. He thought that they were drawing close to the real thing, and he hoped he was prepared for what would meet them. He kept coming back to feeling responsible for his crew and prayed he was up to the challenge. He fell asleep to dreams of desolate white spaces.

***

The crew gathered in the mess hall the next morning with several other crews who had arrived the evening before. No one said much. They were all thinking of the hours of transit time that lay ahead of them. Apparently there had been a marathon poker game going on the whole flight to that point. Otto didn't want to know how much money was involved.

The ten men gathered their gear and walked to the flight line where the *Mata Maria* stood covered with frost. The ground crew had brought a warmer in under each engine. Otto signed off on the crew chief's form. "We got the roughness out of number four," the chief told him.

"Thank you, sergeant," Otto told him and climbed up to his takeoff position. The engines started readily and Otto thanked God once again that they had not been posted to the Aleutians. *Mata Maria* rolled to the end of the runway, held while Bob ran the engines up and then, with a word from the control tower, took off into the morning sun, headed for England, 1865 miles and eight hours away.

King's precise navigation put them exactly where they wanted to be, at the airfield in Valley, Wales. From there, they loaded on a train for London and then were driven from there seventy-five miles to the home field of the 34th Bomb Group in Mendlesham, on the northeast coast of East Anglia, a few miles from the English Channel and less than 100 miles from the continent. They were finally where they could do what they had trained for. Still, Otto couldn't keep a whole flock of butterflies from inhabiting his stomach. Training was one thing, practice missions were one thing, but soon they would encounter the real thing. He hoped they were up to the challenge.

***

The crew jumped out of the truck that had brought them up from London. The air base was strangely quiet. There were no aircraft on the ground, none in the air. A group of senior officers was standing on the second story of the wooden control tower, binoculars in hand, scanning the skies to the east.

"They're waiting for a mission to come back. From the time of day, it must have been one to Germany," Donovan offered. The ten men stood there, waiting with the rest of the base.

Finally, they heard a faint hum from the east. Then, one by one, the black bombers in trail appeared, one after another. Some appeared to be completely undamaged; others were missing parts of their wing or tail plane. Occasionally an engine would be feathered, although the Fortress could fly on two.

Several ships shot off red flares, meaning they had injured aboard. They landed first, and fire trucks and ambulances rushed out to meet them. The rest of the bombers came in one by one. Otto didn't know how many had gone out, so he had no idea of how many were lost. His stomach tightened at the thought that soon he and his crew would be on one of those bombers, either making their way back, perhaps undamaged, perhaps torn up but still flying…or they could be one of those shot down, either parachuting to capture and imprisonment or not escaping the Fort's death spiral or sudden explosion. There were so many possibilities, and he grew dizzy thinking about them.

Well, nothing to be done but find out where they would be billeted. Otto picked up his B bag and led his crew over to operations. It would probably be a while until the operations officer showed up, but they could wait. The Army was all about waiting.

Chapter 25

Set to Go—Mid-September, 1943

Dear Mata,

Well, we've been here for three weeks, and it has been training, training and more training. We must be the best-trained air force in the world, but I suppose it's for our own good. We're eager to get into the fight, but watching the bombers come back torn up or realizing that some have not come back at all tempers that eagerness somewhat. Still, this is what we have trained (there's that word again!) for.

I haven't said much about our living arrangements. About 3000 people are housed on the base, 500 of them airmen. The enlisted men live in barracks, about thirty-two to a unit, while the officers live in Nissen huts, which are rounded metal structures about thirty feet long and sixteen feet wide. Donovan and I are in a hut with four other officers, so it's not so bad. We have a coal stove in the center of the hut, and each of us has a space with a cot, underneath which we put our foot locker, and a place above the cot to hang our uniforms.

We have an ablution hut for daily bathing needs and, further away, a shower hut which we visit once a week.

I'm writing this in the ready room while the rest of the troops are out on a mission. It's so tense to wait for them to come back, to hear the first sounds of engines and then to count them as they come in one by one. Some of the ships are badly shot up. Some have wounded. Some don't come back. That's the hardest of all, not knowing what happened to them unless someone saw the aircraft explode or go down without parachutes appearing.

I don't mean to upset you. It's just the way things are here. Soon we will be joining that flight of bombers and I pray that I will always come back, and that I will, God willing, come back to you and Mama and Papa.

About time for lunch so I'll close.

Your brother,

Otto

Otto held the *Mata Maria* in a hard left turn, keeping in position with the Fort ahead of and above him. The little thirty-ship formation cruised through a spotless English sky. They were on another formation practice mission. Their instructors stressed the importance of staying in formation as a life saver. In formation, one ship could protect others. Alone, the big bombers were easy prey for German fighters. Otto prayed that he would never fall behind the formation or get separated out somehow.

This should be about the last training mission, he thought, and he in fact was itching for some real action. The formation began the long descent into the air base. One by one the bombers peeled off and landed. Otto was next to last and he brought the *Mata Maria* in for a smooth landing, taxied to the hardstand and chopped the engines.

"Next time for real," Donovan said.

"That's what I hear," Otto replied, flipping the switches as indicated on the shutdown checklist.

"You want to go with us tonight? We're going to a pub to sample British hospitality and celebrate going on combat status."

"I don't know, Bob," Otto demurred. "I need to write some letters and finish my book."

"Ah, you can do that any time. Your crew needs you."

"Well…all right."

"There's a bus leaving at 2000 hours. We'll see you then."

Donovan dropped down into the hatch. Otto as the captain of the ship was the last to leave. He walked back to their hut from the flight line. He really didn't want to go to a pub. Although the Brits were their allies, there was tension between them and the Americans. The British attitude was somewhat warranted, he thought. Some American troops acted in an arrogant manner not calculated to win friends and influence allies. But he needed to support his crew. He'd go for one drink and then turn in early. Four AM would come soon enough when they were awakened for their first combat mission.

***

Otto climbed aboard the olive drab bus precisely at 2000 hours. His crew was already in place, with a seat saved for him. The rest of the bus was overfilled, with three men crowded onto a seat meant for two. The sergeant who drove the bus got on, started the engine, and put it into gear. They started for town.

The bus made stops at several pubs. Donovan and Frederick had conducted reconnaissance, as they called it, and told the rest of the crew to get off at a seedy-looking pub called the King's Head Inn. Donovan called. "This is it, fellas! Drink up."

The crew filed through the door into the dimly lit interior. They stood for a moment waiting for their eyes to adjust to the darkness. Otto became aware the pub was populated by about a dozen rough-looking Englishmen. Donovan moved forward to the bar. "I'd like a Guinness," he said.

The bartender didn't move from the other end of the bar. Men that Otto assumed were regulars moved away from them, leaving the Americans standing in an open space.

"I said, 'I'd like a Guinness,' " Donovan called in a louder voice.

The barkeeper answered, "I suppose you would."

Donovan slapped some bills on the bar. "Does this change your mind?"

The bartender looked at the money and then at Donovan. "It does about the drink. It doesn't change my mind about you Yanks."

Otto stepped up. "We don't want to change your mind, friend. We just want to have a drink or two."

One of the men standing by the wall spoke up. "Why don't you leave and then have your drink?" The rest of the Brits laughed.

Visibly irritated, Donovan growled, "What's your problem?" He was asking everyone and no one.

"Our problem is that you Yanks are here."

"We're here to help."

"Yeah, and there are just three problems with that; you're oversexed, overpaid and over here."

"That's clever," Otto said. "I hadn't heard that before. Bet you had to think all day to come up with that." He thought, we've worked too hard to be here to put up with this.

"You calling me stupid?"

"You said it: I didn't."

The fliers instinctively moved into a ring, facing out and raised their fists.

"Look, we don't want any trouble," Otto said, feeling the situation escalating out of control.

"Well, leave."

"We will," Donovan said. "You don't deserve being saved from the Germans."

"Go have some tea," one of the regulars called.

"Kiss my ass!" shouted Briscoe, and then they were through the door onto the street.

"Let's find another place," Donovan told the group.

"I'm going to walk back to base," Otto said. "I've lost my thirst. You guys be careful and I'll see you in the morning."

The crew walked off down the street. Otto turned in the direction of the base. He normally had a good sense of direction and walked slowly down the wet streets. The cobblestones were hard to see with the blackout, but his eyes soon adjusted to the surface. He thought of all he and the crew had been through to get to this point. It was a slap in the face to be rejected by those they had come to help. But he had heard of some pretty big fights between hot-headed G.I.'s and equally hot-headed natives, and they certainly didn't need that.

As he walked on, he thought about Mata and Mama and Papa. It would be about 3 o'clock in the afternoon at home, and they would be ready to start afternoon chores. Suddenly he thought of Betty and wondered what she was doing. Probably sitting at her teller station at the bank. He thought he had handled their last meeting poorly and had started to write her several times, but thought better of it and never did.

Lost in thought, he looked up and realized he had no idea where he was. The labyrinth of old streets, in the dark, had turned him around, and he had lost his orientation. He kept walking, thinking he would find someone to ask directions from. But the streets were deserted.

Otto wandered around for half an hour, thinking he would come across something familiar, but he had not been off base and had not paid attention to the bus route. Then, far down a street, he saw the bus pull through a cross street. "Hey!" he shouted, trying to run on the uneven cobbles to catch up. The bus went on without stopping. Otto slowed to a walk and then stood there.

"You shouldn't run on cobbles, you know. You're likely to stumble."

He turned toward the voice and saw a young woman in a British Red Cross uniform. "Are you lost?" she asked.

"Yes, ma'am, I am. I'm trying to get back to the air base."

"First of all, don't call me 'ma'am': it makes me feel old. And secondly, you're headed away from the base. I'll show you how to go."

"I would appreciate that, M—Miss—?"

She put out a tiny hand. "Dodgson. Alice Dodgson, Red Cross volunteer. And you are?"

Otto shook her hand, feeling its coolness. "Otto Kerchner, second lieutenant, Eighth Air Force."

"Pleased to meet you, lieutenant."

"Likewise."

"Let's be off, then. Do you have a mission in the morning?"

"Yes."

"All the more reason to proceed with dispatch."

As he walked with her, Otto could see well enough to tell that Alice was a beautiful woman with the clear skin possessed by many British women, and regular features. The top of her head came up to his shoulder, and she wore her brown hair in a fashionably short cut.

"So, what's a girl like you doing wandering around at this time of night?"

"I could very well ask you the same thing."

"I went with some buddies to a pub and we received a less than hospitable welcome so I left to walk back."

"And I got off duty and am going home."

"Doesn't it worry you to walk alone through here?"

Alice laughed, a melodious silvery laugh. "I've lived here all my life. I know practically everyone, so there's no problem."

"I see. Hey, it just occurred to me that your last name is the same as Lewis Carroll's real name. If he had married Alice, her name would have been yours."

"Well, fancy that! An American who knows British literature. We're distantly related to Mr. Dodgson, although he never married, as you probably know."

"Yes. *Alice in Wonderland* is one of my favorite books."

"Mine, too."

They walked on in silence for a while.

"Are you a reader, Alice?"

"Yes, anything I can get my hands on. You?"

"Same thing."

"Look," she said. "We're coming up to the base." Otto saw that they were approaching the flight line. "Well, I'll leave you here. I'm sure you know where you are now."

"I'll be fine. Thank you for your help."

"It was nothing. Glad to help an ally."

Alice offered her hand. Otto shook it and she started to walk away, saying "Ta ta for now."

"Good-bye, Alice." Otto stood there wishing he had asked if he could see her again. She was attractive and a good conversationalist. He could tell.

"In the words of the song, 'we'll meet again.' You'll see me at some point, I'm sure," she called back over her shoulder.

He walked around the flight line area to reach the road that separated it from the living and administrative buildings. He crossed the road easily with its light traffic and presented his ID to the M.P. at the gate.

"Good evening, sir," the M.P. said.

"Good evening, sergeant," Otto returned, and made his way to his hut. He got ready for bed and read a little Shakespeare. He kept thinking of Alice and hoped he would see her again soon. He turned out the light and was fast asleep when Donovan and Frederick came in.

Chapter 26

First Blood—Late September, 1943

Otto was flying. He held the stick of the J-2 he had learned on, high above the autumn Wisconsin fields. He flew toward the sun, and all was golden—the air, the fields, the sun low on the dawn horizon. He smiled, completely relaxed as the little engine pulled him along.

He felt a hand on his shoulder, which didn't make sense because he was flying solo. A voice came to him: "Wake up sir. Time to get up."

Otto opened his eyes not to a golden morning but the dimly lit interior of his hut. Mission time. It was the real thing this time.

He went to the ablution hut and stumbled through the 4 A.M. darkness with other shadowy forms. He couldn't tell who anyone was until they got inside the lit interior of the hut. He saw Donovan just ahead of him. "Bob! When did you get in?"

Donovan rubbed his eyes. "About 2 A.M. Too late. Christ, I feel like hell."

"Can you fly?"

"Oh, yeah, I can fly."

He and Donovan washed and shaved at a long line of sinks where other airmen were doing the same thing. No one spoke.

Otto finished and went back, dressed and headed for the mess hall, Donovan walking silently beside him. They came into the warm steamy space of the mess hall and loaded up their plates. One thing, Otto thought, we'll fly with full stomachs. The mission would take about five hours, and they would have sandwiches but he wanted to load up before they left. He hoped he wouldn't lose it all from nerves.

He and Donovan ate quickly and then headed for the ops building where they would receive their briefing. About 200 officers filed into the wooden structure and took seats on wooden benches. Precisely at 0500 hours, Colonel Rackham strode on stage, followed by his aides. The officers sprang to attention. Rackham gave them a dismissive wave of his hand. "At ease. Be seated."

"Today's mission," he began, "should be an easy one. It's right over in France and we expect minimal flak and fighters. You'll be targeting a rail yard. Good luck and good flying."

Navigators stayed for weather briefing while the rest of the officers went outside to take a brief break. Many of them lit cigarettes and stood around in small groups. Otto noticed once again there was very little conversation.

Donovan said quietly, "There's the rest of the crew." They were standing about thirty yards off, smoking and stamping their feet to ward off the early chill.

Otto and Donovan walked over. "Good morning, guys," Otto said and was greeted by a variety of responses, including grunts and lifted hands. "Ready to fly?"

This time the crew mumbled assent. "Do you think this is going to be as easy as they say it will, Lieutenant?"

"I hear the intel on that's pretty good, but we'll have to be sharp anyhow."

The navigators started coming out of the briefing room. King joined them and they walked over to their jeep. Somehow they managed to cram ten men onto one jeep. Otto took the passenger seat; Donovan drove. "You know how to drive this thing, Bob?" he asked.

"It's only got one engine and it doesn't get off the ground. Piece of cake." Donovan threw the jeep into gear, and they lurched forward, the men on the back holding on for dear life.

The flight line was shrouded in mist, but it lifted quickly as the sun came up. Donovan stopped in front of the *Mata Maria*. The crew climbed out and, one by one, took their stations in the aircraft. Otto signed off with the crew chief and pulled himself through the hatch. Donovan was already strapped in the left seat, looking over the checklist. Otto slid into the right seat.

"Let's do it," he said. He and Donovan ran through the checklist.

Donovan called each item and Otto answered in a kind of litany.

"Form 1 A?"

"CHECKED!"

"Controls and Seats?"

"CHECKED!"

"Fuel Transfer Valves and Switch?"

"OFF!"

"Intercoolers?"

"Cold!"

And so on down through the items on the list. Donovan called, "Preflight?"

"Complete!" Otto answered, and pushed his throat mike. "All right, crew, engine start is coming up. Preflight stations, everyone." The replies came back:

"Nav, here."

"Nose, check."

"Flight, yeah."

"Radio, roger."

"Waist one, I'm here."

"Waist two, likewise."

"Ball here."

"Tail present and accounted for, sir!"

Otto sighed. Why did he have a bunch of clowns for a crew? Still, they were a good one, and he supposed that he had to expect some monkeying around.

Donovan fired up the inboard engines. The aircraft next to them pulled forward and turned onto the taxiway. They followed and held as the

Fort in front of them turned onto the runway, held, ran up each engine and started its takeoff roll.

"We're next," Otto said, thinking, could I say anything more obvious? *Mata Maria* surged with the power of the four Wright engines. Bob and Otto ran them up, studying their instruments.

"Engineer here, everything looks good. Let's roll," came Frederick's voice through the intercom.

"Crew, prepare for takeoff!" Otto called as he advanced the throttles and released the brakes. Fully loaded, *Mata Maria* started her takeoff roll slowly, then more and more quickly as the broken white center line disappeared with growing rapidity under the nose.

"Rotate!" called Donovan at ninety-five knots, and Otto pulled back on the wheel. They were airborne.

Otto climbed out, following the previous bomber to the holding area where they would join up. The sky was a perfect blue, and the yellow sun hung low over the horizon. It would have been a great day for flying were it not for a few flak cannons and fighters who were aching to spoil it for them.

Otto realized he was concentrating on the mission too much to be nervous. *Mata Maria* joined the other planes in formation. When they were all assembled, the flight of twenty "boxes" of ten planes each headed for the coast, not far away. They crossed the Channel at 20,000 feet and climbed to their operational altitude of 30,000. Otto had ordered the crew on oxygen at 10,000 and had the gunners test their weapons. Even with a mask on, he could smell the reek of cordite as the chatter of machine guns echoed through the ship. The guns fell silent and the armada of aircraft droned on to the coast.

"Stay alert, crew," Otto said into the intercom. "We're feet dry and that's enemy territory down there." Again stating the obvious, he thought.

"Waist one, I've got a few puffs of flak off to starboard." Otto and Donovan looked off to the right, but the bursts were too far aft for them to see.

"Tail here, wish you guys could see this. The whole sky is filled with aircraft. Wow!"

"Wonder where our escort is," Donovan said.

"Top, little friends incoming, six o'clock high."

"There's your answer," Otto said.

The Mustangs wove over the formation, since they were faster than the lumbering heavies. The escorts would go all the way to the target with them since it wasn't that far into France.

"Top, I've got a couple of bandits circling out of range, nine o'clock low."

"Keep an eye on them, top. Sing out if they make a move," Otto cautioned.

"Top, wilco. Stay where you are, you stinkin' Huns."

Otto started to chide Marx for extraneous chatter but decided to let it go. They were all keyed up.

An hour later, King called, "Navigator, we're two minutes from the I.P."

"Bombardier, got it," came Detwiler's reply.

Otto flew straight and level. He could see the marshalling yards ahead with the lead bombers already dropping their loads. A few random clouds of flak exploded off to the right. His stomach tightened.

"Navigator, we're at the I.P."

"Bombardier--I have the aircraft."

Otto and Donovan took their hands off the controls. Detwiler would fly the Fort during the bombing run from his Norden bombsight.

The *Mata Maria* continued straight and level for what seemed like an eternity but which in reality was about five minutes. The aircraft lurched as Detwiler called "Bombs away!" Otto and Donovan grasped the wheels and put the plane into a turning dive to port. All the formation flying practice paid off as the aircraft in the box moved as one, making a 180 and streaking for home.

"Whew," exclaimed Donovan. "Glad that was easy."

"We're not done yet," Otto reminded him, and, on the intercom, "Stay alert on the way back, crew."

"Top, little friends coming in again."

"That's good news," Otto said.

The formation flew through the clear late morning air. The Channel soon came into view as they let down past 10,000 feet. Otto could see the base as the bombers moved into their holding pattern. When it was their turn, Donovan racked the aircraft around and followed the plane in front of them onto the runway. They taxied back to the hardstand.

"Anyone see any flares?" Otto called to the crew. These would indicate wounded aboard the airplane.

A chorus of negatives came back through the intercom.

"All right, then. We'll be parked in a minute, and we're just in time for lunch."

A chorus of cheers greeted this announcement.

Donovan swung the bomber around, set the brakes and cut the engines. The crew assembled outside the aircraft, shaking hands and smiling. Otto noticed that their faces looked strained and thought, we have to do twenty-four more of these. I hope they're all this easy.

"C'mon," Briscoe said. "Let's go eat!"

"Well, that's one," Donovan said as they walked to the mess hall. "Hope they're all this easy."

"My thoughts exactly," Otto told him.

Chapter 27

Sweet Alice—Early October

"Otto," called Donovan. "You going to the dance?"

Otto looked up from his book. They didn't have a mission the next day, so it was a nice chance to relax and read. They would fly mission number three in a couple of days. So far, so good—they had come through without a scratch. But it was early to assume it would always be that way.

"What dance?" he asked absently.

Donovan sat on the edge of the bed. "The USO dance! They're bringing in Glenn Miller!"

"Who's Glenn Miller?"

"My friend, you spent entirely too much time with the cows on the farm. Glenn Miller is the heppest jive cat around. His sounds are over the moon. You know, 'Moonlight Serenade' and 'In the Mood.'"

"Sometimes I think you don't speak English, Donovan. I have heard of those songs." He and Betty had danced to them, but he hadn't paid much attention to the orchestra. "I'd rather read."

Donovan pulled the book out of Otto's hands and held it out of his reach. "C'mon, son, you need to get out some. All you do is fly and read."

Otto grabbed unsuccessfully for the book. "I like flying and reading."

"Well, now you'll like this. There are going to be Red Cross girls there."

Otto perked up. "British or American?"

"What does it matter? They're *women!* Hubba hubba!"

"Tell you what, Donovan, I'll go if you stop using strange language."

"You got it, my man. Let's go."

It seemed as if everyone on the base was headed for the hangar where the band had set up. Some were watching and listening; some had chosen partners from the women scattered through the crowd and were lindy hopping to "In the Mood." Otto scanned the crowd. The ratio of men to women was about ten to one.

"Hey there, lieutenant, care to dance?"

Otto turned around and there stood Alice, resplendent in a blue dress. He momentarily couldn't speak. After a few seconds, he found his voice as she studied him with those brilliant green eyes.

"Alice! Aren't I the one who's supposed to ask *you* to dance?"

She bowed her head slightly. "Ask away."

"May I have this dance?"

"You may, leftenant."

Just then the orchestra went into "Moonlight Serenade." Otto took Alice by the hand and led her to the small dance floor in front of the band. She slipped into his arms and they moved as if they had been dancing together all their lives.

"Where have you been?" Otto asked her.

"Oh, around. I've been here."

"I haven't seen you."

"Maybe you didn't look hard enough. So, have you gotten lost any more?"

"No—I have a navigator to show me the way."

She laughed. "You looked pretty desperate the first time I met you the other night. I felt sorry for you."

I don't feel sorry for me right now, Otto thought.

"Do you live in town?"

"Yes. I live with my dad and mum not too far from the base. We've lived here for generations. It was a nice little town until the war came and brought all you Americans in."

"Do all British girls have sharp tongues like yours?"

She laughed again. "We just tell the truth. We don't skirt around it like you Americans do."

"All right, truce then. Let's not fight the War of 1812 all over again."

"Agreed," she said, and they danced in silence for a while, listening to the strains of the music. The song finished and they parted and applauded. The band went into "The White Cliffs of Dover."

Alice moved back into a clinch with Otto. They had danced a few steps when Otto felt a tap on his shoulder. A huge lieutenant towered over both of them. "Cutting in," he said.

Alice looked at him calmly. "Maybe later, buster. Not now." The lieutenant walked off.

"Why'd you do that?" Otto asked.

"Because I want to dance with *you*," she said, wrinkling her nose. They danced on.

The show went on for about an hour. Otto and Alice danced every dance. At the end, the orchestra reprised "White Cliffs of Dover."

> *There'll be bluebirds over*
> *The white cliffs of Dover*
> *Tomorrow, just you wait and see*

Otto sang along with the song as he and Alice danced close to each other. She looked up at him. "You dance better than you sing," she laughed.

"I know," he admitted. "Someone else told me the same thing once."

"A girl back in the States?"

"Yes."

"Your girlfriend?"

"More like a friend."

"Yes, I see."

The song ended; the couples applauded and everyone started to drift off.

"I enjoyed dancing with you," Otto told Alice.

"Yes, you're quite a good dancer."

"Thank you."

"Will you see me home? That is, if you think you can find your way back."

"I'll count on some nice British girl helping me find the way."

Alice laughed. "If you're lucky, leftenant. If you're lucky."

They walked along the cobbled streets, wet with rain which had fallen while they were at the dance. Alice lived about fifteen blocks down the High Street and a couple of blocks east. Otto knew that he could find his way back easily. Alice was in a reflective mood as she walked along holding Otto's arm.

"So, what was your life like before the war?" she asked.

"I grew up on a dairy farm, so I spent a lot of time around cows."

"Did you like that?"

"Not at all. I wanted to fly at an early age. An airport went in next to the farm and I spent my free time hanging around there. One thing led to another and I got a job there and learned to fly."

"Is that typical of American pilots?"

"I don't know. Things just fell into place for me."

"Do you still enjoy flying?"

"There's not much time on a mission to think about whether I like it or not. There are moments of beauty but also times of sheer terror. We've had two missions. We need twenty-five to be rotated back home. That's a lot of missions."

Alice was silent for a moment. "Are you ever frightened on a mission?"

"I'd be lying if I said I wasn't but I keep it under control by thinking about how I can protect my crew and my airplane. It's worked out well so far, but I think it's a matter of luck. Or divine protection. I'm not sure which." Otto stopped for a second. "Now it's my turn to ask you some questions."

"Fair enough."

"How long have you been in the Red Cross?"

"Since 1940. A lot of girls signed up after the Battle of Britain. It was a way we could serve, and of course Her Majesty Elizabeth joined up as well."

"What did you do before that?"

"I was in school: what did you expect?"

Otto was silent for a moment. "I'm sorry," she said. " I didn't mean to be short with you. It's just that the past three years have been terribly difficult with food and everything else rationed. I think we Brits tend to say what we're thinking anyhow and sometimes it comes out harder than I intended. I am fond of you already and really hope we can be friends."

"I bet you have a lot of guys wanting to be your friend."

"Not as many as you would think. I'm on the plain side."

"Now, come on, Alice, you're no Jane Eyre."

"Well, aren't you literary, leftenant? I'll take that as a compliment."

"I meant it as one. I think you're beautiful."

"Well, thank you. I suppose I'll do in a pinch, but if you pinch me, I'll slap you. Here's my house."

They stopped in front of a yellow two-story with flower boxes on all the windows. "I'll say my good-bye here. Thank you for a lovely evening."

They stood there for a moment, reluctant for the evening to end.

"I'd like to see you again," Otto said.

"I'm conveniently at the base in the afternoon dealing doughnuts and coffee to the returning airman," Alice said.

"I've never seen you," Otto told her.

"I don't think you ever came in. We're in the mess hall."

"To tell the truth, I never wanted doughnuts and coffee after a mission. I might be starting to develop a taste for them, though."

'I'll be there the day after tomorrow. I'll see you then. We can have tea afterward."

"Well, how very British! Pip, pip, cheerio!"

"You are such a Yank, Otto," Alice smiled. She moved toward him and kissed him on the lips. Otto staggered backward with surprise and then returned the kiss. After a while, she broke away, saying, "I have to go in." She took a key out of the pocket of her coat, opened the door and hesitated. "Good night, dear Otto, and thank you for a wonderful time."

"Good night, sweet Alice," Otto said as she disappeared. He started his way back, feeling not so much that he walked as he floated above the ground. What a wonderful girl—young woman. The future looked brighter suddenly. Now all he had to do was survive the next mission. And the ones after it.

***

Otto searched the crowded mess hall crammed with fliers after the mission. This one had not been so bad, and they were back in five hours. He finally spotted Alice handing coffee out at a table off to one side. He shouldered his way through the crowd and approached her table. She had her eyes down and absently held out a coffee cup in his direction. He took it and then took her hand. Her eyes flashed up, and then she recognized him. "Otto! So good to see you! I'll be done in half an hour and we can go out then."

"I'll change out of my flight clothes and be back in half an hour."

"All right. See you in a bit."

He rushed back to the hut and changed in record time. As he came into the mess hall, he saw most of the troops had left. A thin lieutenant stood talking to Alice. She did not appear to be enjoying his attentions. She looked at Otto with relief. "Here's my date. Are you ready to go, darling?"

"I'm all ready for you, sweetheart," Otto returned. The lieutenant slunk away, disappointment on his face.

Alice and Otto walked through the living area, across the road and by the flight line. They crossed the street into the town.

"May I say you look very beautiful in your uniform?"

Alice smiled and took his hand. "And you in yours, leftenant."

Otto pulled on the bill of his hat. "Thank you, ma'am."

They soon came to a somewhat neglected looking tea shop called "The Tea Shoppe."

"Imaginative name," Otto opined as they walked in.

"Oh? How are you at naming things?"

"Well, about the only thing I've named is my aircraft."

"What's it called?"

"*Mata Maria.*"

"Is that your girlfriend's name?"

"It's a combination of my sister's name and my mother's."

Alice grew serious. "How was the mission today?"

"Not bad. Of course, it can be a good mission for everyone else and a bad day for you. It was a good day, I'm happy to say."

"I'm happy as well."

A portly woman in a stained white apron indicated they could sit at a table near the smudged windows. "We'll have the tea, please," Alice told her.

The woman grunted, went into the back and came back a few minutes later bearing a tray holding two teacups, a teapot and an assortment of scones. She set it before them and walked away.

"Sociable, ain't she?" whispered Otto.

"I'd say," Alice replied out of the side of her mouth. "That's the mother. Usually the daughter does the serving and she's simply lovely. I don't know where she is. Here, let me pour."

She took the teapot and deftly poured two cups full of the tawny amber liquid. She handed one to Otto. "Now to have a proper tea, we must converse on matters of the mind. Or gossip if we can't think of any."

Otto put sugar in his cup and squeezed a lemon into it. "Well, we can talk about literature. What about poetry this time?"

"Oh, good. Don't you just love the Romantics?"

"Wordsworth, Keats and Shelley are some of my favorites."

Otto recited,

> *"I wander'd lonely as a cloud*
> *That floats on high o'er vales and hills,*
> *When all at once I saw a crowd,*
> *A host, of golden daffodils;*

> *Beside the lake, beneath the trees,*
> *Fluttering and dancing in the breeze."*

Alice clapped her hands, "Lovely!" she said. "Do you know more?"

"I have quite a few memorized, but I don't want to bore you. Why don't we talk for a while and then I'll recite some more."

"Fair enough," Alice returned, "but just one more poem. Do you ever think of a poem on a mission?"

"Funny thing," Otto told her. "I thought of one on the way back. We're too busy on the way in to think of much more than flying the aircraft. But I did think of part of one by the American poet Emily Dickinson,

> *Because I could not stop for Death—*
> *He kindly stopped for me—*
> *The carriage held just ourselves*
> *And Immortality."*

Alice let out her breath. "How keenly intelligent that is. She makes Death sound almost…cordial."

"The rest of the poem carries that out. He's a suitor taking her on an outing."

"One she won't come back from."

"I think that's why I thought of it. Death stops for so many airmen. I'm not sure it's as cordial as in Miss Dickinson's poem."

They both sat silently for a moment. "Here," Alice suddenly said. "Try a scone."

"Where are the cookies?"

"You mean the biscuits? There aren't any. It's wartime."

They sat silently for a moment. Alice said, "What you Yanks call a biscuit is entirely different, isn't it? What is a 'biscuit' across the Pond?"

"Well, it's kind of like a baked muffin, but made from dough."

Alice wrinkled her nose. "Sounds perfectly awful."

"They're great with butter and jelly. They're usually served with breakfast, though, so we wouldn't be eating them now anyhow. These scones are good."

"Glad you like them."

They smiled at each other, and Otto took her hand. "I'm glad you came to the dance the other night."

She smiled. "To tell the truth, I don't usually go to the dances. I went hoping I'd see you there."

"I wasn't planning on going. My co-pilot persuaded me. I was so glad to see you again."

"I think we make a great couple. You're different from the other Americans I've known."

Otto sat still for a moment. "In the words of that famous philosopher, Popeye the Sailor Man, 'I yam what I yam.'"

Alice laughed again. "On that note, I think we should leave. I need to go help my mum with the grocery shopping."

"I'd like to meet your parents some time," Otto said, helping Alice with her coat.

"You will, Otto. Why don't you come over Friday evening about six and have dinner with us? It won't be much, but it would give you a chance to meet my parents and for them to meet up."

"All right," Otto said as they reached her house. "See you then."

She kissed him, and this time he responded eagerly. "Be careful and come back to me."

"I will," he said.

Chapter 28

Building Time—Early February, 1944

Otto and Donovan walked wearily from the hardstand where the *Mata Maria* was parked. One more mission down, Otto thought. Number eighteen. Seven more to go. Maybe. There seemed to be the same superstition as in baseball that you didn't say aloud how many were left, be it missions or outs.

Otto was glad he was having dinner with Alice that evening. It would be a welcome change from the all-male company he kept all the time. He found his thoughts slipping to her and had to force himself to concentrate on the mission. She was so easy to relate to. It was as if they had known each other all their lives. She was like, well, she was like Betty in that respect. He wondered briefly what Betty was doing and then thought that he didn't care.

He and Donovan went back to barracks and took a nap. Donovan got up to wash for dinner. "You ready to go?" he asked Otto.

"I've got a date."

"That British girl?"

"Yep."

"She's a looker, all right."

"She's a very nice girl, Bob."

"Right-o," Donovan, gave him a half salute, and went off in the direction of the mess hall. Otto made his now-familiar way to the little yellow house. He stopped by a flower shop on the way and bought a bouquet of mixed flowers. He got to the door and knocked twice.

There was the sound of feet coming to the door, and Alice opened it, smiling radiantly as she saw him. She was wearing an apron. "Otto, come in. I'll put these in water. They're *lovely*."

Otto stood in a small vestibule. "Come on in and meet Mum and Dad." He followed her to a small living room with a sofa and an overstuffed chair facing a large radio.

"Mum, Dad, this is Lieutenant Otto Kerchner, the friend I've been telling you about."

Otto shook hands with Mrs. Dodgson and then with Mr. Dodgson, murmuring words of introduction. They all sat down.

"So, Alice tells us you're a pilot," said Mr. Dodgson.

"Yes," Otto told him. "Eighth Air Force, B-17."

"Grand outfit, I hear. I was with the Grenadiers in the Great War. Bloody mess, that."

Mrs. Dodgson cleared her throat, and Mr. Dodgson looked contrite. "Sorry, didn't mean to offend anyone."

"I'll see if the roast is done," Alice said, going into the kitchen.

"So, young man, what part of the States are you from?"

"I'm from Wisconsin, sir, a little town called Pioneer Lake."

"So, what do you think of Britain?"

"To be quite honest, I think it rains a lot."

For some reason, this struck Alice's father as funny, and he roared with laughter, slapping his knee and growing very red in the face. Alice came in to see why he was laughing.

"We're ready to eat. What's so funny?"

"The rain in the British Isles," Mr. Dodgson said, wiping his eyes.

They all crowded around the dining room table. Otto watched Alice as they ate and the conversation flowed around them. He was content to listen and didn't say much. When they had finished, they adjourned to the living room where Alice and Mrs. Dodgson served tea. They listened to the BBC News and then Mrs. Dodgson stood up. "We old people need to go to bed, but you young folks stay up as long as you like."

Otto stood up as they said their good nights and went up the stairs. He sat on the sofa with his arm around Alice. They watched a large lump of coal burn in the fireplace.

"My parents like you," she told him.

"How do you know?"

"You're not loud and pushy like some Americans and you're very polite."

"That's good to know," Otto said, "because I intend to see a lot of their daughter."

They fell asleep sitting together on the couch. Otto woke up as the coal burned out and a chill overtook the room. "Wow, it's 2 AM," he said. "I'd better get back to base."

Alice took both his hands. "Thank you for coming."

"Thank you for a pleasant evening." He kissed her and then she helped him on with his coat.

"Be careful, my brave pilot."

"I will, my darling," and with that he slipped out the door into the rainy streets.

Chapter 28

Day In and Day Out—Late February, 1944

Otto gripped the wheel of the *Mata Maria*. They were high over Germany and had been pounded by fighters all the way in. The Focke-Wulfs and Messerschmidts had fallen off now, but not before they had taken down two bombers in Otto's box. The remaining Forts formed up as best they could, and flew on toward flak blossoming ahead of them. Otto wondered that the formation could fly so calmly into high explosives.

The flak was "walking" right toward their formation. He hoped the Jerries had the wrong altitude setting, but it didn't look like it. Just then, an errant falk burst caught the ship to starboard in the bomb bay. The aircraft exploded, and Otto heard the metallic ping of shrapnel from the hapless craft hit the fuselage.

"Holy sh—!" came over the intercom. Normally he would have called down the crew member who said that, but those were his sentiments as well. Suddenly he felt weary and sick but he kept her straight and level. A hymn from his boyhood came to him.

> *Ein' feste Burg ist unser Gott,*
> *Ein gute Wehr und Waffen;*
> *Er hilft uns frei aus aller Not,*
> *Die uns jetzt hat betroffen.*
> *Der alt' böse Feind,*
> *Mit Ernst er's jetzt meint,*
> *Gross' Macht und viel List*
> *Sein' grausam' Ruestung ist,*
> *Auf Erd' ist nicht seingleichen.*

"A mighty Fortress is our God…" He hadn't thought of the hymn in years. Here he was in a Fortress flying above Germany. God help us all, he thought.

"One minute to the I.P.," came King's voice over the intercom. Then, from Detwiler, "I have the aircraft."

Otto and Donovan took their hands off the controls, waiting for the familiar lurch as the bombs fell away. Donovan grabbed the wheel as soon as they felt the aircraft lighten and put the Fort into a steep turning dive to port. "Time to get out of Dodge," he remarked grimly.

Then it was back through the flak and the fighters, with several more ships downed in front of them. The gunners kept up an incessant fire. As the Channel approached, Espinosa called in. "Waist two, Cousins has puked in his mask."

Otto keyed the intercom. "Get him out and get him cleaned up. Is he choking?"

There was a delay while the other gunners got the ball out of the turret.

Espinosa came on again. "No, sir, he's not choking but he does look green…we got him. I think he's OK"

Thank goodness we're over the Channel, Otto thought as the ship lowered toward a landing. They circled and waited their turn and landed after the aircraft bearing wounded had touched down. There were a lot of them.

Donovan parked the big bomber and shut the engines down. "Rough one," Otto said.

"You got that right," Donovan agreed and flipped the switches on the checklist.

The crew jumped out of the Fort and walked around it, looking at the bullet holes in the skin. Otto stopped counting at 100. Cousins fell to his knees and was sick again.

"Cousins, are you OK?"

The ball gunner shook his head. "I don't think I can take this any more. Can you get me out of it, Lieutenant? I can't take it." He dissolved in tears. Espinosa came over and put his arm around his shoulders.

"We're here with you, buddy. Let's get you to the infirmary and get something for that stomach." He and Adams helped him to his feet and headed off to the medic hut. The rest of the crew watched them go.

"Well, that was number twenty. Is it bad luck to say how many we have left?" said Donovan.

No one answered. They shouldered their kits and started walking back to quarters.

Chapter 29

Come Live with Me and Be My Love— Mid-March, 1944

Otto was whistling as he got dressed. Donovan was sprawled on his bunk reading a letter from his wife.

"How are things at home?" Otto asked.

"Just fine…three weeks ago," Donovan answered. "Another date with Alice? Man, this must be serious."

"Yes, we're going out for dinner. There's apparently one good place in town and that's where we're going."

"Have a good time. Be home by midnight."

"Right," said Otto. "No mission tomorrow, so I might not come home at all."

"You dog," Donovan joked, and threw a shoe at Otto.

Otto ducked and went out the door. He continued whistling as he walked to Alice's house, carrying the canned ham he had liberated from the mess hall. He felt bad that he continued to eat at Alice's house when he knew they were using their ration points to feed him. The ham was a little hostess gift.

He knocked on the door and Alice answered dressed in a fabulous blue dress. Otto whistled. "Hello, Miss Dodgson."

She struck a pose. "Come on in, airman. I changed my mind and decided to cook for us here. My parents have gone to London to visit my aunt who's not feeling well."

This is my lucky day, Otto thought. He handed the ham to her. "A little gift for you from the people of the United States."

Alice took the ham. "Thank them for me, will you?"

"I will." He walked through the door, immediately embraced her, and kissed her passionately for a long time. After a while, she pushed him back and said, "Not so fast. I have a roast in the oven."

"Let it burn," Otto murmured, kissing her neck. She pushed him away decisively.

"Go sit in the living room and calm down. Dinner's almost ready."

"I hear and obey," Otto told her and sat on the sofa.

"Do you fly tomorrow?" Alice called from the kitchen.

"No, we don't."

Alice had put flowers on the table and lit candles as darkness fell. Otto thought how the candlelight lit her features with a soft golden glow. As they are, they talked of inconsequential matters. When they finished, she stood up and took his hand.

"Come with me," she said. She led him to the downstairs bedroom which he assumed was hers, turned to him, and started unbuttoning his shirt. "I've waited a long time for this," she whispered.

He reciprocated by unbuttoning the buttons down the front of her dress. He shrugged out of his shirt and stood there, bare-chested. She let her dress drop, lifted the straps to her slip from her shoulders and let it fall to the floor.

"Come to me," she said, holding out her arms. And he did.

***

The next morning, they were awakened by sunlight coming in the window. Alice stretched and yawned. "Good morning, my love," Otto said.

"Oh—I didn't know you were awake—good morning, *my* love."

"Thank you for last night. And I forgot to thank you for a lovely meal."

"You're welcome. And now the whole day is ours. What shall we do?"

"I have some plans," Alice said. "But let's get dressed first."

A few minutes later they sat down at a huge breakfast Alice had fixed. "I thought we could relax here for a while and then visit some bookstores and have a picnic in the park. Have you ever been to the park?"

"I haven't seen much of the town except for a few pubs and the buildings between here and the base."

"Very good, then: I'll give you a tour."

"Sounds good. First, though, let's relax some more." He drew her to him.

***

"Look, Alice! Look at this copy of *Bleak House.*" Alice had disappeared around a corner in the tiny book shop they had stopped in. She looked at it with a practiced eye.

"I wouldn't pay that much for it."

"I don't even know how much it is. I can't figure out pounds and shillings and pence." Otto put the book back. "Have you done enough looking? I'm getting hungry."

"It is quarter to twelve. Let's go back by my place and get our picnic stuff."

"Sounds good."

They walked back through the rain-dampened cobbled streets holding hands.

"'You know," said Otto, "I haven't been on a picnic since the senior picnic in high school. As a family we weren't much given to eating outside. That might have been because we spent so much time outside."

"Well, I hope you like what I fixed. I have some ham sandwiches, some fruit, and some wine I think you'll like."

He gave her a hug. "Whatever you have will be great. Say, tell me what is Mendlsham's claim to fame?"

"Not much. It's old but not as many things happened here as happened in Ipswich. There was an old silver crown they found in the seventeenth century, and a gold ring that turned up in the eighteenth.

Supposedly, we were once the residence of Redwald, a king of the East Angles."

"That all so sounds so ancient."

"We do have plenty of history."

They had reached her house by then. She ducked in and came out quickly, carrying a picnic basket and a blanket. "Here—if you'll carry the basket, I'll take the blanket. The park's not far, in this direction."

They walked on in silence and soon came upon a smallish patch of green with a pond near its center. "Here we are!" exclaimed Alice, spreading the blanket on the ground. Otto put the basket on it and helped her take the food out. The sun had come out after the rain, warming things up nicely.

They arranged their meal between them, and Otto leaned over and kissed Alice. "Thank you," she said.

"No, thank *you.*" They both laughed at this exchange and started eating.

"Do you fly tomorrow?"

"Yes. It's our twenty-first mission. I've heard rumors it's going to be a tough one."

"How do you do it?"

"How do I do what?"

"Go out and do something so dangerous?"

"I look on it as a job. We're all doing our jobs so we can go back home again and resume our lives."

"And how does the rhetoric enter into it, you know, fighting for democracy and against oppression and all that?"

"That's part of it, but I think we're more motivated by looking out for each other. You're fighting for ideals, but you're also fighting and doing your job so everyone gets back safely. Although lately I'm more motivated by coming back to you."

"How sweet. I love you, Otto."

"I love you, Alice." They kissed tenderly.

"I have a poem for you since you have recited so many for me."

"Yes?"

"It was written by a pilot, John Gillepsie Magee, an American who joined the RCAF to get into the war. He died in a mid-air collision in 1941.

"It's called, 'High Flight.'

Oh! I have slipped the surly bonds of Earth
And danced the skies on laughter-silvered wings;
Sunward I've climbed, and joined the tumbling mirth
of sun-split clouds, —— and done a hundred things
You have not dreamed of—— wheeled and soared and swung
High in the sunlit silence. Hov'ring there,
I've chased the shouting wind along, and flung
My eager craft through footless halls of air....

Up, up the long, delirious, burning blue
I've topped the wind-swept heights with easy grace.
Where never lark, or even eagle flew ——
And, while with silent, lifting mind I've trod
The high untrespassed sanctity of space,
Put out my hand, and touched the face of God."

Otto did not speak for a few seconds.

"Do you like it?" Alice asked.

"It's something…I've felt the same way myself, when you're up there and there are split seconds where you aren't thinking about the mission and you're aware that, somehow, you're very close to God. I wish I could explain it better."

"No, I understand."

They finished eating, packed the remains of their lunch and stood up.

Just before they were ready to walk off, Alice took Otto's hand. "I have something to tell you."

He looked at her quizzically. "Yes?"

"Please sit down." They sat back down on the blanket. Otto took both her hands. She looked at him directly.

"You should know I was married before."

"Yes?"

"He was an RAF pilot who was shot down in the Battle of Britain. We were both so young—I was only 16, probably too young, but he was so handsome and dashing. It has been a horrible three years, but then you came along. You were somehow different, and my heart was yours the first time I saw you wandering around lost and soaked to the skin."

Otto gazed into her eyes. "I am so sorry for your loss."

She reached for him and held him in a tight embrace. "But now I have you."

"Yes, you do."

They stayed that way for a while. "I've got to be going," Otto said. They stood up and walked quietly back to the house.

"Can you come in?" Alice asked.

"I'm sorry, I have to get back to base. I have a twenty-four hour pass. So I'll just say so long for now."

"Thank you for a wonderful time."

"It was wonderful, wasn't it? Thank you."

He kissed her one more time and then walked down the street, turning back to look before he went around the corner of a building. She was standing there, holding the basket. She lifted her hand and he raised his to her. Then he turned the corner and began walking rapidly back to base.

Chapter 30

Mission 23: 0603 hours Zulu, Late March, 1944

The sleepy men filed into the briefing room, cigarette smoke hanging in a haze above their heads. They sat silently in the rows of folding chairs, either too sleepy or too preoccupied to talk. This was the beginning of a process that would, at the end of the day, either bring them back to base or have them prisoners of the Germans, or worse. Much worse.

Colonel Rackham stepped into the room and onto the stage, followed by his aides. The fliers jumped to their feet, and Rackham motioned them down with an impatient motion of his hand. He grabbed a pointer and nodded at the sergeant who stood at the pulley which moved the heavy black curtains in the front of the room. The curtains parted, revealing a long red line of tape leading deep into Germany. Groans and cat calls arose from the ranks. Rackham motioned them to silence.

"I know, men, I know. This is an important mission. We're going deeper into Germany than we've ever been before. You'll have Jugs with you all the way in and back, but expect Jerry to throw everything he has at you. Remember to keep your formations tight and cover each other. We're really taking the fight to Hitler with this one. Form up on Kerchner. Takeoff is at 0600 hours. Time hack—" he held his left wrist up, fingers poised over the buttons on his watch—"Now! Weather briefing will follow for navigators. Good flying and good luck!"

He tucked his pointer under his arm and marched off the stage. The crews again jumped to their feet, and then dissolved into a hubbub of conversation and complaints.

Otto sank back down into his chair, lost in thought. This would be the hardest mission yet, and he would be at the point, the lead bomber out of three hundred the Eighth would put into the sky this day. He and his crew had trained for a week for this role. Three hundred bombers would release their bombs when Detwiler, their bombardier, pushed the "pickle switch" on his Norden. He had a tighter feeling than usual in his stomach. He tried to push his anxiety aside and think of Alice, lovely Alice, who lay sleeping not a mile from where he sat.

He and Donovan went outside to meet up with the rest of the crew. A new member named Riley, from Boston, was the replacement for Cousins, the ball turret gunner who had invalided out with stomach ulcers. It was a wonder they all didn't have them. Riley stood stiffly at attention, holding a rigid salute. Otto waved a casual hand. "At ease, Riley, you don't have to do that."

Riley moved to the "at ease" position. Otto sighed and stood up. "Just relax, son," he said, although Riley was only about three years his junior. "I hear you're the new ball."

Riley relaxed his posture imperceptibly. "Sir, yessir, I just wanted to introduce myself. It's an honor to serve with you, sir. Scuttlebutt has it that you're the best and the luckiest pilot in the Eighth."

"Thank you, sergeant. And don't call me 'sir'. 'Lieutenant' will do."

Riley grinned. "All right, Lieutenant. The rest of the crew says they call you 'Lt. OK' because, well, you're OK Glad to be aboard, Lt. OK!"

Otto winced. "Yes, I'm aware of that, Riley, and call me that if you want on the ground. But don't use it on a mission. It gets confusing if we have nine people shouting 'OK' into the intercom. Just call me 'pilot' when we're in the air. All right?"

Riley came to attention and held another salute. "OK, Lt. OK! Will comply, sir, don't cha know?"

Otto waved a salute, dismissing Riley, who went off to find the other crew members. He sighed again, picked up his flight case and joined the last few stragglers filing out of the B-hut.

Dawn was barely breaking, illuminating the golden fields of wheat that surrounded the base. It was almost harvest time, and a slight chill hung in the air. Otto found the jeep with his crew already crowded on. He climbed in the passenger seat as the crew chorused, "Good morning, Lieutenant OK!"

"Good morning, troops," he returned and grabbed the windscreen as Donovan put the jeep in gear and lurched off toward the flight line.

The *Mata Maria* sat on the first hardstand on the flight line. The crew, headed by Sergeant D'Agostino, had finished servicing the Boeing and was standing in a rough line waiting for the flight crew. Donovan whipped the jeep around in a tight turn and killed the ignition. The nine other members of the bomber jumped out and headed for their stations. Otto went over to Aggie D'Agostino. "She's all set to go, Lieutenant. Number three was running a little rough but we got her back to spec." He handed Otto a clipboard. Otto scribbled his signature without looking at the form. Aggie ran a car repair shop in Brooklyn before the war, and there wasn't anything mechanical he couldn't fix. They shook hands and he did a quick walkaround. All was in order.

Otto lifted himself through the front hatch and made his way to the left seat. Donovan was already at work, flipping switches. He and Otto ran down the preflight checklist. Satisfied, they moved on to engine start.

Donovan punched the start button for the inboard starboard engine. The big Pratt and Whitney turned over a few times, belched a puff of white smoke and then caught, running up to its cruise setting. *Mata Maria* lurched to the right, held by wheel chocks under the main gear. Donovan punched start for the number two engine and it caught, joining its companion on the other side of the fuselage. Donovan and Otto studied the gauges. "We're good," Otto said, nodding to the crewmen on either side of the bomber, who pulled the wheel chocks out. Otto advanced the throttle on the port engine and pulled the control on the starboard to idle. The B-17 made a slow turn onto the taxiway.

They ran out to the end of the runway where a spare B-17, inboard engines turning, sat in case *Mata Maria* couldn't go. Otto caught a quick glimpse of other bombers moving out of their hardstands and onto the taxiway. They always reminded him of fat black ducks waddling along the ground. But these ducks packed a punch.

Otto turned to the set point, locked the brakes, and hit the start button for engine one, which fired and promptly ran up. He hit start for number four. It turned over two, three, four, five times and did not catch. He tried again, with the same results. A crew chief sitting in a jeep beside the replacement hustled over. "We're going to have to put you in the spare, sir. You know the rules."

Otto was already undoing his seat belt. Mission rules held that if the lead bomber couldn't go the crew had to switch to the reserve. Crews didn't like flying a spare. *Mata Maria's* crew felt theirs was a lucky bomber and they had a lucky pilot. Otto keyed his mike. "Pilot to crew. We're switching to reserve." He heard the protests and profanities before the mic cut out. Nothing to do but change.

The ten men repeated the loading process and the engines started promptly on the bomber with the red tail showing that it was a lead aircraft. Otto's call sign remained the same, and as he and Donovan stood on the brakes, he contacted ATC. "Sudbury control, this is Mike Alpha Tango Alpha, ready for takeoff."

The reply came promptly in his earphones. "Roger, Mike Alpha Tango Alpha, you are cleared for takeoff. Good luck, fellas."

"Roger that, control. Thank you." He keyed the intercom. "Crew, takeoff positions. Out."

Otto advanced the throttles to takeoff setting and as he called, "Release!" he and Donovan let off on the brakes. The big Boeing began its takeoff roll, slowly at first and then accelerating through the early English morning with increasing speed. Donovan called out the airspeeds. Otto could feel the heaviness of the aircraft and its bomb load. He saw the ambulances parked at the end of the runway.

"95!" Donovan said. "Rotate!"

Otto pulled back on the control column and the bomber pulled into the air. Donovan was on the gear lever almost as soon as they cleared the ground. The pilots could hear the main gear motors whine, followed by a solid thump from both sides as the wheels locked into place. "We have two greens on the gear," Donovan said quietly.

The bomber strained and creaked as it clawed for altitude against its load of bombs and fuel and men. The crew was uncharacteristically silent on the intercom. Otto supposed they were spooked by having to take the reserve. He would have preferred the *Mata Maria* himself, but procedure was procedure. He supposed that the Army had a procedure for everything. Not that they were always followed, especially in the Air Corps.

The lead aircraft pulled through 1,000 feet, 2,000, straining upward to its operational altitude of 30,000 feet. At 10,000, Otto ordered the crew on oxygen. The cold crept through the thin aluminum skin and he was grateful for the heated electric flight suits they all wore. Detwiler, the navigator, called out headings as Otto flew a "racetrack" in the sky to allow the other bombers to form up on him. They did this for half an hour, finally reaching their assigned altitude. One last turn, and they were headed east toward Schweinfurt and its bearing factories. They had been told to expect heavy resistance from flak and fighters.

"Tail to crew, wish you guys could see this. There are Forts from horizon to horizon. What a sight." That was Stone in the tail gunner position.

Otto heard the whir of the turret motor behind and above him as Schmidt, the top turret gunner, swiveled to the six o'clock position to look at the aerial armada. He felt the vibration of Riley's ball turret in the belly of the airplane as the new man followed suit. "Wow! Lieutenant OK, wish you could see this!"

Donovan rolled his eyes above his mask. Otto punched on the intercom, "Riley, identify yourself by position and don't use 'OK' on the horn. It creates confusion. Do it again and I'll have you busted to private." There was a long pause.

"Ball here, sorry, Lieutenant—"

"Pilot," Otto interjected.

"I mean 'pilot,'" Riley stammered. "All this is new to me."

Adams, the right side gunner called out, "Right waist, little friends, four o'clock low, P-47's." He paused, then exclaimed, "What the hell—they don't have drop tanks! What the f—"

"Someone screwed up somewhere," Otto intoned calmly, but he was not happy at the prospect of going unescorted the last part of the run. The Jugs could have gone the whole way with the tanks. Without escort, the bombers would be left vulnerable during the hairiest part of the mission. Well, what could you say besides S.N.A.F.U.?

The Channel lay far beneath them. Time to have the gunners do their test. "Gunners, weapons check," he called into the intercom. The cockpit was filled with the sounds of explosions of six pairs of .50 caliber Browning situated at several points in the aircraft, punctuated by the tinkle of shell casings hitting the floor. The stink of cordite reached his nostrils. Yep, the '17 was aptly named, all right. Flying Fortress. Still, it just took one hit from a Messerschmidt cannon or from a flak shell and they were all history.

"That's enough, gunners," he called as the firing went on a little too long. "Save it for Jerry."

The air armada bore onward toward the French coast. They could expect fighters first, particularly as they got closer to the target, then flak and then the fighters again after the bomb drop. Otto wondered how the Germans figured out where they were going. Although it was pretty hard to hide 300 bombers laying down contrails like directional signs pointing to them.

A thick cloud deck loomed over the continent. This wasn't in the plans. "Nav, this is pilot. Did the forecast include a cloud deck?"

"Pilot, nav here. No sir, broken clouds was the forecast. I see it, too, sir, and I don't like it."

I don't either, thought Otto as the flight bore on.

Chapter 31

Into the Mix—1027 hours Zulu

The cloud bank stretched from horizon to horizon.

"Nav, is there any way around this thing?

"Don't think so, sir. We can try to climb over it."

Otto debated. Going higher meant going up through the overcast. Going under it meant exposing the flight to attack. Or at least more of an attack than if they stayed at altitude. The big engines on the Forts operated best at altitude. He made a decision: they would go up and take their chances on a letdown to the target. He keyed his mic.

"Nav, I'm going to take her up. Ball, tail, top, watch to see that the flight follows."

He heard a round of "Rogers" from the stations and porpoised the aircraft to indicate a change in altitude. The flight observed radio silence at this point in the mission. Otto advanced the throttles to full military power and pulled back on the wheel. The B-17 nosed upward.

It wasn't enough. The cloud deck was building, and soon they were in a thick overcast. Damn, Otto thought.

"Pilot, tail. I've lost sight of everyone."

"Roger, tail. Thanks. Let me know if you catch sight of them again." They were somewhere beyond the front line over Nazi-occupied Europe in a cloud bank with three hundred aircraft loaded with fuel and explosives. Some days it doesn't pay to get out of bed. He considered aborting the mission by firing off a flare but knew he would have to answer to that decision. Better to press on.

Otto held his course steady, and the clouds suddenly parted to an area of clear skies. The call came from tail: "BANDITS! BANDITS! 5 O'CLOCK HIGH!" The chatter of the tail gun was joined by the top and starboard waist. He could see the nose gun swivel to the right, loosing bursts of .50 caliber shells. The Me109's tore past the bomber, tiny in comparison, moving so quickly, quickly, pulling Immelmanns and coming back toward

Otto and his crew. Generally, they avoided frontal attack, but these guys were *good,* blasting away and then peeling off just as they entered the range of the American guns. A cannon shell struck the starboard wingtip and shredded it. Otto and Donovan pulled the ship back to port and adjusted trim to compensate for the additional drag and loss of lift. As he did many times every mission, Otto thanked God for the toughness of the Forts. He had seen some limp back to base with incredible damage, a dozen feet of wing torn away, stabilizers and rudders almost completely shot up, engines charred lumps of metal. But they still brought their crews back.

"HERE THEY COME AGAIN," screamed Riley, and once again the gunners opened up. The ship shook with the recoil of thousands of shells pouring into the sky.

"Short bursts, lead your target," Otto called out, uncertain whether anyone could hear him. They knew what they were doing, but in the excitement of being shot at, they might do anything. He just hoped no bomber was within their range. There were too many cases of bombers being shot down by friendlies.

The attacks came in wave after wave for the next twenty minutes. Otto silently cursed the lack of escorts. What good was it having P-47's with drop tanks if they weren't used? Someone had screwed up, that was for certain.

As suddenly they began, the swarms of black fighters fell away. Otto called for a crew report.

"Crew, damage report," he called. The voices that came back were tense and higher pitched than usual.

"Top, right wingtip is shredded."

"Waist one, a few holes in the fuselage here and there. Nothing serious."

"Bombardier, a hole in the glazing."

That was all. Everything considered, not too bad.

Ahead, a curtain of black puffs of smoke littered the sky. Flak. That meant they were near the target. The fighters had peeled off so they wouldn't be hit by their own AA fire.

"Into the valley of death rode the ten thousand…"

It was Detwiler, the literature major. "Det, keep your Tennyson to yourself, will you?" Otto scolded.

"You got it, pilot. 'We who are about to die salute you!' "

Otto and Donovan scanned what they could see of the sky. "Tail, who's with us?" Otto called.

"Tail here. I see maybe a dozen a/c, and the formation is pretty ragged."

Otto cursed silently. The other ships were supposed to form up in order to protect each other. Maybe they would after the bomb run.

"Pilot, nav, we're at the I.P."

Flak shells began exploding on either side of them.

"Bombardier, you have the aircraft." Otto said, as he and Donovan lifted their hands from the controls. Detwiler, the bombardier, flew the aircraft from his Norden bombsite. The Fort had to fly a straight and level course for what seemed like an eternity but which was really only a matter of minutes. Otto kept his hands poised over the wheel, waiting for Detwiler's call.

The bomber jolted and slewed to the left as a flak shell punched through the wingtip on that side, exploding fifty feet up from them. Shrapnel pinged against the fuselage. Otto could see Detwiler correcting with what control he had.

The last ten feet of the port wing was gone and the number one engine was smoking. "Shut down number one," Otto called, and Donovan hit the "kill" switch on the panel to his right. The prop windmilled and stopped as Donovan feathered the blades.

Otto dialed in more trim to compensate for the damage.

"Bombs away!" Detwiler called, and the aircraft lurched upward, free of its load. The flak was so heavy that it looked like, as the saying went, Otto could have gotten out and walked on it. He grabbed the controls and firewalled the throttles on the remaining engines, diving down and to the left, headed into a U-turn that would take them away from the murderous AA all around them.

"Tail, someone's hit. They're going down." There was silence on the intercom.

"Count the chutes, tail."

More silence. Finally, "No chutes, Captain. Poor fellas couldn't get out."

The bomber rattled and shook as it was pounded by concussions from shells bursting all around.

Over the intercom: "O my God."

Otto keyed his mic, grateful that Donovan had his wheel in both hands. "What is it?"

"One of our guys took a shell in the gas tank. He just exploded. There's nothing left."

God rest their souls, Otto thought. "OK, stay alert."

The rest of the flight pulled ahead of them since they only had three engines. Otto watched grimly as the remaining ships formed up and grew smaller and smaller. Those were the rules. Don't risk your ship to cover a crippled craft.

The flak bursts grew less and less frequent, but that only meant the fighters would make another appearance, having landed, refueled and rearmed. He could see them swarming over and through the formation ahead of them and knew they would pounce on his crippled ship.

"Overspeed on number four!" shouted Donovan. He reached up and killed that engine.

Crap, Otto thought. Slower and slower. "All right, crew, we've lost two engines. Jerry's going to come after us with all he's got. Check your chutes and be prepared to bail out if I sound the horn."

Otto pulled out the flak jacket he sat on while over the target. Since most AA came up, the jacket did precious little if worn as intended. It probably wouldn't do much anyhow, but it didn't hurt to sit on it. He put it on.

He steered for a cloud bank ahead, but hadn't reached it when top sang out, "Bandits! Twelve o'clock high! Jesus! There must be thirty of 'em!"

Otto could hear shells perforating the aluminum skin of the fuselage. Detwiler called out, "Schmidt's down. I'm checking him right now."

Otto calmly replied, "You know what to do, Det."

"Roger that. He's hurt pretty bad."

Otto thought quickly that he had never had a crew member injured. Well, *Mata Maria* was a lucky ship, but they weren't flying her today. Damn the luck.

Machine gun fire rang from all stations as the Germans bore in time after time. The cloud bank was only a hundred feet away. The B-17 bucked and shook as if a giant fist has struck it. All the bullets hitting the skin sounded like a hailstorm.

"Damage report!" Otto called.

"Jesus, Lieutenant, a shell punched right through the fuselage! The hole must be three feet in diameter!"

Donovan was sweating profusely as he wrestled with the controls, which had gone mushy. Otto pushed into a gradual descent to keep from stalling. He didn't know if he could recover from one if that should happen.

Wisps of cloud closed around them and then they were in the cloud bank, safe for the time being. Now if they could avoid running into another aircraft.

All Otto and Donovan could see was gray. At least the Germans couldn't see them. The '17 kept losing altitude gradually, so Otto had some hope of making the Channel. They could bail out and be picked up by the coastal patrol. He didn't want to have his crew come down in German territory.

"Pilot, power's out to the ball. We can't get him out."

"All right, Detwiler, take the fire ax and chop him out. Be careful not to chop him up when you do."

Amidst the din of laboring engines Otto and Donovan could hear the ax ringing against the metal of the ball turret. After about five minutes, Detwiler called. "Pilot, we got him out. He's white as a ghost."

"Have him lie down. How is he?"

"Not good, sir. We need to get him some real help."

"Stick him with a styrette. We'll get this thing down as soon as we can."

"Sir," Donovan said, "Do we have enough altitude to make the Channel?"

"I don't know, Donovan. Let's pull up as much as we can. Watch for a stall."

The clouds parted and they caught a glimpse of the Channel coastline ahead. A P-47 slid in beside them. Otto pointed to his headphone and shook his head. No radio. The '47 pilot nodded and stayed just off their wingtip.

Otto made a decision. "Crew, prepare to bail out."

Donovan didn't move. "Donovan, that includes you. You stand a better chance by going into the Channel. SP will pick you up."

"What about you, Otto?"

"I'm going to bring it in. If I can."

"Sir—"

"*Move*, Donovan. That's an order!"

Donovan undid his harness and stood. He clasped Otto on the shoulder. "Good luck, Otto. See you back at base."

He went into the back where Otto could hear him arranging for a bail out order. They would send someone out with Schmidt and Riley. Maybe he should keep them on the aircraft. No, they would get medical attention more quickly if they bailed out. And landing in the water would be less rough than the crash landing he was about to make.

Chapter 32

Falling Fast—1227 hours Zulu

The Fort rattled and bucked as it came over turbulence created by the water of the Channel. Otto kept them at a thousand feet, but he was losing altitude faster than he liked. He punched the bailout horn and felt the aircraft lurch up slightly as each man jumped out the side hatch. He counted, one, two, three, four, five, six, seven...where was eight? Then he remembered that Schmidt and Riley had gone out with someone else. A good crew.

His thoughts flickered briefly to Alice and then to his mother and father and to Mata. He wrenched them back to the task at hand. Concentrate, Kerchner, concentrate. He had 35 miles to go to the airfield, and he wasn't sure he could hold it up that long. He would have to. A straight-in approach.

He had plenty of fuel since only two engines were operating, even though they were at full power. He prayed that they would hold up, scanning constantly for potential landing sites. His altitude crept down gradually. He had to be trailing smoke, and surely the Jug in formation with him had radioed ahead about his predicament.

The crew had by now been recovered from the Channel, provided they landed all right. He would find out later. The CP did an amazing job of plucking fliers out of the water.

He saw the airfield from about twenty miles out. Five hundred feet. Otto kept his hands and feet busy, right at stall speed, which was about all he could manage. He didn't have the bomb load, but he had more fuel than he wanted.

Four hundred feet. He was about fifteen miles out. Too soon to shoot the flare that would indicate to the ground that his radio was out and he was coming straight in on an emergency.

Three hundred feet. He had the controls wrenched all the way over to starboard and the big aircraft still wanted to pull to port. He was practically standing on full right rudder to keep what marginal control he had. He pulled the throttles back and the Boeing started to nose up into a stall. He rammed the levers back to full power. If the engines quit entirely it wouldn't be a pretty picture.

Farms slid by, with farmers harvesting what looked like wheat or hay. They used horses. Otto idly wondered what his mother and father and Mata were doing at this hour. It would be about 8 AM in Wisconsin, and they would have been up for hours.

Two hundred feet. He had the field in sight, straight ahead. He dropped the gear, hoping that the hydraulics weren't shot out. The light for the port gear came on. Ah, crap. No starboard gear. He'd have been better off leaving the gear up and making a belly landing. He toggled the gear switch. The light stayed on. Stuck. Crap!

One hundred feet. Time for the flare. As if they couldn't tell he was in trouble by looking at what must have been a smoking, tattered wreck.

Gott in Himmel, help me now, Otto breathed, opening the side window and sticking the flare gun out into the slipstream. He was at 100 knots. Needed to slow down to land. He popped the flare as the '17 slid off to the left. Otto dropped the flare gun outside the window and slammed his hands back on the column. The aircraft wallowed and came back to a mushy, porpoising path. He pulled the flaps lever, to no effect.

The ground rushed up to meet him. He held the plane off the ground as long as he could to bleed off speed, and felt the port gear touch. The aircraft bounced, once, twice and then he was down, jouncing along on one wheel, trying to hold the wings level as long as he could. He could see an ambulance and a fire truck rolling toward him. He chopped the throttles and braced himself.

The starboard wing quit flying and fell to the grass. The Fort wheeled around the pivot point created as the stub of the wing dug into the dirt. The field whirled dizzily by. Otto thought of the ride at the county fair which twirled riders around and around. The aircraft slid around twice. Right before it came to rest, Otto heard the sound of metal tearing. It was probably the tail breaking off. He hit his head on the instrument panel.

Half conscious, he heard an explosion from behind him and then smelled smoke. He was on fire, but he couldn't stir himself to move. He needed to undo his harness and get out, but he was sleepy…so sleepy…

The flames swept up around him. Otto closed his eyes. He did not feel the heat. He felt nothing.

Chapter 33

The White Room

He opened his eyes. He expected to feel pain from his burns, but he felt all right. All he saw was white, and at first he thought he was in a hospital ward. But no, he was standing. Somehow he was standing. As he became more aware of his circumstances, he saw that he was in a medium-sized windowless white room. There were no lights, but the walls themselves were luminous. A door stood in the wall across from him, so he went over, opened it and stepped outside.

He was in a small, carefully cultivated garden. The air was soft and fragrant with the scents of flowers he did not recognize. And there, seated at a small table with two chairs, sat his father, wearing a long white robe. He wasn't the old man Otto remembered: he looked like the pictures taken during the war. And he was smiling.

He gestured to Otto. "*Kommen Sie*, Otto. Be seated. We have much to talk about." He did not speak out loud, but Otto heard the words in his head.

Bewildered, Otto took the chair across from his father. "Papa, is that you? And is this—"

Hans put his hand on Otto's shoulder. "Yes, ist me, Otto. And this is whatever you think it is."

"It's very nice…and am I--?"

Hans shook his head. "Nein, you are not dead. Why you are here I do not know. But you must return to your life. You have much left to do."

Otto sat quietly for a moment. "And what do you do here?"

Hans laughed heartily. "I tend die Kühe, of course! It is what I do best!"

"But why do you have cows here? Do you need to eat?"

"We don't need to, but it is pleasurable, so we do it."

"This is unreal."

"I assure you, mein Kind, that this is far more real than what you call reality."

"How?"

"My cows are never sick and they never die. I have to tend them, but you know I love mein kinen. They are fed and milked."

"Milked?"

"Yes, and I cannot tell you how or why, but in doing this I enable cows in your reality to produce milk and feed hungry children."

"So you have a purpose here."

"Yes, and so do you, dear Otto. That is why you must return, to play out your purpose until it is your time to join me here. Me and all our relatives."

"Where are they?"

"In your partial state here you cannot see them, but they are here."

"And what is my purpose, Papa?"

"I think you know, Otto." The figure of his father wavered and gradually grew transparent.

"Auf weidersehen, mein Sohn. Take care of your mother and sister…" and he was gone.

Otto sat at the table for a few more seconds. Wow. This must be some load of morphine they had him on. Soon he would wake up. He closed his eyes.

Chapter 34

The Burn Unit—April, 1944

When he opened his eyes, he saw all white again. He thought he was back in the white room, but he felt tremendous pain all over his body. He reached up with his hands, which were wrapped in some sort of cloth, and put them to his eyes. There was a soft covering over his eyes. That was why he saw white. He called out, "Help me! Help me, please!"

He heard a rapid click of footsteps and felt someone by his side. He was lying on a bed.

A soft voice spoke, "All right, Lieutenant. Are you having pain? Nod your head if you are."

My God, Otto thought, am I ever having pain. His whole body felt like it was on fire. He nodded his head as best he could and the pain became more intense in his neck when he moved.

"I'll increase your drip, then."

He heard the clink of metal against metal, felt something cold flowing into the vein in his arm. Darkness reached up and took over the whiteness.

***

Otto felt like he was swimming in a dark sea. He thought he turned his head upward and he could see the surface of the water as a brighter glow. He swam upward, noting with bemusement that he could breathe underwater. These must be some strong drugs, he thought. He made a long slow climb toward the light, surfacing, breaking the water.

The pain slipped in again, about as bad as before. He opened his eyes and saw darkness this time. He called out, "Is anyone there?" His voice was muffled and his lips flared with pain as he moved them to speak.

He heard the same rapid footsteps and then the soft voice. "I'll increase your drip, Lieutenant."

"Don't put me totally out. Where am I?"

"You're in the hospital. You were badly burned in the crash. You need to lie quietly and rest."

"What about my crew?"

"They were all rescued. They'll be in to see you when you're feeling better."

Otto felt the darkness creeping up on him again but he fought it. He was barely conscious when he heard heavier footsteps and the voice of what must have been a doctor.

"How's he doing?"

"He's in and out. He's on a lot of morphine. I don't think he'll make it."

"All right. What a shame. Keep him comfortable and inform me if there are any major changes."

"I will, doctor."

Otto slipped into dark dreams. He was back in his fifth grade classroom. Miss Smith was there, looking stern, and Dr. Carter, who appeared to be very sad, and his father, who sat with his arms folded. Miss Smith spoke first:

"I warned you not to have anything to do with airplanes. They are death machines. But you wouldn't listen, would you, Otto? Now look where you are! Well, you'll never fly again!"

Dr. Carter nodded. "That's right, Otto. Even if you recover from your burns you won't be able to hold the controls. I told you what happened to my son. But you persisted. And you see what it got you."

His father looked at him sternly. "You should have been a dairy farmer like me, Otto. I should not have let you go to that airport so much. Now who will help run the farm? Your mother and sister are struggling. And you will be no good to them, if you survive."

His last words echoed, "If you survive…"

***

Otto opened his eyes. He saw white and knew that it must be day. "Is anyone there?" he called. The pain was perhaps a bit less intense, but still present, still burning all over his body. He was hungry.

The nurse came up to his side. "Yes, lieutenant. Are you in pain?"

"Yes," he said, "but I'm hungry. Can I have something to eat?"

"What would you like?"

"Some applesauce and milk, please."

"I'll check with the doctor to see if it's all right. You'll have surgery tomorrow." She clicked off.

Otto tried turning his head from side to side. The pain shot through his neck. His skin felt so tight. He couldn't imagine what he looked like. He shoved the thought out of his mind and tried to guess how many days had elapsed since the accident. His skin was itching where his beard had grown, so he supposed it had to have been several days at least. He couldn't tell.

The nurse returned. "All right, Lieutenant. I have the applesauce. I'll take some of the bandages off so I can feed you. Let me know if it hurts too much."

"What's your name, ma'am?"

"I'm Lieutenant Robinson."

"I meant your first name."

She hesitated. "It's Doreen."

"Pleased to meet you, Doreen. My name is Otto. Please call me that."

"Well, all right, Lieu—Otto." He could feel the bandages being unwound from around his jaw. "Open your mouth."

Otto did so, and pain coursed through his mouth and lips. He felt the cool sweetness of the applesauce and the metallic taste of the spoon. The food tasted wonderful. It was worth the pain to have it in his mouth.

"Is that all right, Otto?"

"Yes, Doreen, it tastes very good."

"OK. And now some milk. I'll put the straw in your mouth."

Otto thought that milk never tasted so good. He sucked the cold liquid and felt it cool his mouth and throat. Everything else on him felt as if it were burning up.

"How badly am I burned?"

"You're burned over 50% of your body. We thought you weren't going to make it. You'll stay here for a while and then we'll send you back to the States. I'm sorry, but you're going to have to have a number of surgeries to remove dead skin. It's a painful procedure."

"What do I look like?"

"I'll let you judge that for yourself, Lieutenant, when the time comes."

That didn't sound good. Otto fell back on the pillow. "May I have some more morphine?" The pain was starting to build.

"Certainly, Lieutenant." He felt the familiar coldness creep up his arm and then he felt nothing at all.

***

Doreen removed the bandages from his eyes a couple of days later. She had dark hair, bright green eyes and a small, pretty face. Otto's vision took a while to clear. He was in a bay separated by white curtains from other beds in what seemed to be a large ward. Other soldiers lay in their beds, wrapped from head to toe as he was.

"Are all these fellows burned?" he asked Doreen.

She nodded as she adjusted his IV. "Yes. This is the burn unit. You're in the hospital in Taunton." Most of the soldiers lay still. Some groaned from time to time. I know why, Otto thought. His skin felt tight all over his body. Doreen said that was scar tissue forming.

"Would you like to see your crew?"

"Yes, very much."

"I'll let them know. They can come in this afternoon. Now, they'll be shocked when they see you, but they've asked about you every day since you're been here."

"How long have I been here? I've lost track of time."

"About two weeks."

"And my parents and sister? Do they know?"

"They were notified only that you were injured. You can write them or I can write a letter for you."

"Thank you. I'd like that."

"All right, lieutenant. Try to rest now."

"Doreen?"

"Yes?"

"Has a British Red Cross worker named Alice been here?"

"Oh, your girlfriend? Yes, she's been here every waking moment that she could. She has helped with your care. She'll come in this afternoon after your crew. I sent her home to get some sleep. She's quite stricken with you."

"Yes, ma'am."

"Now get some rest. That's an order."

"Yes, ma'am, I will." Otto lay back on the pillow and drifted off into sleep again.

Chapter 35

Conversations—April 8, 1944

"Lieutenant? Lieutenant Kerchner?"

Otto felt like he was at the controls of the *Mata Maria*. They must be in a cloud bank because all he could see was white around him. He reached for his throat mike but felt a soft material. He pressed it anyway. "Identify yourself by position, crew."

There was a moment's hesitation and then he felt a hand on his shoulder. "Lieutenant, it's me. Bob. Bob Donovan, your co-pilot."

The fog bank cleared, and he saw Donovan's face looking at him, and, standing behind him, the rest of the crew, looking young and afraid. "How are you, sir?"

"I'm doing as well as expected. How are all of you?"

They greeted him with a chorus of "Fine…never better…doing great…"

"So," Otto said, "How do I look?"

"Like a mummy," Riley piped up. "We're glad you're alive, sir, don't cha know?"

Robinson elbowed Riley. "Actually, sir, we came by when you were out and you had those white pads over your eyes. We said you looked like Little Orphan Annie."

"Well,' leapin' lizards,' Robinson." He turned sober. "It must have been a pretty bad crash."

"It was," Detwiler said, holding his hat in his hands. "We saw pictures of what was left of the wreck. There wasn't much. It was all burned up."

"Sir," Riley offered, "We want to thank you for what you did."

"What did I do?"

201

"You held the aircraft up so we could jump out. We were all picked up and on boats within ten minutes. If you hadn't stayed with the ship, who knows what would have happened. We're sorry you were injured."

Otto grimaced. "Just a little bad luck and some so not so good pilotage. And a contribution from battle damage. I think it was a good landing because I was able to walk away from it. Or, more accurately, be carried away."

Donovan regarded him gravely. "You're getting the Distinguished Flying Cross for what you did. The colonel is coming in tomorrow to give it to you. We all got commendations, but you're the real hero. We were just doing our jobs."

"So was I," Otto returned. He felt a wave of weakness come over him and closed his eyes for how long he didn't know.

He opened them again. "You'll have to excuse me, fellas. I need to rest. Thanks for coming by."

The crew looked at the floor and shuffled off, murmuring good-byes and promises to return.

Nurse Robinson came in and increased his drip. Whiteness overtook him again.

***

"Otto? Otto? Wake up, my darling." The voice was soft and melodious and in his state, Otto thought it the voice of an angel.

He felt the soft pressure of a body leaning over his and the warmth of a face close to his bandaged head. Lithe fingers removed the pads from his eyes.

Alice. It was lovely Alice come to see him. Tears filled his eyes. His eyes came into focus and there she was, smiling at him while tears ran down her cheeks.

"Alice, is it really you?"

She looked at him with those deep blue eyes. "Yes, Otto, it's me. I've been here before, but you were asleep. How are you feeling, darling?"

"Well, I've been having a lot of pain, but right now I feel great. Sit beside me and just let me look at you."

She pulled up a chair and sat beside the bed, holding his bandaged hand. "You're quite the hero, you know."

"I don't know why. I lost the ship."

"But you saved your crew. Aircraft can be replaced."

"Alice, will you tell me something."

"Anything, my love."

"How do I look? I know I have to be scarred, but how bad is it?"

"I haven't seen, Otto. I can ask to be here when your bandages are changed. I'm sure you're handsome as ever."

"They tell me I will have to have several surgeries to cut away the dead skin."

"Don't worry about that now. I'll be here. I promise."

"Thank you, Alice. I love you."

"And I love you." She stood up and bent over to kiss the bandages on his face. "You need to rest, dear Otto. I'll be back." Her hand lingered on his chest for a moment and then she was gone. He could not hear her footsteps. Ah, a goddess floats above the ground, he thought. Once again unconsciousness overtook him.

***

The next morning, Otto was lying back, staring at the ceiling. Doreen came in. "You have some special visitors," she smiled.

Otto sat up. He recognized the general from picture in *Stars and Stripes*. He gulped. It was General Arnold. He was followed by an entourage of officers, including Colonel Rackham. Otto's crew brought up the rear, looking cowed with so much brass around.

Arnold stopped by the bed and saluted. Otto belatedly returned the salute. "Pardon me for not getting up, General," he said.

Arnold smiled. "Rest easy, son. The normal protocols are off here."

He turned to an aide, who opened a wooden box and held it for him. Arnold took a medal out of the box. Facing Otto, he intoned, "For meritorious service and incomparable airmanship, I am pleased to award you the Distinguished Flying Cross." He reached over and pinned the medal to Otto's pajamas. "And there's something else."

He took something else out of the box and pinned it to Otto's shoulders. Otto couldn't see what it was, but when Arnold straightened up, he held out his hand. "Congratulations, Captain Kerchner!"

Otto was stunned. He was nowhere due for a promotion. His crew clapped and whistled but quickly fell quiet when Arnold and his entourage turned to walk out of the ward. The nine men crowded around his bed.

They started to clap him on his shoulder, but stopped in mid-gesture, mindful of the pain he felt. "Way to go, Skip!" Riley exclaimed.

"Thank you, Riley. And thank you all for being here! You earned this as much as I did."

Just then Doreen came up to the bed. "Gentlemen, you'll have to leave. It's time to change dressings. You can come back tomorrow."

"We have a mission tomorrow," Donovan said.

"Really?" Otto queried. "I thought you were on leave."

"We were," Donovan said, "but it was up last week. We flew number 24 then and this is 25. We go home after this one."

"That's great, fellas. I'm going home, too. Eventually"

"We'll be sure to stop by and see you before we ship out."

"Thanks, guys."

Each member of the crew shook his hand, offering congratulations and wishing him good luck.

Doreen had a basin of water with her, a sponge and a roll of gauze. She wet down each section of the bandages, unrolling each one carefully. When she got to the bottom layer, it stuck to the healing skin. Otto winced as the bandage pulled off pieces of scar tissue. Doreen rewrapped each section, working from his feet up. She unwrapped his head, taking her time since the skin there was the most sensitive. Otto's head was completely exposed, and she gently patted it with a wet sponge.

The curtains around the bed rustled and Alice came in. She stood there, wide-eyed, staring at Otto.

Doreen froze. Alice was able to get in because of her Red Cross uniform, but generally no one witnessed the bandage change. Otto couldn't even have a mirror until he had time to grow used to the idea of his appearance.

Alice's hand flew to her mouth. Tears rolled down her cheeks. Otto saw horror in her eyes, and worse, pity.

"Oh, no," she choked out. "Oh, no." She turned to go. "I can't take it. I'm so sorry. I just can't take it." And she was gone.

Otto and Doreen stayed in their positions for a long moment. Doreen finally spoke. "I was afraid of that."

It seemed to Otto that she was speaking from a long way off. He didn't understand. Was he so hideous that Alice, gentle sweet Alice, couldn't stand to look at him? What would happen? He raised his eyes to Doreen's face. Tears ran down his cheeks. "You were afraid of what, Doreen?"

"Of her reaction. I've seen it happen when friends and relatives of burn victims see the damage for the first time."

"But we were more than friends. We were—"

"Yes, I know. I'm sorry." There was a long pause. "Let me finish this."

She quickly rewrapped Otto's head. He wanted to disappear, to never come back here, to go far away. His mind was filled with a thousand despairing thoughts.

Doreen gathered up the old dressing and her basin and sponge. "She'll be back, Otto. I just know she will. You'll see."

Otto turned away from her. He heard the rapid click of her heels as she walked away. He lay still and then darkness overtook him.

***

"Captain Kerchner? Captain? Wake up. It's time for your pills."

Otto lay still and kept his eyes closed. He didn't want medicine. He didn't want company. He didn't want to wake up. He wanted whoever it was to go away.

Someone touched him on the shoulder. A ring of pain formed around the touch. "Ow!" he exclaimed. "Jesus! That hurt! Don't touch me!" His eyes flickered open and he saw it was Doreen. "What you do want?"

"To give you your medication. You have a debridement surgery this morning and I need to get you ready."

"I'm not having the surgery."

"You have to, Otto. If you don't you'll get a skin infection and die of it."

"Good. I want to die."

"No you don't. Now take these pills."

"Go to hell."

Doreen paused. "I know you're hurt now, but you've got to think of yourself and your family. If nothing else, get well for them. These things happen. It happened to me last year."

Otto looked at her. "You? As good-looking as you are?"

Doreen blushed. "Well, it wasn't the same. I was engaged to a captain in the infantry who was killed in a training accident. I was a mess for months. I'm still sad, but life goes on. This is war, after all."

Otto reconsidered. "I'm sorry, Doreen. Give me the pills." He took them and swallowed them with the water she offered from a glass. "I thought Alice and I had something going on. I guess we didn't."

"She'll be back, Otto. I just know it."

"I don't think so, Doreen. I don't think so."

***

The next day, an officer showed up at Otto's bedside. Otto could tell he was a chaplain. He didn't want to talk to him. He quickly closed his eyes and pretended to sleep.

"Captain Kerchner?" The man's voice was sonorous and deep. Otto wondered idly which denomination he was. Probably not German Lutheran. Not that it mattered. Not that anything mattered.

"I'd like to talk to you, Captain. May I sit down? "

Otto gestured with his hand to the chair beside the bed, keeping his eyes closed. "Suit yourself."

"Lieutenant Robinson thought it might be helpful if I stopped by and we talked some. How are you feeling?"

"To be honest, padre, I feel like hell. How else should I feel?"

"I'm Chaplain Higgins. Well, it's certainly understandable you would feel like that. You've had a couple of rough blows recently, and I'm sorry I have to add to your troubles. We received word that your father passed away."

Otto sighed. "I know."

Higgins looked puzzled. "Did someone else tell you? How---"

Otto waved his left hand. "I just know, Chaplain."

Higgins put his hand on Otto's shoulder. "He contracted pneumonia and died before anything could be done. I'm sorry. This is so difficult. Is there anything I can do for you?"

"You can give me new skin and bring my girlfriend back."

The chaplain smiled sadly. "I wish I could, Captain, but I can't."

"When did my dad die?"

"It was about the time of your accident. It takes a while for notifications to get to us."

Otto nodded silently. Higgins sat there for a while.

"Are you religious?" Higgins asked. "You're listed as German Lutheran."

"That's the church my parents belonged to. I went as a kid but I haven't gone much since I went into the service."

"Would you like for me to have a prayer with you?"

"I'm not much on praying, Chaplain. You'll have to excuse me if I don't want to talk to God right now."

"I understand, son. So what do you see happening to you?"

"I guess I'll ship stateside and spend some time in a hospital and then go back to the farm and help my sister. No one will be around to see me but her, my mother and the cows. It will be ideal," he added sardonically.

"May I share some scripture with you, Otto?"

Otto waved one hand in resignation. "Be my guest. That's what chaplains do, isn't it?"

Higgins took out a small Bible and opened to a place near the middle. He cleared his throat and announced, "From Psalm 139, a psalm of David. I think this has a lot to do with your situation.

> *O lord, thou hast searched me, and known me.*
> *Thou knowest my downsitting and mine uprising, thou understandest my thought afar off.*
> *Thou compassest my path and my lying down, and art acquainted with all my ways.*
> *For there is not a word in my tongue, but, lo, O Lord, thou knowest it altogether.*
> *Thou hast beset me behind and before, and laid thine hand upon me.*
> *Such knowledge is too wonderful for me; it is high, I cannot attain unto it.*
>
> *Whither shall I go from thy spirit? or whither shall I flee from thy presence?*
> *If I ascend up into heaven, thou art there: if I make my bed in hell, behold, thou art there.*
> *If I take the wings of the morning, and dwell in the uttermost parts of the sea;*
> *Even there shall thy hand lead me, and thy right hand shall hold me.*
> *If I say, Surely the darkness shall cover me; even the night shall be light about me.*

> *Yea, the darkness hideth not from thee; but the night shineth as the day: the darkness and the light are both alike to thee.*

He closed the Bible and stood up. "You are in a dark place, now, Otto, but God is light and God is with you. Bless you, my son. I will be praying for you."

Otto lifted a hand. He didn't want any more religious talk, but he thought of a question as the chaplain turned to go.

"Chaplain?"

Higgins turned back to him. "Yes, Otto?"

"Why is God punishing me? Have I done something terribly wrong?"

Higgins looked down for a moment. "I don't think God is punishing you, Otto, and you probably haven't done anything worse than the rest of us. These things happen to the best people, but even through the valley of the shadow of death, God is with us. I hope you can find a way to believe that."

With that, he turned and was gone. Otto lay in the bed for a long time, thinking.

***

Doreen came in the next morning with his pills and some water. "This is my last day here, Otto. I'm being transferred to the Italian campaign. There's heavy fighting and a lot of casualties."

Otto felt a pang. "I'm sorry to see you go, Doreen. You've been very kind to me."

She laid a hand on his arm. "You're going to be fine, Otto. I just know it."

"I wish I were as convinced as you are."

"Some nice lady is going to snap you up, you big war hero."

Otto said nothing. Tears formed in the corner of his eyes as he thought of Alice.

Doreen leaned over and kissed him on his bandages on the top of his head. "Good-bye, Otto. I will miss you." And she was gone.

***

Doreen's replacement was a short, stocky woman who was all business. She was competent, but had no time for extraneous conversations. That was all right with Otto. He didn't feel much like talking.

Otto was sitting in the sun room looking out over the grounds of the estate that was being used as a hospital. His burns still pained him and parts of his body itched terribly. He looked up from his book to see Riley coming toward him.

"Captain OK!" Riley called as he got nearer, a broad smile plastered on his face.

"Hi, Riley." Otto said absently.

"How are you, sir?"

"I'm here, Riley."

"Well, everyone has to be somewhere, Captain. Listen, the other fellows told me to come by. They're getting ready to ship home and do bond drives. Since I only have four missions, I've been assigned to another crew to finish out, don't cha know?"

Otto could not help feeling that now his crew was deserting him. Still, they were a good crew and had earned their way home.

"We heard about your girl and your father, Captain." Great, Otto thought. Everyone knows all about me.

"Yeah, it stinks, Riley."

"I'm sorry, sir. I had something similar happen to me. In basic I got a 'Dear John' letter from my girl back home in Boston. My brother later wrote me that she was steppin' out with every 4-F in sight. So good riddance to that bitch. Before I got the letter from my brother I went AWOL on a three-day drunk. I was busted back to private. The captain said he wished he could create a lower rank because being a private was too good for me. The next week I got word my dad had died, so I did it again. I spent a week in the brig for that one."

"Humph," Otto grunted.

"Anyhow, what I'm trying to say, sir, is that I got over that, and I'm sure you'll get another dame. They're everywhere. And you'll remember the good times with your dad. Did he take you hunting and fishing?"

"No, he was always working, so I was always working. I wish I could be as optimistic as you are, Riley."

"It's not so much optimism as it is the way things are. People come and go in our lives. If you're lucky you get up with someone special. And life goes on."

"I'm not feeling too lucky these days."

"It'll come back to you, sir. I know it will." Riley stood at attention and saluted. Otto returned a half-hearted salute.

"So long, sir. You're an excellent pilot. Hope to see you stateside."

Otto waved one hand. "See you, Riley."

Otto watched him walk away down the long sunroom. An orderly was walking his way, carrying the day's mail. He came to Otto and handed him a V-mail envelope. Otto saw it was from Mata, and he knew it had to be her first letter to him since she had been notified of his accident. He tore it open eagerly.

Mein Lieber Otto,

We received the telegram that told us you had been wounded in action. We have not received any more details, and so we hope and pray that your injuries are not serious and that you will soon finish your missions and come home. We hear that the war is going better, but it is hard to know what to believe. There are so many stories and rumors.

I do not know if you have been notified, but Papa passed away last week. He caught pneumonia and only lasted a couple of days. He was so weak he couldn't fight much. We had a German-language service for him at the church. The services are in English now, but they made an exception for him. The neighbors have been wonderful, but now it's just me and Mama in the house. I know you were not able to come back, even if you had not been injured. I miss Papa, and I know you will, too.

The farm is doing well. Old Mr. Pierce died last month, and his wife did not want to live there alone, so I bought their holdings. It is perhaps a terrible thing to say, but we are doing very well financially because of the war. The Army buys all the milk we can produce and would buy more if we had it. Of course, when it gets to you, it's nothing like the milk we know! So we are continuing on.

I do not wish to worry you more, but Mama does not do much these days. Even before Papa died, she sat in the kitchen and sometimes stirred herself to clean something or make something to eat. This past week she has stared out the window. She does not seem to be herself, and I fear her mind is not right. I do what I must, and Johnson is a help, although he is of course feeble himself and old, but we are getting things done.

I saw Betty Ross when I went into town yesterday. She asked about you. I don't know what happened between the two of you before you left, but I think she would like to hear from you. I hear that she is dating a fellow who works at her father's bank. He's considered necessary to the war effort. I also hear he's not very nice, so I hope Betty will not do anything rash. You might try writing her and see if she'll answer. I know you two have always been close—or you used to be.

Well, time for evening milking. Please let us hear back from you. We think of you often and pray for you and all our brave servicemen.

Your sister,

Mata.

Otto folded the letter and put it back in its envelope. The news just gets better and better, he thought, and stared out the solarium windows without really seeing anything.

Chapter 36—May 15, 1944

Don't Sit Under the Apple Tree with Anyone Else But Me

After four more surgeries to remove dead skin, Otto's doctor deemed him well enough to travel. On a rainy morning, a nurse he had never seen before helped him pack his bag and helped him into a wheelchair. She was entirely too cheery for Otto's taste, so he just grunted when she chirped, "Well, aren't you the lucky one, Captain, getting to go home?"

Yep, Otto thought, I'm about the luckiest guy I know.

Since he was ambulatory, he was able to climb aboard a waiting Army bus with various other wounded soldiers. Some were missing arms and legs; one poor fellow had part of his face blown off. Well, maybe he looks worse than I do, Otto thought, but I doubt it. He still had not been able to bring himself to look in a mirror.

The bus jolted and pitched along a small country road for about an hour until they came to a paved highway. Obviously the Brits weren't spending a lot of time or money on the roads with the war on. The passengers rode in silence. There was a nurse who sat at the front and came by periodically to check on the men. She passed by Otto. "How are we doing, Captain?"

"As well as can be expected, ma'am," Otto returned.

"We'll be there in about another hour."

Otto stared out the window at the rainy landscape. Most of the traffic was military—jeeps, trucks, flatbeds with tanks and jeeps on them. It seemed as if everyone was going to war. He smiled ruefully. Well, they were going to war. There were rumors of an invasion and there did seem to be much more traffic than usual. Well, he wouldn't be part of it. He wouldn't be part of anything. And so he fell asleep, his head against the window.

He awoke with a start as the bus braked to a halt. A corpsman came up the stairs and started helping the wounded off. They were parked on some sort of dock, with a huge ship towering over them. Otto recognized it as a

Liberty ship, one of those manufactured in 42 days. It had obviously brought materiel to the front and now was taking wounded back.

The docks were a beehive of activity with huge cranes offloading pallets onto waiting trucks. Otto saw tanks held high in the air and then lowered onto flatbeds and driven away.

The wounded soldiers made their way up steep stairs to the main deck of the ship. Those who could not walk were carried on stretchers by corpsmen. Otto walked with a cane.

A sailor with a clipboard stood at the top of the stairs, directing each of the wounded as they came on board. "Captain," he said, looking at the tag that hung from Otto's pajamas, "you're on deck 2, cabin B. Go down this gangway and turn left. There'll be someone there to help you." Otto joined the flow of people moving down a narrow stairway.

The interior of the ship was painted gray. Bare bulbs covered with wire cages provided light. Another sailor directed Otto to cabin B. He opened the door and stepped through. Four cots filled most of the space, and someone had deposited his B bag on one of them. The sailor who had directed him to his cabin stuck his head in. "Head's down the hall, Captain. We'll get underway at 1400 hours."

"Thank you," Otto said, and sat on the bed. He could feel the vibration of distant engines beneath his feet. So this was home for a while. He went over to the porthole and looked out. From there he had a reversed perspective on what he had seen from the dock. A steady line of soldiers was proceeding slowly up the gangway.

"Sir, lunch is in the wardroom in ten minutes." A young nurse leaned in the doorway. "Go down this hall and then up one level. You'll be able to smell the food." She smiled at him.

"Thank you," Otto said.

***

Back in his cabin after lunch, Otto found the other beds occupied by an Army major, an AF lieutenant and a Navy ensign. This must be officers' territory, he thought. The three other men lay on their cots. Each lifted a hand at him. No one seemed to feel like talking.

Otto felt the vibrations increase beneath his feet and surmised they were getting underway. The ship moved sideways, stopped, and then went forward at a slow pace. Otto made his way to the main deck, which was crowded with ambulatory patients. A tug pushed the ship out into the Channel. The proceedings were strangely quiet, with those men who could stand lining the rail.

When the ship was in the Channel, the tug backed away, sounding a long blast on its whistle followed by two shorts. Otto felt the vibrations under his feet increase. They proceeded slowly down the waterway, the docks and warehouses dreary and gray in the falling rain. Otto looked behind (six o'clock, he thought automatically) and saw a line of similar vessels.

They proceeded this way for about half an hour and came to a headland. The Channel was choppy with whitecaps. The deck began to pitch and Otto decided it was time to go back to his room. He noticed several destroyers in position to join their little fleet. The escort, he thought. The Battle of the Atlantic had slowed down, but there was still a threat from U-boats. The line of cargo ships moved into the Channel, with the destroyers falling in along the length of the line.

Back in his cabin, Otto noticed immediately that not only was the ship pitching, it was corkscrewing as it plowed through the waves. And then it abruptly changed direction every half minute or so. Otto knew these measures were to foil German attacks.

He had never been airsick, so the motion didn't bother him, but it got to the Army officers in the room. After a few minutes of motion, they bolted for the head, their faces a pale shade of green. Otto looked out into the passageway to observe that not everyone made it to the head. Some victims were using their crash helmets as basins, while others struggled to reach the main deck where they could be sick over the side. Otto was grateful he didn't have that to contend with that. He lay down on his cot and fell fast asleep.

He was awakened by a nurse who handed him a glass of water and some pills. "What time is it?" he asked, having no idea how much time had passed.

"It's about 2100 hours, Captain. You slept through supper. Do you want me to get you a sandwich?"

"That would be nice."

"We have Spam, Spam, and Spam."

"Spam would be great, if you have it." Otto smiled, although it stretched the skin around his mouth and hurt like the dickens.

"If you don't mind my asking, Captain, how did you get burned?"

"That's OK," Otto said. "I destroyed some government property, namely one B-17, 'G' model."

"I've heard you're a hero," she smiled, and he thought with a pang that she looked like Alice.

"I don't know about that."

"I'll get you your sandwich. You're fortunate that you feel like eating. So many of the fellows are seasick."

Otto watched her walk out of the cabin. He lay back on the bed.

***

The convoy plowed on through restless seas for ten more days. Occasionally, Otto went on deck but there wasn't much to see: the line of gray transports butting through swells and whitecaps with destroyers running along the edges like sleek greyhounds guiding their charges. The convoy was fortunate in that it was not attacked, but they had several drills. Everyone who could put on a life vest and helmet and came out on deck.

The sky was gray, the ships were gray, the sea was gray, and so there wasn't much to look at. Otto generally didn't stay long in the cold wind and squalls of rain. He spent most of his time on his cot reading or sleeping. The nurse who offered him the sandwich the first day, whose name was Joanne, said they would ship into New York and then go by rail to a hospital in Boston where he would be further treated. Otto wondered how much they could do for him. He still hadn't looked into a mirror.

The day came when the ship's loudspeakers announced that they would be sailing into the New York harbor that afternoon. Otto wanted to see the city, and so he joined most of the ambulatory patients who crowded the rails. They proceeded up the Lower Bay in line with the other ships, and steamed into the Upper Bay. The skyscrapers of Manhattan came into view, and Otto felt a lump in his throat as the Statue of Liberty passed on the port side.

Tugs met the ship and guided it into place at a dock near mid-town. Otto went back to collect his bag. He had walked and strengthened himself enough that he could carry it unassisted. He was dressed in fatigues. Joanne came in to see if anyone needed help.

"Well, I'll go with you as far as the hospital, and then I turn around and go back to England," she told him.

"You ought to fly back," Otto said. "It's faster, with less seasickness."

She laughed. "Seasickness doesn't bother me. My dad was in the Navy, and I think I inherited his sea legs."

"If I don't see you, Joanne, thank you, and good luck."

"You, too, Otto. Say hello to your mom and sister for me when you get home."

"I will." She walked out into the corridor.

Otto joined the masses of wounded soldiers moving down the gangplank to waiting Army buses. He tossed his B bag into the cargo compartment underneath and carefully climbed the few short steps, taking a seat near the front. He idly watched the parade of soldiers and MP's as they found their way to their transport.

A short sergeant came on and sat in the driver's seat. "Who wants to go to Boston?" he called. A chorus of light boos greeted his question. "No one for Boston then," he muttered as he closed the door and started the engine. "I'll take youse as far as the train station. You're on your own after that."

The bus crept through heavy traffic. Otto had never been to New York before, and he thought he might like to return, if his appearance could be disguised or fixed so he didn't frighten people. The transit buses were packed with people hanging off them, and Otto saw people piled into the few cars in the traffic mix. Most people were walking, thronging the sidewalks, everyone walking quickly, purposely. *I hope they're working on the war effort*, Otto thought as the Army bus inched through the crowded street.

About half an hour later, the driver pulled the bus to the entrance to Grand Central Station and shouted, "Here you go, gents! Track 42! It ain't the Chattanooga Choo Choo, but it'll get you where you need to go. All ashore that's goin' ashore!"

The troops unloaded, with orderlies unloading the bags from underneath the bus. Otto retrieved his and walked through the doors, coming into the cavernous lobby. He saw the famous clock where people met. Several people were standing expectantly at its base. They had people to meet. He didn't. He did have a train to catch, though.

The knot of soldiers moved toward Track 42, melting into a sea of uniforms, with very few people in civilian clothes. Otto thought all the troops were overseas, but it was obvious there were still a bunch at home, if the station were any indication.

An olive drab line of Army railroad coaches stretched into the distance at Track 42. Otto went about halfway down the line and climbed into the coach. He settled himself into the last seat after lifting his bag onto the overhead rack.

The other troops were silent as they filed into the coach. No one seemed to feel like talking. Their war was over, and they were headed for months, maybe years of treatment. Otto hoped that at the very least he would be in a hospital closer to home. He wanted more than anything to see Mama and Mata.

The car loaded up, and Red Cross workers came down the aisles passing out box lunches. Otto opened his and saw that it had a ham sandwich and an apple, along with a Coke. Well, he guessed they couldn't keep milk cold enough to make that the drink. So warm Coke it was. He bit into the slightly dry sandwich, thinking that he wasn't really that hungry.

The train lurched and began sliding out of the station. They were enveloped in the darkness of a tunnel for several minutes, and then burst back into sunlight. From his navigation experience and the sun, Otto knew they were headed north.

The train traveled through closely packed stores and apartment buildings for a while, and then ran along the shore. As had been the case the entire journey from England, the soldiers were silent. Their war was over, and what they had to look forward to were long rehabilitations and an uncertain future. Otto preferred not to think about it.

The scenery soon resolved itself to a long gray shoreline and gray waters of bay after bay. Otto tired of looking out after a while, wishing he had a book. The ship he had come back on had a small library of castoffs, but nothing had interested him. As if reading his thoughts, a Red Cross girl came through the carriage bearing a basket loaded with books.

She stopped at each seat, offering the occupants an opportunity to choose something to read. Most of them declined, but when she reached Otto, asking "Would you like a book?" he said, "Yes, please." He dug into the layers of books in the basket after she had deposited it in the seat, coming up with a copy of *Gone with the Wind*. He had heard about the movie but had not seen it. He didn't know if he would like it. He would have to find out.

Half an hour later, Otto found himself impatient with the book. If the characters would just stop dallying and *do* something, that would be all right. Instead, they chattered endlessly. He put the book down on the seat beside him and stared out the window. He wished he had a newspaper. He could do the crossword and catch up with Little Orphan Annie. Leapin' lizards, but it had been a long time since he had read any comics, except for those *The Stars and Stripes* carried.

He had had a few books in his foot locker, but whoever had packed his things up had taken them back to the base library. They weren't there, anyhow. Not that they were his to begin with.

His head dropped forward, and he nodded off. The train bore on up the coast.

Otto was awakened by the sudden jolt of the train braking to a halt at the station. The silent soldiers gathered their bags and filed out. They were greeted by another sergeant with a clipboard. "Aww raght, troops," he barked, "Follow me!" They fell in behind him, making their way through crowds which had very few civilians mixed in.

They emerged into the gray twilight in front of the station where more olive drab buses awaited them. Otto climbed on board the first one after handing his bag to a corporal to be put under the bus. The driver came on board and a few seconds later they were making their way through heavy

221

traffic. They crept through the backups for about a half an hour before coming to a stately brick building. On it a new sign read, "U.S. Military Hospital, Boston District." Letters cut into stone above the entrance read "Boston City Hospital." The building looked old, and like much else, had been taken over by the military. Well, it would be home for a while. Otto hoped it wouldn't be too long.

The wounded soldiers filed off the bus and up the steps. An orderly led them down a long hall to a large atrium with metal chairs arranged in rows. Otto took a seat near the window.

A doctor in a white lab coat came in with a corporal in uniform. "Attention!" he called, and the men rose to their feet.

"At ease, men. Be seated," the doctor said. "I'm Major Lynch, and I want to welcome you to the burn unit of the Massachusetts Military Hospital. We're relaxed about military matters here, so there's no saluting and we don't pay much attention to rank. We do pay attention to getting you to the point you can get out into society. That involves not only physical healing but also psychological healing. You've all been badly burned and scarred as a result. We'll help you cope with the reactions you're going to get when you are in the outside world. But for now, you'll be here for a while. We can't say how long, but it will be a while. Now, Corporal Smith will pass out telegram forms so you can notify your families where you are. The hospital address and ward name has been typed onto the form so they'll know where to send mail."

The corporal passed out the forms. Otto took the pencil he was offered and carefully printed,

IN HOSPITAL IN BOSTON WITH BURNS STOP DON'T KNOW WHEN I WILL BE RELEASED STOP WRITE TO ADDRESS BELOW STOP

He handed the form to the corporal who took it along with the others.

The major spoke again. You've been traveling so you wouldn't be aware of what has been going on. This morning, forces of the Allied nations landed along the coast of Normandy in France. They have met with heavy resistance but have gained a foothold. I will bring you further information as it becomes available. I hope you will join me and the staff here in praying for the success of the mission. This is what we've been waiting for."

Well, what you know, Otto thought. The invasion has started. He wondered how his bomber outfit was involved. He knew they would be doing something. He'd have to find out more. He'd have to get hold of a newspaper and see if there was a radio.

"Corporal Smith will take you to your ward. Good afternoon and good luck."

The corporal led them down another long hall to a ward much like the one in England.

"Choose any bed you want," he called. "No fighting over the beds. They're all alike. Dinner is at 1700 hours. I'll come back to show you where the dining hall is."

Otto chose a bed by the door and dropped his B bag on the covers and then settled himself. Large floor-to-ceiling windows looked out on a nondescript courtyard. He sat on his cot. So this was it for the next several months. He wondered what those months would hold. He lay on the bed and waited for the dinner call.

***

The next morning, after a dinner and breakfast that left Otto thinking that all Army meals were much the same, no matter where he was, Corporal Smith came into the ward. "Attention, troops!" he called. "Assembly in the solarium! Follow me!" The soldiers, dressed in their regular uniforms as opposed to hospital robes, rose and filtered out of the ward, down the hall to the same large room Dr. Lynch had greeted them in the day before. About fifty chairs had been arranged in a circle, and on each chair lay a mirror. Dr. Lynch stood expectantly in front of the wall away from the windows.

The men shuffled in. Each one found a seat, took the mirror and sat down. Otto did not look in the mirror. He had not looked in a mirror since the accident and he didn't intend to start today.

"Good morning, men," called Major Lynch. "Here is my first order to you: look in the mirror at your seat."

The soldiers slowly complied. Otto could hear gasps. Some of the men began crying. Evidently he wasn't the only one who had not seen himself in the mirror. Smith came over to him. "You heard the major, Captain. Use your mirror."

Reluctantly, Otto lifted the small mirror and looked into it. What he saw made him gasp. He looked like a mummy from a horror film with its bindings off. His hair had been burned away; he had no eyebrows; and his nose and ears were half burned away. Most of his face was covered with a tight shiny layer of scar tissue, light brown in color. The only feature that was anywhere near the same were his green eyes. Tears trickled from the corners of his eyes. Dear God, how could he ever go out in public? He wanted to go somewhere and hide. No wonder Alice had run away from this horrible sight.

Major Lynch gave the soldiers time to quiet down. "You see what you look like to the outside world. We want you to get used to that. You will receive stares and unkind comments. But you are the same inside. You are, to a man, brave soldiers who have served your country. Let no one take that away from you." He looked around the room. "Captain Kerchner, would you please stand?"

Otto was puzzled as he stood. The major continued. "Captain Kerchner was a B-17 pilot on a mission in which his bomber took heavy damage from flak and fighters. He kept the ship up so his crew could bail out and attempted to bring it home. It crashed and burned with the results you see when you look at Captain Kerchner. He is the winner of the Distinguished Flying Cross, and in my book, an authentic hero. I salute you, Captain Kerchner." He snapped off a smart salute.

Otto stood there for a second, embarrassed by the attention. He returned Major Lynch's salute and sat down.

Lynch continued. "Remember who you are and remember what you have done. We'll get you fixed up as best we can and then get you home to your loved ones. And now, if you'll return to the ward, the doctors will make their rounds."

As the men stood to go out, Lynch came over to Otto. He stuck out his hand. "I just want to shake your hand, Captain. That was a fine piece of flying you did."

Otto shook his hand. "Thank you, sir. I just wanted to take care of my crew and bring the aircraft back. I guess I batted .500 on that one."

"You batted 1.000 in my book, Kerchner. I'm proud to know you. We'll get you out of here as soon as we can."

Otto turned and walked back to the ward to see what the day would bring.

***

Mein Lieber Otto,

We were so glad to get the telegram from you and have an address to write to. All we knew was that you had been injured. We didn't have any details. I am sorry to hear that you were burned. I hope it was not too badly. We look forward to seeing you soon when you are allowed to come home.

Mama is about the same. She does not seem to be any worse, but then she does not get any better. The farm continues to do well. If I had 1000 more cows I could sell every bit of milk they would produce. I am thinking of continuing to expand the herd and hire more people to help. When the war ends, there will be plenty of babies born after the servicemen come home. You know what I mean (blush). So I think we will do pretty well.

Your allotment continues to come every month and I am saving it for you to do as you wish. Perhaps we can use it to buy a cow or two…or a thousand!

Continue to be brave, dear Otto. We are here waiting for your return.

Your loving sister,

Mata

Chapter 37

Going Home—Late July, 1944

Otto stared out the window of the train at the trackside buildings which seemed to move backward with the train's motion. He was really going home and that was exciting. Over six weeks of treatment were behind him. It hadn't been easy—there was painful physical therapy, occupational therapy and what they called just plain therapy to help him and the other burn patients adjust. Or maybe cope was a better word. He understood that he was angry about what had happened to him, even though he didn't necessarily feel angry, but he was. He was angry about his crash, he was angry about his appearance, and he was angry about Alice leaving him. He settled into his seat and tried not to think about it.

The train surged ahead through the New York countryside. The fields were brown, and he saw few cars on the rural roads. Gas rationing would account for that, he thought.

The car he was in was filled with men in uniform. Some of them glanced at him as they came into the coach and quickly looked away. He was more or less resigned to his appearance now, but he wished someone would look at him without looking away quickly, or staring or flinching. Maybe that was asking too much.

He had written Mata with the train he would be arriving on. He would go through Chicago and then up the lake shore to Milwaukee and over to Madison and up through Eau Claire to Pioneer Lake. He would continue his rehab in the hospital at Madison. He thought he could fly down there and back if he could stand to be in an aircraft. He hadn't flown since the accident. Ah, well, there was always the train.

A popular song came into his head for some reason. It seemed to pertain to his situation, in that way that pop songs do.

> *I don't want to walk without you, Baby;*
> *Walk without my arm about you, Baby;*
> *I thought the day you left me behind,*
> *I'd take a stroll and get you right off my mind,*

But now I find that
I don't want to walk without the sunshine
Why'd you have to turn off all that sunshine?

There was plenty of sunshine falling on the fields, but he certainly didn't have anyone to walk with. Oh, well, it was just a song.

He thought how it would be good to be home, to be able to help on the farm and to be away from curious eyes. It was about harvest time, a time of work and beauty.

He closed his eyes and the train rolled on into the twilight.

***

The braking of the train awoke Otto. He had slept fitfully through the night, waking each time the train stopped at a station. The first gray light of dawn was filtering through the windows. Then they plunged into a tunnel. A conductor came walking down the aisle. "Chicago! Chicago! Union Station! Transfer here for points north, west and south! This station is Chicago!"

Otto stood and pulled his B bag off the overheard rack. He was stronger than he had been when he came to the hospital, but he had lost weight during his recovery. He waited while the other soldiers got their bags and joined the line shuffling off the train.

A blast of hot air hit him as he came down the steps. The interior of the coach was hot as well, but it was hotter outside. Wind swept down the platform and tore pieces of paper out of the hands of those who did not have a tight grip on them. A low hum arose from the crowd as they commented on the heat. Maybe they had forgotten what the Midwest was like in late summer.

Otto came to a schedule board and studied the departures. All right, his train didn't leave for an hour so he could get some coffee and something to eat. He chose a walk-up hamburger stand so he wouldn't have to endure the curious stares of waitresses and other diners in a sit-down eatery. It was as good as anything for breakfast. The old man who ran the hamburger stand looked at him curiously for a moment but his eyes did not linger on Otto's face. That was a small saving grace anyhow.

Otto took his coffee and burger over to a bench across from the stand and ate it slowly. A constant stream of men in uniform with a few women mixed in surged past him in both directions. They all seemed intent on getting somewhere, walking purposely. They were part of the war effort. He wasn't any more, unless he wanted to count producing milk for the troops. I also serve who stand and wait, he thought bitterly. He finished his burger and threw the wrapper away in a nearby trash can and returned the coffee cup to the stand. The board showed his train was loading so he headed in the direction of Track 45.

The line of cars was shorter than the one he had come in on and the engine was a small dirty steam locomotive. Well, it would get him home. He climbed the steps into the coach. With half an hour until departure there were a few soldiers scattered around the worn seats. Otto took one near the end of the car. A couple of men idly glanced at him and then went back to reading or looking out the window. Otto settled himself in and watched people walk past the car.

Promptly at 9 AM the train lurched forward and they rolled into a tunnel, coming out along the shoreline. Shortly they were past the buildings and streets of the city and into farmland. Most of the fields were brown but Otto knew they had just been harvested. The soil would sleep over the winter, but all it needed was sun and warmth next spring to burst forth into green shoots. Well, good for the soil and the plants. He would remain brown and withered the rest of his life.

He fell asleep, exhausted from the night before.

They pulled into Milwaukee on time, and a few of the troops got off there. More left at the stop at Madison. There was a brief layover at Eau Clair for lunch, but he wasn't hungry and didn't get off the train. Everyone else left and didn't come back, so he was the only one left in the coach as it continued to Pioneer Lake. About 4 o'clock he recognized landmarks around the town, and the train pulled into the small station about 4:30. He lifted his bag from the overhead rack and eased down the steps. The conductor steadied him as he stumbled, giving him a little salute as he stood on the platform. He saw Mata at the other end of the train. She recognized him immediately and ran down the length of the cars, crushing him in a tight embrace, laughing and crying at the same time.

"Otto, mein Otto, I'm so glad you're here! Let me look at you!" She held him at arm's length and studied his face. She did not flinch or look away.

He only saw joy and affection in her shining eyes. "You've lost weight! I'll have to fatten you up!"

"It is so good to be back home, Mata. I can't tell you."

They started walking toward the parking lot. Mata was uncharacteristically chattering a mile a minute. "There's so much to tell you that I couldn't write. The farm is doing well. I've acquired some more acreage and about a hundred more cows. The Army continues to buy everything we produce and I am thinking there will be more demand after the war so I think we should continue to expand our operation. We can hire some more men to help us when the war is over, and…"

They had reached the car by this time, a 1938 Model A Ford sedan. "This is new," he said.

"Well, I bought it used. The T was getting old and I needed something reliable to drive."

Otto threw his bag in the back seat and let Mata's words wash over him. She put the car in gear and smoothly backed out of the parking space.

"Hey, sis," he said when she paused for breath. "When did you learn to drive?"

"Shortly after you left for overseas. It was a matter of 'had to' so I did it. Am I doing all right?" She shifted into the next gear.

"You drive like you've been doing it all your life." She glanced over and smiled at him. "I can't tell you how I've dreamed of this day."

As they went past familiar farms, Mata told him what had happened to each property. "The Wilsons' son didn't want to farm, so their farm is vacant…the Turners died, one after another, so I bought their farm at auction…the Smiths just quit after Steve was killed in the Pacific…"

"I didn't know that," Otto said. He couldn't help thinking that it was poetic justice. Still, the death of a fellow soldier was sad.

"We only got the news shortly before you got here. It devastated his parents."

"So, did you buy their farm?"

Mata nodded and looked straight ahead.

"Mata, how many farms have you bought since I've been gone?"

"Just three," she said in a small voice.

"Well…" Otto started. "I hope we can afford them all."

"We can Otto, and more. We don't spend much otherwise, and I saw some opportunities. You told me I was in charge when you left."

"I think it's great, Mata. I think you should be in charge of the war. Can we stop by the church? I'd like to see Papa's grave."

"Certainly," Mata said. A few minutes later she steered into the gravel lot of the old stone church. She and Otto went into the graveyard next to the church. Hans' tombstone was in the second row, toward the end.

Otto put his arm around Mata, and they stood there for a moment. "He was a good man," Otto said finally. Mata wiped a tear away.

"Yes he was," she said.

They got back into the car and drove home in silence.

"I'll show you the books after supper," Mata told him as they walked in. I've got some chicken fixed . . . just the way you like it."

They came to the long driveway which was now graveled. Otto felt an emotional surge as the farm house and barn came into sight. Home. He was finally home. Not the way he would have liked, but he was home.

He was preparing to climb out of the car when Mata touched him on his sleeve. "I have a couple of other things I need to tell you before we go in."

"OK, go ahead."

"One is that Betty Ross married a fellow who is a vice-president in her father's bank named Brown. I think she just settled for him and she isn't very happy. I know you and she were close."

Otto said nothing. He had a relationship with Alice and he was sure Betty knew about it. So she was free to do what she would. They didn't have an understanding or anything.

"Second, Mama is worse. Mostly she sits and stares but it seems she's in another world. I didn't want to worry you by putting too much about it into a letter. I hope all this doesn't ruin your homecoming."

Otto looked down for a moment. "Well, she's still with us. Maybe in her condition she won't be as upset by how I look."

"She probably won't know who you are, Otto. She thinks I'm her sister most of the time."

"Well, let's go in."

Mata led the way through the familiar kitchen door. "Mama, look who I brought home," she exclaimed.

Maria sat at the kitchen table, but her hands were not busy as they usually were when she was there. She held her hands in her lap and looked up absently.

"Yes, Rose? Who is it?"

"See for yourself!" Mata said, standing to one side.

Otto stood still. There was no sign of recognition in Maria's eyes. Finally she brightened. "Hans! It's you! You've come back, my darling!" She rose unsteadily to her feet. Otto stepped over to keep her from falling and as she embraced him, he felt how frail and thin she was.

"Yes, I'm here," Otto murmured, looking at Mata, who had tears rolling down her cheeks. "I'm finally here."

"You're so young, Hans. I thought you were older like me. But you look the same as you did the day we were wed." She sat back in her chair and resumed absently gazing at the table.

Otto sighed. There was not much to do. He followed Mata into his bedroom, which had not changed since he had left for basic. The pictures and models seemed childish now, given all he had been through. He sat on the bed. Mata went out, closing the door. "I know you probably want to be alone and rest for a while. We'll eat in about an hour."

Otto suddenly felt very tired. He lay back on the bed and stared at the ceiling.

***

The next morning, Otto rose early, made himself some coffee and went out to look around the farm. Mata would be up soon, but he wanted to see what she had done in his absence. He went into the barn where the cows were beginning to stir, anticipating feeding and milking. All was in order and perhaps cleaner and neater than when he had left. He went back out to walk around the barn and saw a new building, a kind of shed. Then it occurred to him. The Model T was not in its place in the barnyard. He idly wondered what had happened to it. It was old, but cars were not being made for the duration, so he couldn't imagine that Mata would have gotten rid of it. He pushed open the shed doors and the T was there, covered with dust. Next to it was a 1936 Model A pickup. Mata had probably forgotten to mention it to him with all the other news she had.

He went back into the kitchen. Mata was there fixing sausage and eggs for breakfast. "There you are," she smiled.

"Yes, I've been checking out the property to see how the farm has been run in my absence. I would say it has been run very well. Apparently it is quite a prosperous farm because the farmers have acquired a new truck."

Mata's hand flew to her mouth and her eyes widened. "Oh, Otto, I'm sorry, I forgot to tell you. I bought the truck from the Hansens when Roger joined the Marines."

"It's a wonderful truck."

"The T was getting so old, but I kept it and we use it to transport hay for the herd and other things. Actually, I learned to drive on the A, before I bought the sedan. I thought you'd like to have something newer to drive when you came back."

"So we're a three car family now."

"Looks like it."

"I'm proud of you, sis, for all you've done here."

"And I'm happy you're home, brother."

"So am I," Otto said.

233

Chapter 38

Fall and Winter—1944-45

Otto soon became aware of just how greatly Mata had expanded the scope of their little dairy farm. He spent some time visiting the farms she had acquired. Each farm had its own manager, and the roads leading to them were busy with tanker trucks coming to load the milk produced by the dairy herds. In truth, there was not much for him to do, so after a few days, he stayed put on the family farm and helped with small chores. He didn't want to go to town and be exposed all over again to stares and questions.

The summer passed into autumn. The three of them had a small Thanksgiving. They ate; Mata cleaned up, Maria continued to sit at the table and Otto retired to the living room and listened to the radio. The Allies continued to move into France, headed for Germany. He thought the war in Europe might be over by the end of the year. Then the Germans counterattacked in mid-December. The news called it the Battle of the Bulge. As he followed accounts of the fighting on the radio, even on Christmas Day, Otto was concerned that weather prevented air support. The weather broke shortly thereafter, aircraft could fly support missions, and the Germans were pushed back.

The heavies continued to pound German cities and manufacturing. It was still just a matter of time until the Third Reich was destroyed. How much time, he couldn't tell. He supposed no one could.

New Year's passed quietly.

***

Otto stumbled on the frozen rutted mud as he came in from the barn. Christ, it was cold, even for the first week in February. Maybe he could prevail on Mata to buy some electric heaters for the milking barn. The cows would appreciate it and so would he.

The weather had turned exceptionally frigid a week ago and had stayed that way. He thought back to a brief warmup, when was it, the second week of January? That was the week Mama had died. She just continued to decline in front of their eyes. The doctor could find no reason, other than to say she was not in her right mind and seemed to have given up the will to live. Mata came in from the barn one afternoon and found her sitting in her usual place in the kitchen chair, staring straight ahead but seeing nothing. They had a traditional service at the church and buried her beside Hans in the graveyard. Mata wanted *Ein Feste Burg* in German sung at the end. Otto thought of the English words:

A mighty fortress is our God
A bulwark never failing
A helper He, amid the flood
Of mortal ills prevailing…

He couldn't sing that without thinking of his aircraft, the *Mata Maria*. He wondered where she was now and if she was still flying. She had probably been assigned to some other crew, and her name had been changed. There had been a lot of changes brought on by this war.

Maria's service was in English, and afterwards Mata told him that the church had switched to English in 1940 except for some funeral services for the older folks like Hans when it became clear that anything in German was suspect. Even the German-language papers that Hans read when he was alive had changed over.

Otto thought it ironic that he had fought for a freedom that his friends and family at home did not have. Well, that's how it went sometimes.

Otto remembered how they had followed the wooden casket carried out the church door to the graveyard where his father's grave was. A freshly dug hole lay in wait, and the minister said a few words of commitment and that was it. They all turned to go back into the church basement where the women had prepared a funeral meal. The old people who were left came by, murmuring their sympathies, trying hard not to be obvious about staring at Otto's appearance, telling him they were glad he was home. They probably were, but Otto felt like he was just getting through a decent interval of time until he could leave. Mata kept looking at him anxiously. Finally people started leaving and he and Mata did as well, to go home to the quiet and empty house.

So it had been the two of them for the past month or so. Days they did what was necessary to manage a rather large dairy farm. In the evenings, Mata worked on the finances and sewing while Otto listened to the radio, war news mostly, or read the newspaper from Minneapolis that came by mail. They went to bed early since they had to get up early, "with the chickens," as Mata said. Otto just grunted. Getting up at 5 AM was easy compared to rolling out in the cold not knowing if it would be his last morning.

The war seemed to be distant, although there was news of the progress on both fronts, along with rumors and speculation. Otto was most interested in the progress of Allied troops through Europe. The bombers continued to pound strategic targets. Otto knew they were inflicting incredible damage on the German war machine.

They went into town on Saturdays. Otto kept a scarf around his face up to his eyes, which was easy enough in the winter. He thought idly what he would do in the spring and decided he would think more about that when the time came. Maybe people would just have to get used to it. They said he was a war hero, after all, so wasn't he something special? Deformed and grotesque, but special.

Otto had noticed after a couple of days at home that there weren't any aircraft going into the field next door. He supposed that limitations on fuel and pleasure flying made the difference, and so did not get by the field to see for himself for a couple of weeks. When he pulled up to the office building and hangar, he was in for a shock. Clearly no one had used them for quite a while. Some of the windows in the office were broken, and the door hung from one hinge. He got out and went into the office. A layer of dust covered everything. He went into the hangar. The Fleet stood in one corner. It was not damaged, but Otto could hear mice scurrying along the walls. What had happened to Wilson? To Sparky? He didn't know who to ask since those two kept to themselves at the airport. Maybe Mata would know.

He found her in the kitchen, working on lunch. She smiled when she saw him come in. "Everything all right at the airport?" she asked brightly.

Otto shook his head. "It looks like it has been abandoned."

"Oh."

"Do you know what happened to Mr. Wilson and Mr. Duncan?"

"Wilson I haven't heard anything about. I think I heard somewhere that Mr. Duncan died. Apparently he had quite a drinking problem and they found him in the hangar one day. I didn't think to tell you."

Well, that was too bad about Sparky. He was a good pilot. Wilson, he didn't know about. What could have happened to him? Otto began to have an inkling of an idea, but there was work to be done so he turned to it.

***

Two weeks later, Otto was coming in from the barn when he saw a large black car making its way down the drive. He didn't recognize the make or the occupants. The limo stopped outside the farmhouse and a liveried chauffeur jumped from the driver's side and opened the back door. A distinguished looking man climbed out of the back seat. He spotted Otto and said, "Captain Kerchner?"

Otto stepped toward him. "I'm Otto Kerchner."

The man plucked a business card from an inside pocket. "Allow me to introduce myself. I am James Potter of Potter and Jensen, attorneys-at-law in Minneapolis. Is there some place we can talk?"

Otto shook hands with the man. He had a firm grasp. Otto didn't know what to think. Maybe they were being sued. But why come all the way from Milwaukee to do that? He motioned toward the door. "We can talk in the kitchen. Come on in.'

They filed into the kitchen where Mata was washing dishes. "Mr. Potter, this is my sister Mata."

Potter tipped his hat and then removed it. "Delighted to make your acquaintance, Miss…Kerchner?"

Mata quickly dried her hands and took Potter's outstretched palm. "Nice to meet you, Mr. Potter." She looked at Otto quizzically.

"Mr. Potter is an attorney from Minneapolis," Otto explained.

"Our taxes are paid up, Mr. Potter," Mata began.

Potter smiled. "Oh, I'm not here about taxes. May I have a seat?"

"Certainly," Otto said, and indicated a seat at the table. Ross sat and opened his briefcase. Otto took one of the other seats and Mata the third. It was Potter's turn to look quizzically at Otto.

"Mata and I are partners in the farm," Otto indicated. "We make all the decisions together. She takes care of our finances."

"This does not have anything to do with the farm, Captain," said Potter, drawing a thick sheaf of papers from his briefcase. "It has to do with the airport."

"The airport? It's in ruins."

"Well, it's yours now, Captain."

"It's what?"

"It's yours. Our client, Mr. Wilson, passed away suddenly last November. It took a while to straighten out his affairs. That's why I'm only now getting to you. Mr. Wilson left you the airport property and everything on it in his will."

Otto was speechless for a moment. Then he spoke. "What am I going to do with an airport?"

Potter chuckled. "Anything you wish, Captain. It's all yours. Please sign at the X's and that will take care of the paperwork."

Otto took the huge black fountain pen from Potter and signed his name where he indicated. Potter gave him a copy of the deed to the airport made out in his name, collected his papers, put them in his briefcase. He stood up and offered his hand first to Mata and then to Otto.

"Thank you for your time. Now if you'll excuse me, I need to be on my way back to Minneapolis."

"Won't you have some coffee," Mata asked him. "I should have offered you some earlier. It's just…"

Potter waved one hand, on which a huge diamond sparkled. "No thank you, Miss Kerchner. That's a kind offer, but one which I feel I must refuse. Now if you'll excuse me, I'll be on my way."

Otto opened the door and Potter strode toward the limo where the chauffeur stood by the car. He opened the rear door and Potter slid in the back seat. The chauffeur got in, started the car and drove off. Potter gave them a brief wave and then they were gone down the driveway.

Otto and Mata were quiet for a moment. "Well," Otto said after a while.

"Yes?" Mata asked.

"Well, I have work to do. We'll talk about this over lunch." He headed back to the barn.

"As you wish, dear brother. As you wish."

***

A couple of hours later, at lunch, they sat in silence for a while. Finally Otto said, "So?"

"So what?" Mata answered.

"Is this a game?" Otto said.

"What kind of game?"

"A game where you answer my question with another question."

"Well," Mata said, "if it is such a game, you started it by asking a question."

"And you continued it by answering with a question."

They were both smiling by this time, and then broke into waves of loud laughter. After a while they laughed themselves to silence. Otto broke that silence.

"So, what do you want to do with the airport?"

"It's your airport, Otto, what do you want to do with it?"

"Help me decide. We could turn it back into pastureland."

"We have about all the acreage we can manage right now without getting bigger than I want to."

"I could run it as an airport if you'll help me with the finances."

"I can do that easily, brother." She reached across the table and took his hand. "I want to see you happy. You have seemed so down and quiet ever since you've come back. I think flying would be good for you, and meeting people who come to fly."

"I'll see," Otto said. "When do we eat?"

Mata laughed and shook her head.

Chapter 39

A Letter Arrives—February, 1945

Otto came home for supper the week after Potter's visit. Mata was in the kitchen, working on the meal. She smiled when she saw Otto and then assumed a serious expression. "A letter came for you today."

"Oh?" Otto rarely got mail.

"Yes. It's from England." She handed the thin envelope to him.

Otto studied the return address. "A. Franklin, 43 W. Eads, Wembley." He didn't know any "A. Franklin." He tore the envelope open and took the single sheet of thin paper out. Mata went into the living room to leave him alone. He read:

Dear Otto,

I am writing to you to say how truly sorry I am that I could not stand by you. It was simply too much to bear and I feel awful about running away. I pray that some day you will forgive me.

The second piece of news I have is that we have a son. He was born June 30, 1944. He looks like you and I hope that you may meet him some day.

I married a RAF leftenant to give our son a father. Roger is good to me and to young Otto (that's his name).

Things are hard here, as they have been. I hope that you are recovering well and that you do not think too badly of me.

I am,

Your Alice

Otto held the letter in his hand for a moment. Mata came back into the room. "Is it from—" she started.

Otto handed her the letter and looked at the floor for a minute.

Mata read the letter. "Are you going to answer her?"

Otto took the piece of paper and crumpled it in his fist. "When do we eat?" he said.

Chapter 40

A Chance Encounter—early March, 1945

Otto drove over to the airport to look at it with a closer eye. It wasn't too far gone. He could have it repaired. They had money from his disability and Mata had accumulated a nice little nest egg with careful management of their finances. He nodded to himself. It was worth a try.

He drove into town, stopping first at the lumber yard, wearing his hat pulled low over his face. He knew by this time how people would react to his appearance. They had taken "field trips" at the hospital in Boston to public places to become accustomed to the reactions they would receive. These ranged all the way from people who gasped or looked away quickly to children who asked "Mommy, what's wrong with that man?" There was one bright spot during these excursions. A well-dressed older man came up to him and studied his face for a long minute. He stuck out his hand. "Captain, I want to thank you for your service to our country. You've obviously sacrificed a great deal and I salute you for it."

Otto returned the handshake. "Thank you, sir. That means a great deal to me."

This episode was the only one like it in his time at the hospital.

People in the town were marginally better. They knew him, after all, or at least what he had been. Still, some of them looked at him a little too long. Otto came out of the lumber store with his order completed. They would deliver the next day.

He turned to go down the street to where he had parked the truck when he saw her—he saw Betty making her way across the street, clad in a yellow dress the same color as the one she wore when they practiced dancing for the prom. She saw him standing there on the sidewalk and smiled broadly, quickening her step to come over to him. Otto waited. Uh oh, he thought. Here it comes.

"Otto! How are you?" There was no sign of shock or aversion on her face. She embraced him and reached up and kissed him on his cheek, which was almost entirely covered by scar tissue. He realized that it was one of the few times a woman had kissed him since his accident.

"Well, I'm a little different from the time you last saw me, Betty. But you haven't changed a bit!"

She cast her eyes down for a brief moment. "Maybe in ways that don't show, I have. But no matter. I heard about your accident and your medal, and Mata kept me up about your treatment. I didn't want to intrude on your time with your family, so I was waiting until I ran across you. It is truly good to see you."

"It's great to see you, Betty. Well, I have to be getting along…"

He turned to go, but she caught him by the wrist. "Otto Kerchner, do you mean to tell me you can't spend a few minutes catching up with an old friend?"

Otto felt himself blushing, although he was sure it wasn't visible. "Of course I can, Betty, it's just that…"

"Just that what, Otto?" She was looking steadily at him with her fists on her hips.

"Nothing, Betty. Is Spencer's still open?"

"You bet. I haven't been there in years. Let's go."

She went over to the same Packard convertible she had driven to prom. With all vehicle production turned to wartime uses, the cars did not look that much different from those Otto was familiar with when he left. Betty looked at his "new" pickup. "You've moved up in the vehicle world, Otto."

He smiled. "This was Mata's doing." Betty laughed at this, a laugh that sounded like silvery bells. Otto got into the pickup and followed Betty to Spencer's. They parked and went inside. The waitress waved them to a table. There weren't many other customers at that hour, so they sat down in the seats closest to the door. A few eyes turned their way and then quickly looked away.

Betty sat across from him. She hadn't changed much in the time he was gone. Maybe a little more mature looking. He wondered how he looked to her.

"You haven't changed a bit, Betty." She blushed and looked down.

"Why, thank you." There was a moment of silence.

"I'll say it for you. I have changed a lot."

She reached across the table and took his hand. "I was so sorry to hear about your accident and injury. But Otto…"

"Yes?"

"Your eyes are still the same. They are still as wise and kind as ever. It's still the same you inside."

"I'm glad you feel that way because I don't feel the same."

"But you are. I can tell." She took her hand off his as the waitress came up.

"What'll it be, folks? Ladies first." They hadn't noticed the waitress.

"I'd like water to drink," Betty said, "and a tuna salad on whole wheat."

"And you, sir?" Otto saw the familiar flicker in the waitress's eyes.

"I'll have a cheeseburger done medium well with mayonnaise, mustard, lettuce, tomato and pickle, and a soft drink. Thank you."

The waitress took their menus and walked off rapidly.

"So, Betty," Otto began as she got out of earshot. "How are you?"

"I'm all right," she said, but Otto saw she dropped her eyes as she said this and knew she was not all right.

"Are you still working at the bank?"

"No, I stopped that when I got married. I stay at home most days and supervise the staff. I do sing in the choir at church and sit on the library board. I think music and books are so important."

"I agree. Go on, please."

"There's not much left to tell."

"What about the lucky fellow you married?"

"To be honest, and we always have been honest with each other, I don't see much of Tom. He's either working or at the club or on a business trip. I don't want anyone to know how things are, so I don't say much, but honestly, I'm starting to think this marriage business was a mistake."

"I'm sorry to hear that. I'm still not married and probably never will be now."

"Don't be so sure. Some smart girl will snap you right up."

"I doubt it, but thank you for saying that."

She took his hands again. "Dear Otto, do you ever think that things could have been different?"

"Different how?"

"With me and you?"

"Betty, I don't think much about the way things could have been. I try to think about the way things are and accept them. It's part of the way I deal with my situation."

"I see." Just then the waitress came back with their order. She set them down and they ate for a while in silence.

Betty spoke. "Let's get together again soon."

Otto hesitated. "Betty, it's really great seeing you and talking to you, but really, you're a married woman."

He could not read her expression. "If you can call it a marriage," she said. "I rarely see Tom and if I say anything to him, it turns into a big argument." Tears filled her eyes. "I should have waited for you. We had—have something special."

"I'm sorry, Betty." He reached out and took her hand. "I'm still your friend. That hasn't changed."

She smiled through her tears. "Thank you, Otto. That means the world to me."

They finished and got their check. Otto insisted on paying. They walked out to their cars.

"Otto, one more thing…"

"What is it, Betty?"

"Would you give me flying lessons?"

"I'd love to, but I haven't flown since the accident. I'm not sure I will ever fly again."

"I know you will. You were born to fly."

"I'll think about it and let you know. Great seeing you, Betty." He stuck out his hand.

"Oh, Otto," she said and reached up and kissed him on the cheek. "It was so nice talking with you. We'll have to do it again."

"I hope so," she said, getting into her car. "Good-bye for now."

"'Bye, Betty." He started the truck, got in and drove home. Life was interesting. And sometimes amazing.

Chapter 41

Teach Me Tonight—Late March, 1945

Betty was true to her word, and the next Friday she showed up midmorning at the airport. Otto recognized her Packard as it pulled up beside the hangar. The airport wasn't that busy, so Otto hurried over and opened the driver's door for her. "Otto!" she exclaimed. "So good to see you again!" She gave him a hard hug and kissed his cheek. "When do we start flying?"

Otto looked down sheepishly. "Actually, I meant to call you. There's no flight instruction for the duration. All the fuel and materiel go to the war effort. I'm sorry."

Betty's bright blue eyes flickered briefly. "Well, let's go flying anyway. Are you OK with flying? Which one is your plane? Is it the silver one over there?"

"No, we own the yellow Cub and the red-and-white J-5. I'd use the J-5 for instruction if we could, so let's take the J-2 up. I can give you informal instruction and some flight time, but nothing official. We do have a small fuel allotment and there's not much business. I think I'll be all right since you'll be with me. "

"Let's go," Betty said.

She took his arm and they walked over to the yellow Piper. Otto went over the parts of the aircraft with her and showed her how he inspected each part. Betty watched with the same kind of concentration on her face that Otto remembered from algebra class. Finally he said, "All right, you climb into the pilot's seat and I'll prop it."

"'Prop it' as in 'prop it up?'"

"No, as in 'turn the prop to start the engine.' This aircraft doesn't have a self-starter like the J-5 does." Otto helped Betty into the cockpit, showed her the controls and had her pull out the throttle and the choke. "Close the throttle when the engine starts but not all the way, and I'll come up and trade places with you."

Otto went around to the front of the aircraft and pulled the prop through and then gave it a hard tug as he stepped back. The engine caught and Betty cut the throttle to idle. She got out of the front cockpit and got into the back. Otto climbed into the front. He shouted back to Betty over his shoulder. "Ready?"

"I'm ready," Betty said.

"Let's go, then!" Otto advanced the throttle and the little yellow plane moved forward to its takeoff position.

"Is it always this bumpy?" Betty asked, leaning up so Otto could hear her.

"Not once we take off. It should be very smooth today." Otto lined up on the familiar runway and advanced the throttle. The Cub trundled forward, slowly at first and then faster and faster.

He heard Betty squealing from the back seat, which she never did as far as he knew. The airplane's tail came up, and they were running level to the ground. Otto waited until the airspeed reached the rotate velocity and pulled back on the stick. The Cub lifted off and they were flying. They climbed a little more slowly than usual, because of Betty's extra weight, although Otto thought she didn't weigh that much at all.

Otto heard Betty from the back seat as they climbed. She was both laughing and crying. "Betty, are you all right?"

"I'm more than all right, I'm wonderful! What an experience! Otto, why didn't you tell me it was like this. It's amazing. Thank you! Thank you! Thank you!" She reached up and hugged him around the neck so strongly he started choking. He tore at her hands and pulled them off and when he had recovered his breath, said "Don't choke the pilot, Betty! You'll need me to land this thing."

She dropped her hands to his shoulders. "I'm sorry, Otto. I'll try to behave. But you understand how exciting this is, I'm sure."

"I certainly do, Betty." He pulled them into a wide turn and then straightened out.

"This is beautiful," Betty exclaimed. "You can see everything from here. Everything looks like toys—the farms, the houses, the cars. It's a different world up here. I love it!"

They flew on a bit more and then Otto said, "Would you like to fly the plane?"

"Oh, can I? I won't ruin it or crash it or something like that?"

"I doubt it," Otto chuckled. "I have dual controls. I'll take back over if you get into trouble, but I don't think I will have to." He released his controls. "You have the aircraft."

He could hear Betty in back of him, breathless. "Oh, my…oh, my…this is hard…" After a few seconds the Cub skidded off to one side. "Oh!" Betty screamed in a small voice. "What am I doing wrong?"

Otto brought the Cub back on course with a brief touch on the stick. "You're doing well. Just a light touch on the controls is all you need. Not as much as you would use on a fountain pen. The aircraft tends to be stable unless you persuade it otherwise." The noise of the Cub engine sounded like one of the power lawn mowers the groundskeepers used at Betty's house. It was nowhere near the thunder of the four Wright Whirlwinds of the Fortress. But, then, no one was shooting at them.

Otto was glad that he suffered no anxiety about taking the Cub up. Having Betty with him made a difference, as did concentrating on helping her fly?

"This is great, Otto," exclaimed Betty as she guided the airplane through a few small turns. Otto took the controls and said, "I have the stick." He brought the Cub over in a hard left turn so that they were almost looking straight down at the ground through the side window. Betty stifled a sharp scream.

"Sorry, should have warned you. We need to get back. I don't have that much of a fuel allotment and I'd like to do this again if you'd care to."

"I'd love to," Betty answered from the back seat. "It's so beautiful and peaceful up here, not like the world below." They straightened out from the turn. The newly planted fields stretched from horizon to horizon. Otto put the airplane into the approach pattern as Betty followed each turn, looking right and left. Then they were on final, and they dropped until they could hear the whispering of grass against the wheels. Otto chopped the throttle, and they were down, rolling smoothly to a stop. Otto moved the throttle up a bit and they rolled up to the tie-down close to the hangar.

Otto opened the side door, climbed out and helped Betty out of the front. She was flushed and smiling, and when her feet hit the ground, she enveloped Otto in a huge hug and kissed him on the mouth. He nearly lost his balance but steadied himself on one of the Cub's struts.

"Otto! That was terrific! Let's do it again soon! I don't think I've ever been so excited!"

"It was fun, Betty. How about next Saturday about the same time?"

"You got a date, mister!" she called as she swung off to her car. She waved with one arm extended as she got into the car, fired up the engine and made a quick half-turn to be pointed in the right direction.

Otto stood by the Cub, waving as she picked up speed. He got a rag from the cockpit and started wiping down the Cub. That was definitely a good time, he thought, already wishing it was next Saturday.

**

Betty came for her lesson the next Saturday, and the next, and so on. It was soon evident that she was an excellent and sensitive pilot, and Otto spent much of each lesson looking around and enjoying being in the air. They made a cross-country trip to Eau Claire in the big Cub, where they grabbed a sandwich at the snack bar (Otto teased her that he was glad they had tuna fish since that's what Betty always had to eat when he was with her).

After just a few lessons, Otto knew Betty was ready to solo. They were sitting talking about the lesson at an outdoor table by the office door. "So just try to stay relaxed on your approach to landing. I think you're tightening up on the stick and that causes you to over-react when you get some bumps. Light touch, and go with the aircraft and it'll put you down smoothly if you don't try to horse it around."

Betty listened with the same rapt concentration she always gave him when he talked about the lesson.

"This is so much fun, Otto. When will I be able to solo?"

"I'm not sure. I'll let you know when I think you're about ready. Just one thing—"

"Wear a blouse you don't mind ruining next time."

Betty's eyes widened. "I'm going to solo? But—am I ready?—are you sure?"

Otto raised his right hand. "I didn't say anything about soloing, did I? Just wear something old."

Betty leaned over the table and kissed him on the cheek. "You are such a dear! Thank you! Thank you! Thank you!"

Otto blushed, grinned and waved a hand in her direction. "OK, next week, then. We'll see."

"All right, dear Otto. I'll see you then." She walked off to her car and drove off with the top down, waving until he could see her no more."

Otto went over and emptied the trash from the large can beside the table. As he was hauling it around to the dump area in the back, he thought, I'm falling for her. Dammit, I'm falling for a married woman. Maybe I should tell her I can't teach her any more. Well, she'll solo next week and I won't spend as much time in the cockpit with her. We'll see.

***

Betty showed up half an hour early to her lesson the next Saturday. The weather was clear, and Otto told her he'd have to finish some paperwork before her lesson. She stood and looked around the silent airport where there only the planes and the high school kid Otto had hired to help him run the place. It was a contented place for her, unlike her house, which was so big and depressing.

He came out and handed her the keys to the Cub. "Take 'er up," he smiled.

"What!? By myself? But I'm not ready! I can't! I mean…"

"You're ready," Otto told her. "Now get flying, lady!"

Otto sat on the picnic table outside the office and watched Betty preflight the Cub. She was dressed to the nines as usual with a yellow skirt and a nice white blouse that looked new. She apparently had forgotten his warning to wear something old. Maybe she didn't have anything old.

She finished her preflight and climbed into the cockpit. Otto walked over to prop the engine. He pulled it through once.

"Switch on!" Betty called.

"Switch on," Otto answered.

"Clear!"

"Clear!"

"Contact!"

"Contact!"

Otto spun the prop hard, backing away as the engine caught. He gave Betty a thumbs up and she nodded. The engine ran up, and she taxied toward the runway. She held at the end, testing the controls. Satisfied that everything was in order, she pulled out the throttle and started her takeoff roll.

The little yellow airplane started down the field, slowly at first and then faster and faster. Betty pulled back on the stick at just the right time, and she was airborne, climbing for altitude. Otto could hear her whooping all the way from where he stood. He grinned.

The Cub ran through its departure pattern and Betty was off to the west. Otto watched the aircraft grow smaller and smaller until it disappeared over the horizon. He could still hear the engine in the morning stillness. He sat on the table and waited. In a few minutes, the Cub appeared from the southwest, entering the pattern precisely and running through the legs. Betty turned on final and smoothly brought the aircraft down. She flared a little too high and the plane bounced twice before settling to earth. She taxied over to where Otto stood, parked the Cub and cut the engine. Otto came over and opened the door, a pair of scissors in his hand.

Betty jumped out of the cockpit and embraced Otto hard. "It was wonderful! I wasn't concerned at all! I did everything just the way you told me! I'm sorry I bounced on landing! Thank you so much for teaching me!"

Otto staggered backward under the force of Betty's hug. "Nice flight," he said. "And don't worry about bouncing it. You'll improve. Now for the ceremony. Untuck your blouse."

Betty backed up and took the tail of her blouse from her skirt.

"In honor of your first flight," Otto began, and snipped off the end of her blouse, "I initiate you into the fellowship of pilots." He presented the scrap of cloth to Betty. "Now we have to sign the paperwork."

Betty slipped her arm around his waist as they walked over to the table. Otto had the application for her license there and had her sign it. He then took the pen and wrote on the cloth, "Excellent first flight! April 25, 1944. Otto Kerchner, Instructor." He gave the scrap to Betty. "Here! A lot of fellows frame these and hang them on a wall."

For the first time since he had known her, Betty was less than well-dressed, with one uneven edge of her blouse hanging down over her skirt. She couldn't seem to stop smiling. "You did so well! I'm so proud of you!" he told her. "And I have a little something for you—" he pulled out a bag from the department store in town—"something every pilot should have."

"You didn't have to get me anything," Betty exclaimed. "You taught me to fly." She pulled a long white silk scarf out of the bag. "Otto! It's lovely! Just like pilots wear! Thank you!" She kissed him again.

Otto smiled. "You *are* a pilot, Betty!" He wrapped the scarf around her neck. "There—now you're really ready to fly!"

Betty beamed and posed with her scarf. "I'd say this calls for a celebration. How about dinner at my house this evening? You can meet Tom."

"That would be swell. Can I bring Mata?"

"Of course. About seven, then?"

"I'll be there. Thank you for the invitation."

"We'll have something pork-ish if that's all right with you."

Otto laughed. "I was in the Army. I'll eat anything."

She got into her car and took his hand. "Thank you, Otto. You've done so much for me. We'll have to fly together."

Otto shook his head. "You don't need me to fly. It would be fun to do it together, though."

"See you!" She put the car in gear and drove off. Otto stood there a while and then went back into the office.

***

"Mata! I'm home!" Otto called as he came through the kitchen door.

Mata came into the room. "How did it go today, brother?"

"Fine. Betty soloed and she's invited us for dinner tonight. I accepted on your behalf. I hope that was OK."

"That would be wonderful. I've always wanted to see the inside of their house." She stood by the wall, steadily looking at him.

"Why are you looking at me that way?"

"I'm just wondering exactly what kind of relationship you have with Betty."

"She's a friend. And now she's a fellow pilot."

"I wonder, dear brother. I wonder. A woman knows."

"Knows what?"

"What's happening with you and Betty?"

"Which would be nothing. I'm going to help Steve with the milking."

"As you wish. Just be careful."

***

Mata pulled the Ford up in the circular driveway a few minutes before seven. She peered out the windshield at the two-story brick colonial. "Wow," she mouthed. "What a house! And I bet the inside is as gorgeous as the outside."

They got out of the car and went over to the front door. Otto rang the doorbell and they heard a distant ring and then steps coming toward them on the other side of the door. The massive oak door swung open, and Sarah stood before them. "Miss Kerchner, Captain Kerchner, it is so good to see you. Mrs. Brown is expecting you. Please come in."

She showed them into the parlor where Otto and Betty had practiced dancing what seemed like a lifetime ago. They took seats on the sofa as Sarah indicated. "Mrs. Brown will join you shortly. Is there anything I can get you?"

"No, nothing, Sarah, thank you. How are you?"

Sarah smiled briefly. "I am well, thank you for asking. Now, please excuse me."

Mata had not said a word. She was looking around at the furnishings. "So what do you think?" Otto said out of the side of his mouth.

Mata was breathless. "It so…beautiful. I've only seen places like this in magazines. What a gorgeous, elegant house!"

"Yeah, Betty and her family always did have good taste. Her parents gave her this as a wedding present and moved to another, larger place. It's palatial, I hear."

At that moment Betty swept into the room, wearing a black evening dress. Mata looked down at her print dress for a moment. "Welcome; it's so good to see you! Mata, I'm so happy you could come." She kissed Mata on both cheeks and then came over and hugged Otto. "It's my flight instructor! Did Otto tell you I soloed today?"

"Yes, he did," Mata answered. "Congratulations!"

"Maybe I'll be the next Amelia Earhart!"

"I hope you won't disappear," Mata chimed in.

"I have no plans to disappear. Would you like some drinks? Please sit down and I'll have James serve us."

As she rang a small silver bell, Otto noticed that her eyes were puffy and somewhat red. He looked over at Mata, who raised an eyebrow. "Are you all right, Betty?"

Betty looked down at her feet. "I'm sorry. Tom had to go back to the bank on business. He won't be joining us for dinner and sends his regrets."

Otto and Mata murmured words of understanding. "I hope you will be able to meet him another time."

James came into the room bearing a silver cocktail service and three glasses. "Are martinis all right?"

"Fine," Otto said. Mata looked at him quickly. "A martini is a drink made with gin and vermouth. It's quite good. You should try it."

"Yes, do try one, Mata." Betty said.

"I've only had beer," Mata responded. "And I didn't like it very much. But I'll try this martini."

James poured three drinks into chilled glasses and handed one to each of them. Otto and Betty took a sip, from their glasses, while Mata barely tasted hers.

"So, what do you think, Sis?"

"It's…different. I think I could grow to like it."

Otto and Betty laughed.

***

"Would anyone care for coffee? We can have it in the parlor." Betty looked at her two dinner guests, who had pushed their chairs back slightly.

"Yes, please," they both answered.

"Well, let's adjourn to the parlor, then. Captain Kerchner, would you escort us?"

Otto took Mata on one arm and Betty on the other. "You must tell us more about your bomber and crew and your missions," Betty told him as they entered the parlor.

"There's not much to say," Otto offered. "It was a job and we did it and now I'm out of it."

"Otto doesn't like to talk about it much," Mata told Betty.

"I understand," said Betty, looking at him in a way he couldn't figure out. Sarah appeared carrying a tray with a silver coffee service and china cups.

"So, Mata, I hear the dairy is going really well."

"Yes, we've been fortunate that there is such demand for milk. I think there will always be."

They finished their coffee and then Otto stood. "We really should be going. Cows don't know how late we've been up. Thank you for a delightful evening, Betty."

"It was my pleasure. I hope you'll come again soon."

Betty saw them to the door, hugged Mata and after hesitating a bit, hugged Otto. They got into their car and drove away. Betty waved to them from the door.

"What do you suppose happened?" Otto asked Mata.

"I think Mr. Brown didn't want to dine with you. He's probably heard too much about you from Betty."

"What?"

"It's as clear as the nose on your face, Otto. Betty is in love with you—and I'd say you're mighty fond of her as well."

"We're just friends."

"Right."

"Mata…"

"Yes?"

"Nothing."

Chapter 42

Unexpected News—Early April, 1945

Otto came home from the airport one balmy April day. Mata greeted him at the door in tears.

"What is it, Mata? What's wrong?"

"Otto, the President's dead. It just came over the radio. He died in Warm Springs." She sobbed into the handkerchief she held in her hands.

Otto hugged her and then went over to the radio in the living room and turned it on. FDR dead. How could that be? The war must have put an incredible strain on the man. The announcer came on, speaking of the President's death in somber tones.

Otto tried to think. Who was Vice-President—make that the new President? Wasn't it that Truman fellow from Missouri? What kind of leadership would he provide? Only time would tell, he supposed. In the meantime, the noose was tightening around Germany. Otto hoped Truman would prosecute the war with the energy that Roosevelt did.

***

The next morning, Otto went over to the airport. There was some business, but nothing like what it would be after the war. Mata had told him he should buy some surplus aircraft that surely would become available with the cessation of hostilities. That sounded like a good idea to him. Out of all those government-trained pilots, some would want to buy their own aircraft and fly them. That would be good for business.

He opened the office, went in, sat at the desk and started filling out some monthly reports. There wasn't much to report, but the bureaucrats had to be satisfied. The morning sun came through the glass in the door, and suddenly he was aware someone was standing in the light. He couldn't see who it was for the glare at first, but as he stood, he saw that it was Betty, and she was dressed in black. He had never seen her dressed entirely in black. She had an absolutely implacable look on her face.

He caught her by the shoulders. "Betty! Are you all right? Sit down. Let me get you some water."

She sat and stared straight ahead. He got her a glass of water and gave it to her. She drank it slowly and then turned to look at him. "Otto, Thomas has been killed."

"What? Killed? How awful! What happened?"

She smiled a sardonic smile. "The husband of his girlfriend shot him dead. In bed with her. Shot them both. And so I'm a widow. And you know what? I don't care. In fact, I'm glad. Good riddance, I say. Just call me the Merry Widow."

Otto was speechless. "I am so sorry, Betty. What a horrible thing to have happen."

She looked at him evenly. "Don't be sorry, Otto. I'm not."

"When is the funeral?"

"I don't know. I don't care. Do you have something to drink?"

"There's some whiskey in the desk."

"Gimme a shot."

Otto poured one shot after another. Betty was soon out of it, collapsed on the desk, breathing heavily. Otto thought for a bit. He finally lifted Betty up, carried her to the Packard, put her in the passenger's seat and drove her home. As he pulled up, Sarah and James came rushing out of the house. "We were so worried about Miss Betty," Sarah said. "She got the news and just ran to her car and drove off. We didn't know where she was!"

"She was at the airport with me," said Otto as he helped get Betty into the house. "She had a few drinks."

"You gave her drinks?" Sarah regarded Betty somberly.

"Well, she asked for them. I've seen soldiers do this after some sort of trauma."

"I think you know how things were between her and Mr. Brown," Sarah observed. "I would think she'd be drinking to celebrate."

"I don't know her motives," Otto said as they carried Betty up the stairs to her room. They deposited her on the bed and tiptoed out. "She'll be all right," Otto told them. "Just let her sleep it off. She's going to have a hell of a hangover, though."

"We'll take good care of her," James told him.

Otto went back down the steps. He hesitated at the front door. "Do you mind if I take the Packard home? Someone can pick it up later or I can get Mata to pick me up if I return it."

"We'll come get it later," Sarah said. "Thanks for bringing her home." She caught Otto's wrist as he was opening the door. "She's going to need you now as never before."

"I know that," Otto told her, thinking, *What have I gotten myself into?* "One more thing—when is the funeral?"

"Saturday at eleven AM at the Episcopal Church," said James.

"Thank you," Otto told him, started the car and pulled off. What a fine mess, he thought.

***

Word got around town about the manner of Tom Brown's demise and of course most of the town turned out for the funeral. Some wags were calling it "the best show in town," although such sentiments were repeated at places such as the barber shop and the pool hall and not in polite society. Otto put on his dress uniform and Mata the dress she wore to her mother's funeral. Few people had seen Otto since his return, so this would be their first chance to do so.

He and Mata arrived half an hour early and found the sanctuary three-quarters full. They took seats near the back, but Otto could see people looking at him a few seconds more than was polite.

An unseen organist played some familiar hymns; others Otto had never heard before. Must be the difference between Episcopalian and German Lutheran, he thought. Right at eleven, a robed minister came in the back of the sanctuary and called in a sonorous voice, "Will you all rise?" The congregation stood, and the minister led a small procession down the aisle to the front. Six men in dark suits carried in a casket covered with a large white cloth, followed by Betty in black wearing a veil, with her mother on one side and her father on another. She looked over at Otto and winked. Otto hoped no one else saw it, but he thought Mata did, because she sighed heavily. The rest of the procession consisted of people Otto did not know. He assumed they were Tom's relatives.

The group reached the front and the pall bearers placed the coffin on a white-shrouded stand. They retired to places on the front pew and the family filled in behind them.

Otto half-listened to the service. He had seen too many deaths in the air for one more to make an impression, particularly when he didn't know the man. Of course, he didn't know all the crews he saw perish in the stratosphere, but that was somehow different. They were his brothers in arms. Tom Brown was, well, he was what he was. There was no mention of anything about Tom as an individual. Otto wondered if that was true of all Episcopalian funerals or just this one. The prayers were beautiful, he thought.

The service passed quickly, and the congregation stood as the coffin was carried past them. Otto and Mata did not plan to go to the Union Cemetery in town and waited while the family passed by. This time Betty gave him a radiant smile. Oh my Lord, Otto thought. What will happen next?

Mata was wiping tears away. He put his arm around her as they walked from the church. "Are you all right, sis?" he said.

"I'm all right. It's just so sad, and it will be difficult for Betty, the way people talk."

"Yes, people will talk," Otto murmured. They waited outside the church for the casket to be loaded into a black hearse. It pulled away, followed by the cars of those going to the cemetery. Otto and Mata got into their sedan and headed for home.

Chapter 43

Life Goes On—May, 1945

Otto occupied himself with reconstructing the airport during the spring. Betty came out regularly to take the Cub up. Occasionally Otto would ride with her in the J-5. She was building time. He had all the time he wanted for a while. They sat in the office and had long talks through lazy afternoons.

Mata told him that the time he and Betty spent together was the subject of much town gossip. Otto said he didn't care.

***

Betty sat across the table from Otto at the farmhouse. She was also a frequent visitor at the house now that she was a widow, and when Otto had to go over to the airport, sometimes she went with him, and sometimes she stayed and helped Mata. They enjoyed talking with each other.

Today, they were talking about business. Otto had plans and he wanted the two women in on them.

"We need to plan for the end of the war," he said. "There is going to be a tremendous increase of interest in flying and we have to be ready for it."

"So," said Mata, "we buy surplus aircraft and rent or re-sell them."

"You'll need funding," Betty told them.

"Mata is in charge of finances," Otto offered.

"We have some cash reserves," Mata said. "But we also need a bigger barn and some of the milking equipment needs replacing. I've been holding off until the end of the war."

"I think it'll all be over by the end of the year," Otto surmised. "We're on the continent and driving forward daily. And we control the air. The Nazis are finished. It's just a question of how soon."

"Do you wish you were still over there?" Betty asked him, taking his hand.

"I would like to be with the fellows and help with the effort, but if I had made two more missions I would have rotated home and become an instructor." He smiled wryly at what could have been.

Betty patted his hand. "I'm glad you're here."

Mata stood up and got the coffee pot. "Do you want me to leave you two love birds alone?"

Betty giggled. "Maybe later," Otto laughed.

Mata poured more coffee. "I think we need to incorporate the airport, get town sponsorship and sell stock."

"Whoa! Those are big steps!" Otto told her.

"Not all at once, silly. And we'll have to wait until the war's over. It's not like we're going to do all this this afternoon."

"I know my dad's bank would be good for a loan. He really admires you, Otto, and thinks the world of you."

"Are we agreed then?" Otto looked at both women. They nodded and he sat back in his chair.

Betty spoke. "Now I have an idea that's sort of related to business, and it's to have a charity ball to benefit the USO. We can have a band in from Minneapolis and sell tickets and make some money for a good cause. What do you think?"

"I think it's a great idea," Mata said. "Where would you have it?"

"Mom and Dad have said we can use their place. We can have it in maybe late May or early June."

"The war will be over by then," Otto pointed out. "I mean the war in Europe. I believe we're going to have to invade Japan, and that won't happen until late next year unless something unforeseen happens."

"In any case, there will be a need for funds," Betty noted. "So let's get started."

Otto stood up. "Planning social events is not my strong suite, so if you'll excuse me, I have some work to do. I'll help any way I can. Just tell me what to do."

"Oh, you can assure yourself we'll do that," Mata smiled, and she and Betty chuckled.

Otto left them talking about guest lists. He felt more comfortable on the farm or at the airport or in the air than he did at a social event. Still, it was a good idea. They would have to see how it all panned out.

***

Betty and Otto were working in the airport office one day later that week. The airport was quiet. A car came up the gravel drive, and Betty looked out to see who it was. "Otto, it's Mata!" she exclaimed and ran outside to see what Mata was doing there. She never came unless she had told them she would be coming.

Mata got out of the car, leaving the door open in her haste. "Betty! Otto! The Germans have surrendered! The war is over in Europe!"

Betty raced to her and they embraced, jumping up and down like two schoolgirls. Otto came out, wiping his hands. He smiled a broad smile as he embraced the two women. "It's finally over. I don't believe it. Well, one down and one to go." They stood there a while, the three friends, too overcome to think what this turn of events might mean for their lives.

***

The charity ball took place the last Saturday in May. Mata and Betty had enlisted some help, but they spent the better part of the week before at the Ross's mansion, decorating and taking care of final details. Otto had to stay at the farm and supervise the hired men since Mata generally did that. She came home Friday evening, looking tired but satisfied.

"So, how is it going?" Otto asked her.

"We're ready," she told him. "I just have to go over tomorrow morning and help Betty with a few details and then come home and get myself ready."

"With all this business, you haven't told me who your date is." Betty had asked Otto to escort her, and to wear his uniform.

Mata blushed. "It's Pete Johanssen, two farms over."

"Mata, I didn't know you had a boyfriend."

"He's not my boyfriend. We've been out a few times, but nothing beyond that."

"How did I miss this?"

"You've been busy with Betty."

"Yes, well, good for you, sis. I hope you have a great time."

"I know you will with Betty." She winked at him.

***

Otto had had his uniform cleaned, and he dressed carefully the next day. He came out into the living room. Mata clapped her hands. "How handsome you are, brother! Betty will be on the arm of the handsomest man there!"

"Well, I'd better get going. Thank you for letting me use your car."

"Yes, well, this isn't exactly a pickup affair. Pete will be along to get me in a few minutes, so you'd better get going."

Otto drove carefully to Betty's house, parked and knocked on the door. He was somewhat surprised when Betty opened the door herself. She looked radiant in a blue dress with her hair done up. Otto gave a low whistle. "You look wonderful," he told her.

"And you are so handsome," she said, drawing him by the hand into the vestibule.

"Where are Sarah and James?" he asked.

"They're at my parents' helping with the dance. They'll stay there overnight, so after the ball it'll be just us here. Now come in and let's have a little pre-event drink."

Otto followed her into the living room where the silver cocktail service was set up. She mixed up two cocktails, plopped an olive in each one and offered him one. He took it. "A toast!" she exclaimed.

"A toast," he returned, somewhat more weakly.

"To winning the war, to the USO and to us!" She clinked her glass on his.

"To winning the war, the USO and us!" he echoed. They both sipped from their martinis. "Sit down, we have a minute," Betty said. "Are you ready for your coming out in society?"

"Like a deb? I guess so."

"Most people haven't seen you since you got back. They want to see their war hero."

"I'm not exactly something to look at," Otto said.

"If they see what I see, they'll be just fine."

"There were plenty of stares at the funeral."

"Yes. Thank you for coming. What a show that was."

"The minister didn't say anything about Tom. Is that customary?"

"Apparently it is, although he asked me if there was anything I wanted him to say about him. I said no. What I meant was I didn't care *what* he said about the son of a bitch."

"That's so unlike you, Betty," looking at her with a level gaze.

"Yeah, well, no one knows how bad it was. And it was my own damn fault for marrying him."

"Well, water under the bridge."

"You like to say that, don't you, Otto?"

"It helps me get through."

They finished their cocktails and then stood to go. Betty took Otto's arm and they went out the front door.

"Ooh, you have the car," she exclaimed. "Very nice."

Otto opened the door for her and she got in. "Thank you," she smiled up at him.

Betty was clearly excited about the upcoming event. "We've raised over $20,000 from our little town. Can you believe that? Of course, everyone wants to help the boys. Everyone has someone in the war in some way."

She kept up a steady flow of comments during the short drive to her parents' house. They had to line up behind other cars turning into the long circular driveway. When they reached the head of the line, James opened Betty's door and then came around to park the car for them. "Good evening Captain," he said with a slight bow.

"Good evening, James," Otto returned. Betty took his arm and they walked the red carpet that had been laid out for the occasion. They walked through the ornate double doors that Otto remembered from their dance lessons. A uniformed butler announced two couples before them and then it was their turn:

"Mrs. Betty Brown and Captain Otto Kerchner!" he intoned. There was mild applause from couples gathered in the parlor. Otto and Betty stepped into the room. Betty waved to a few people she knew. Otto felt as if everyone were staring at him. They moved rapidly to the side of the room.

The orchestra Betty had hired for the occasion started playing. She looked at him in recognition: "It's 'Teach Me Tonight,'" she said. "One we practiced dancing to in high school. Let's dance, Otto. I want you to hold me in your arms. I'll even let you sing to me."

Otto laughed and took her easily into his arms. "No singing," he promised. "I've given up on that."

Betty laughed and they moved around the small dance floor with a few other couples. "You dance divinely, Captain K," Betty told him, smiling.

"As do you, Mrs. Brown," he returned. "I had the best instruction from two ladies of my acquaintance."

The soloist finished the song,

One thing isn't very clear, my love. Should the teacher stand so near, my love?

Graduation's almost here, my love. Teach me tonight.

They clapped for the orchestra, which swung into "In the Mood," an up-tempo number. The band was good, and played all the popular songs. The soloist took the mike and said, "And now a special trip number for all you guys and gals in the service. This dance is for you and this song is for you. Two other women joined her and they launched into "Boogie-Woogie Bugle Boy." The couples jitterbugged as if they were on fire.

After a couple more up-tempo numbers, the band slowed it down with "The White Cliffs of Dover." Betty had Otto hold her close. Otto couldn't help but think of Alice, who sang along with the song when they danced to it a world and eons away. Betty looked up at him. "Why so serious, Otto?"

"Oh, nothing. This song just reminds me of something."

"Or someone?"

"Or someone."

"Someone like Alice?"

"Well, yes."

"Mata told me you got a letter from her."

"I did."

"And?"

"I threw it away. That part of my life is over. I prefer to focus on what's going on now, including and especially you."

Betty held him closer. "I'm glad."

"So am I," Otto answered.

The band took a break, and the dancers filed into the dining room, which had been set up with a display of Army food. Otto groaned inwardly. He understood that the food was to show support and solidarity with the troops, but he had had enough Army food in the Army. He and Betty took small plates and a few forkfuls of the offerings and made their way to the garden, where tables covered with white linen had been set up. They sat down and were soon joined by Mata and Pete. Otto stood up as Mata sat down. "Good evening," Betty said. "Mata, you look absolutely lovely. Pete, you're lucky to have such a beautiful date."

"I know," Pete answered.

"I can't believe we're actually doing this and it's going so well," Mata said. "I hope we raise a lot of money for the USO!"

"We'll announce a final figure near the end," Betty assured her, "after we've had time to count it."

273

The two couples sat and listened as the orchestra started playing again. This time the song was "I'll Be Seeing You." Betty took Otto's hand as she hummed along with the song. The vocalist came in,

I'll be seeing you in all the old familiar places

That this heart embraces all day through…

Otto smiled at Betty. He couldn't remember being this happy for a long time.

***

Betty took the microphone about midnight to announce the totals. "I am so pleased to tell you that tonight we have raised over $22,000 for our USO. Isn't that wonderful?"

The couples gathered in the garden applauded and then began saying their good-byes.

Otto and Betty went over to her parents. "Mom and Dad, thank you so much for letting us have our soiree at your house. It was the perfect place!"

Otto shook hands with Betty's dad and her mom kissed him on the cheek. "I know you both worked very hard," Mrs. Ross told them. We were happy to provide the place."

"Well, we'll be going," Betty said. "I'll call you tomorrow."

"Good night," they said to each other.

Betty and Otto walked out into the warm evening. Otto opened the car door for her. He came around, got in, started the car, and they drove off.

"I hope you can come in for a few minutes," Betty told him. "And no excuses about having to get up with the cows."

"Well, I guess I can."

"You'd better, mister," and she laid her head on his shoulder.

Otto stopped the car in front of the house. "We'll have a nice nightcap," Betty promised.

She opened the door and they stepped in. She threw her arms around him and kissed him long and hard. "Alone at last," she whispered, and winked. "You sit here in the living room and I'll change into something more comfortable. Take off your jacket."

Otto obediently did as he was told. He sat looking around until Betty came in dressed in what he would call not very much. He gulped.

Betty had a cocktail glass in each hand. "Here's your drink," she told him. "Like my outfit?"

"V-v-very much," Otto stammered.

She took his glass from him and set it with hers on the table. She leaned over and kissed him, and as he responded, began to undress him. His hands slid down her back as he hugged her to him. She broke away from the kiss, stood up, took him by the hands and said, "Let's go upstairs where we'll be more comfortable."

She pulled Otto up and he followed her up the stairs. She lay on the bed on her back. He thought how alluring she looked and then she reached out and pulled him down on her.

***

Later, in the dark, Betty whispered, "Stay with me."

"I really should be going."

"Why won't you stay?"

"People will talk."

"Let them talk. I don't care."

"I have to think of your reputation, Betty." Otto stood and started getting dressed.

"Well, if you must, but promise we'll see each other tomorrow."

"We will. I'll be at the airport about nine."

"I'll be there."

He leaned over and kissed her. "I love you, Betty."

"And I love you, Otto."

He crept down the dark staircase and made his way to the Ford, driving home with a thousand thoughts and a slight smile.

Chapter 44

War's End—August, 1945

The beginning of August was hot in upper Wisconsin, except right by the lake, which always offered cooling breezes in the summer. Otto had tended to airport business all day, and when he pulled up into the driveway of the farmhouse, he was surprised that both Betty and Mata came running out to meet him.

"It's over! It's over!" they shouted, in such a frenzied fashion it was hard to tell what they were saying.

"What's over?" he asked as they hopped around beside him.

"The war!" Mata shouted. "Japan has surrendered! The war is finally over!"

Otto felt his knees go weak and he was glad they were there to hold him up. Almost. They fell over in a heap right there in the driveway, laughing and crying all at once. When they had exhausted themselves, they lay there for a few moments and then got to their feet, dusting themselves and each other off.

"When did you hear the news?" asked Otto.

"It was just on right before you came in." Betty told him. "Isn't it glorious?"

"Let's celebrate," Mata cried. "Let's go to town! I bet people are celebrating in the streets!"

And they were. As they drove up in Betty's car, the streets were filled with enthusiastic townspeople dancing, kissing each other, hugging and drinking out of bottles. As they got out, men ran up and kissed and hugged Mata and Betty. Women Otto had never seen before came up to him, hugged him and kissed him. Otto had to admit that he enjoyed it, and most of all the thought that all the destruction and sacrifice were over. Now, after so many years and so many deaths and so many injuries like his, they could return to leading normal lives. He felt joyful to overflowing. Life was good in so many ways.

Chapter 45

Northwest Airlines—November, 1945

Mata came into the house from hanging clothes late one morning to find Otto studying several sheaves of paper. She recalled a thick envelope that came for him in the mail earlier that week with the imprint of Northwest Airlines on it. Otto had said something about trying for an airline job since the airport was in good shape. He had hired a manager, Jimmy Thomas, from town, who had been in the AAF in the Pacific. He had flown reconnaissance missions and shared Otto's passion for airplanes.

"What are you doing, brother of mine?" she asked.

"I've decided to apply to be a pilot with Northwest Airlines. I think I'd make a good candidate with my war record and multi-engine time. So I have all these forms to fill out. Would you look over them to make sure I did everything correctly?"

"I'd be glad to." Mata sat down at the table and looked over some of the forms. "Otto, you're a shoo-in! Once you fill out the forms, what do you do?"

"The next step is to have an interview in Minneapolis. After that, I don't know."

"My brother, the airline pilot. That is so exciting!"

Otto labored over the forms and took them directly to the post office in town the next day so they would arrive sooner.

He waited impatiently for a return letter. It arrived ten days later. Mata greeted him at the door with it. "Otto! Look what came today!"

He ripped it open eagerly and read down the page. "I have an interview! Next Wednesday in Minneapolis with the chief pilot! This is great news! I have to tell Betty!"

"You know, brother, if we had a phone installed, you could call Betty. That is, unless you'd rather *see* her."

Otto was already running for his truck. "News like this needs to be delivered in person," he shouted. And he was off.

***

Betty's excitement matched his. "Oh, Otto, that is so wonderful! Can I go with you?"

"I'm just going to fly over, have the interview and fly back. I'll need to concentrate and frankly, Madame, you distract me."

She rubbed his shoulders. "Oh, I can distract you all right…"

"Betty…" he started to say but then he said no more.

***

Otto checked the address again. Yes, that was right. Fourth floor of this building. He still found cities a little confusing and intimidating but he reminded himself that being in the city and having an interview was a whole lot easier than taking on German flak and fighters. He pushed open the revolving door and headed straight for the elevator. "Floor, please," the operator said, looking at him longer than was necessary. "Four," Otto said.

Mata had helped him pick out a new suit, and he thought he looked pretty good, considering. He thought about wearing his uniform but decided against it. Northwest would know all about his military record. The elevator doors opened and he saw the logo of the company on the opposite wall.

He went into the office and was greeted by a well-dressed receptionist behind a counter. She looked at him levelly, without blinking. "Good morning, sir. May I help you?"

Otto stood with his hat in his hand. "I'm Captain Kerchner, and I have an appointment with Captain Harrison."

The receptionist smiled. "Please have a seat. I'll tell him you're here."

Otto sat on a sofa that he judged was leather-covered. Pictures of Northwest aircraft adorned the walls. He looked at them, especially noting the newest model. It would be great to fly one of those. It would also be nice to fly without people shooting at him.

The receptionist looked over at him. "Captain Harrison will see you now, Captain Kerchner."

"Thank you," Otto said, and went over and opened the door marked, "Captain Robert Harrison, Chief Pilot."

Harrison was seated at his desk, dressed in a dark business suit. He finished writing on the paper in front of him and then stood up, offering Otto his hand. As he made eye contact, Otto saw a flicker in his eyes and thought, Uh oh. Here it comes.

"Captain Kerchner, Robert Harrison. Good to meet you. Please have a seat." He indicated a chair across from him. Otto shook his hand and sat down.

"Did you have a good trip over?"

"Yes. I flew into the airport. Very smooth flight."

"I have no doubt, with your piloting skills. You were with the Eighth?"

"Yes, twenty-two missions and then I crashed on the twenty-third."

"I was with the 468th in the Pacific."

"Did you know Paul Tibbits?"

"He was with a special group, but, yeah, we all knew who he was. He was a pilot's pilot. Now, let me say first that your record is very impressive. Ordinarily we'd hire you on the spot, but—"

He hesitated, and Otto waited expectantly. Here it comes, he thought.

"Well, quite frankly, Captain, speaking aviator to aviator and veteran to veteran, we have appearance requirements."

"Yes?"

"I'm sorry, but you don't meet them. We have to think of our public image in this business." Otto read genuine regret in his voice and eyes. "Maybe you'd like to try our freight division. I am truly sorry, Captain."

There was no use beating a dead horse. Otto stood and offered his hand to Harrison. The chief pilot shook it, and said, "Perhaps in the future things will change. I'll keep your file active and let you know if it does. Thank you for coming in."

"Thank you for your time," Otto turned and walked back into the reception area. The receptionist looked up.

"I'm truly sorry, Captain. I hope you can fly for us one day." She must have known about the policy since Harrison's thick walnut door remained closed during their conversation.

"Thank you, ma'am. You're most kind."

Otto took the elevator down to the street and lost himself in the throngs on the sidewalk. He was somewhat accustomed to the way he looked by now, but that didn't mean everyone else was. He would have to think about his next step, his plan B. He always had the airport, and maybe something would come of that. He looked around for a cab to take him to the Minneapolis field.

***

Mata heard the sound of Otto's car pulling into the driveway late that afternoon and rushed out to meet him. She stopped when she saw his face. "Otto, what happened?"

He leaned wearily against the car. "They wouldn't take me because of the way I look."

"The way you look? What does that have to do with flying?"

"I don't know, Mata. Something to do with maintaining the image of the airline."

"Well, who is the president of it? We'll fight this! We'll make them see that you are the best damn pilot in the world."

Otto waved his hand. "We won't win, Mata. It's their policy and their company. I'll think of something else. Enlarging the airport or something."

Mata put her arm around him. "If that's what you want," she said.

"Well, I wanted to be a pilot for Northwest, but that didn't work out."

"We'll find something better," Mata told him. "I have faith in you."

Chapter 46

Serendipity—January, 1946

Otto threw himself into the airport with renewed energy. Betty was there most days and they enjoyed each other's company as they worked and as they took breaks. Otto had moved a bed into the back room and sometimes stayed there overnight. So did Betty.

He was going through paperwork early on a Monday morning. Betty had not come in yet, but he heard a car pull up in front of the office. He looked out and saw it was Mr. Ross, driven by his chauffeur. Otto hurried outside.

James opened the door for Mr. Ross, saying, "Good morning, Otto."

"Good morning, James, how are you?"

"I'm fine, sir. Mr. Ross has something to ask you."

Probably my intentions regarding his daughter, Otto thought, but Ross shook his hand as he got out of the car. "Good morning, Otto. I need a big favor."

"Good morning, Mr. Ross. I am at your disposal."

"I need to get to Minneapolis this morning for a last-minute meeting and I want to see if you would fly me there. Libeau moved away last month and I lost my air transport."

"Certainly I can, Mr. Ross, as a favor to you. I don't have a license to fly passengers but I can take you. Give me a few minutes to prep the aircraft and we'll be on our way." At the same time he was thinking, if I get a lot of these I'll need a faster, bigger capacity aircraft and a license. He tucked the idea in the back of his mind. If he couldn't fly for Northwest, he could fly for himself.

"Thank you, young man," Ross said. "And by the way, Mrs. Ross and I are very pleased that you are seeing Betty. We were never impressed with her husband. I don't know why the bank hired such a scoundrel. They did so over my head. The truth will out. It always does."

283

"Thank you, sir. Betty is a wonderful young woman. She should be here in a few minutes. Please have a seat in the ready room and we'll be all set ready to go in a few minutes."

***

Otto made the trip in record time with a tailwind and spent the two hours Ross was gone looking around the airport. He studied the bulletin board in the pilots' lounge and saw a notice for an auction of war surplus aircraft the next month. Some of the aircraft listed, especially the Beechcraft twins, seemed to be ideal for his purposes. He made a note of the date and time and a mental note to talk to Mata and Betty about his plans.

Mr. Ross appeared promptly at the time he had promised. Otto helped him into the J-5 and they were ready to return. "Did your meeting go well, sir?" he asked Ross.

"Very well, Otto, thank you." He looked thoughtful. "I have a series of meetings coming up and would like for you to fly me to them if you don't mind."

"I'll be glad to," Otto replied. "I've decided to start an air taxi business once I do all the paperwork and acquire some bigger, more powerful aircraft."

Ross clapped him on the back. "Splendid! And if you need financing, you know where to come. We'll offer you our best rates on a loan."

"Thank you, sir; that's very generous. I'll talk to Mata and Betty about it and keep you informed. In the meantime we can continue to use the Cub. But I think you'll like the Beechcraft once we get them."

The flight back was uneventful and they arrived back in Pioneer Lake mid-afternoon. Betty came out to greet them as Otto taxied up.

She kissed her father on the cheek as he got out. "Daddy! So good to see you! I got Otto's note about your trip. I hope it went well."

"It went swimmingly," Ross returned. "And your young man has a sound idea for a business flying people around. I'm sure he'll tell you all about it."

James had brought the car back and held the door for Ross as he walked toward the car. He waved to Otto and Betty. "Next Tuesday, same time, Otto. Good-bye for now." He got in and the car drove off.

Betty took Otto's arm as they walked to the office. "So tell me about this business idea. I want to hear all about it."

"I'd rather wait until Mata can hear all the details. How about if you come over about six tonight and have dinner with us?"

"You haven't been to my house for a while. What if you and Mata come for dinner? I'll fix it myself since Mama and Daddy are using James and Sarah now. Just one person doesn't need a butler *and* a maid."

"All right, I'll tell Mata," Otto said. "I'm sure she will be delighted not to have to cook. I'll tell you the basics, though. We're going to buy a couple of twin-engine surplus Beechcraft and use them to run an air service from Pioneer Lake to Minneapolis and maybe a couple of other cities."

Betty clapped her hands. "What a wonderful idea!" she exclaimed. "And that will certainly help the airport grow."

***

Otto rang the doorbell at Betty's house promptly at six. Mata had put on one of her church dresses and Otto wore his suit. Betty promptly opened the door. "Come in, come in," she told them, kissing first Mata and then Otto on the cheek. She showed them into the parlor where drinks were ready. "I hope martinis are all right."

"Just fine," Mata said. "I've acquired quite a taste for them."

"They're better than dark beer, I'd say," Otto noted. He raised his glass. "A toast: to our airline business."

"To our business," the other two echoed, clinking their glasses with his and taking a quick sip.

They chatted for a while and then Betty stood up. "Dinner's ready," she said. "Let's eat."

They talked as they ate.

"I think we can operate as a charter so we can see what kind of business is out there," Otto said. "This beef is delicious, Betty."

"Thank you, Otto. Sarah showed me how to make it."

"I've checked over the finances, and the income from the airport will fund the purchase of the aircraft," Mata said. "I'm going by average price at auction from last week."

"How do you find these things out, Mata?"

"I have my ways."

"I know that."

"So, anyhow, I'll file papers for our incorporation as a business. We need a name for the Department of Financial Institutions, though."

There was silence as they contemplated various names.

"What about 'OK Airlines,'" Betty asked. "You know, after your nickname, Otto."

"That sounds like a cowboy airline. Not the image we want, I think."

"What about the initials of our first names?" Mata said. "You know, 'MOB Airlines.'"

Otto made a wry face. "We lost our mob connection when Wilson died."

"Oh. You're right."

"What about Pioneer Lake Airlines?" Betty asked.

"Well, that says something about where we fly from. It doesn't say where we fly to," Mata offered.

"Wisconsin Airlines, then," Betty said.

"We wouldn't fly to Wisconsin only. We'll be flying to Minnesota as well," Mata told her.

"W and M Airlines, then?" Betty said.

"I've been thinking of M and M Airlines." Otto said thoughtfully. "That could stand for 'Mata and Maria' in honor of you and Mama, Mata, and for my B-17. It also could stand for Milwaukee and Madison since we could fly to those places."

"I like that," Betty said.

"So do I," Mata added.

"Well," Otto told them as he raised his glass, "To M and M Airlines, then. May we prosper."

"Hear, hear," the other two said.

Chapter 47

M & M Airlines—June, 1946

Six months later, M & M Airlines was thriving. Word got around that Otto would provide a fast, comfortable trip to Madison or Milwaukee for local businessmen, and for hunters and fishermen who came out to Pioneer Lake year 'round to enjoy their sports. Initially, Betty and the Kerchners operated the service as a charter, with flights flown as needed. Otto found he was flying himself ragged, so he scheduled first one flight at noon, and then two other flights at ten and two. The Beechcraft was almost full for most flights, and about six months in, Otto realized he needed another pilot and also realized his airport manager had multi-engine experience. He hired Mata's Pete as the airport manager and gladly gave up some of the runs to the cities to Jimmy.

Otto was at his desk one Friday morning. Betty was at her place in the outer office. She came in to where Otto sat and closed the door.

"Hey, good-lookin'," Otto said.

"Don't flatter me, Otto. We need to talk."

"Those words usually mean I'm in trouble."

"You're not in trouble. I just want to talk seriously about something."

"And what would that be? Business is booming."

"I want to talk about us, you wonderful man."

"Us?"

"Yes, I want to know where you think we are going."

"I hadn't thought much about it, Betty. I guess overseas I got used to just getting through the next few minutes or the next hour or the next day. I had general dreams and plans for after the war, but the accident changed all that."

"Otto, I love you and I will stay with you no matter what. I just wanted you to know that." She stood up and went back to her desk.

Otto sat there for a while, puzzled. Then he realized what Betty was saying. He arose from his desk and went out to her.

"Yes?" she said, looking up at him.

"We're going flying, Betty."

"Right now? I have all this paperwork."

"I'm the boss and I'm giving you the rest of the morning off to go flying with me."

Betty stacked the pile of papers on her desk in a neat pile. "Well, OK, boss."

She walked with him to the J-5 which had some age on it but was kept in pristine condition by the A&P man Mata had hired. They were soon drawing repair and overhaul jobs from 100 miles around.

Otto climbed in first and then Betty after him. He ran a quick check of the controls and cranked the engine. It seemed puny by comparison with the B-17 or even the M&M Beechcrafts. They taxied out and held at the end of the runway to allow two aircraft on final to complete their landings.

Otto took off smoothly, and soon they were at ten thousand feet amid scattered clouds and brilliant sun. Otto fished around in his pocket and, holding the stick with his right hand, held the box out to Betty with his left.

"What's this?" she asked.

"Something I should have given you months ago. Betty, will you marry me?" He pulled off the top of the box to reveal a brilliant diamond.

Betty's hand flew to her mouth. "Oh, yes, Otto! Yes, my love!" They went into a long passionate kiss. Only the Piper slipping off to one side brought them back to where they were.

"Whoa," Otto exclaimed, "We'd better straighten up and fly right."

"Let's land! I want to tell everyone! My parents will be so pleased! They think the world of you, Otto."

Otto set the J-5 down on the smooth summer grass and taxied to the hangar. They worked together to secure the aircraft. Otto went over to tell Jimmy they would be away for a few hours. He and Betty hopped in her car and took off.

"Who should we tell first?" Otto asked her.

"Mata! She's like a sister to me."

"Me, too," Otto chuckled and Betty smacked him in the head.

They soon were at the farmhouse. They walked in to find Mata cleaning the kitchen floor. She looked up as they came in, alarmed.

"What's wrong? Has something happened? Tell me!" She quickly relaxed when she saw their faces were relaxed and smiling.

"Sit down, Mata," Otto told her. "We have some news." They all sat at the kitchen table. Otto put his arm around Betty. Mata looked expectant.

"Should you tell her?" Otto asked Betty.

"I can, if you want."

"OK, then."

"Mata, your brother and I are engaged."

Mata screamed and launched herself out of her chair, reaching to take Otto and Betty in her arms. They embraced as Mata babbled what seemed like a hundred questions.

"Where will it be? *When* will it be? What will your colors be, Betty? What about attendants?" Mata was flushed and smiling.

"Hold on, Mata, this just happened about an hour ago. We'll have plenty of time to plan, but we haven't talked about any of the details. I do know that I want you to be my maid of honor."

"Oh," said Mata breathlessly, "I'd love to. I'd be honored, in fact."

"We can have the reception at my parents' house. They adore Otto so I know they'll say yes!"

Mata and Betty were soon caught up in a whirl of plans and ideas. Otto excused himself to go outside and walk across the pasture in the warm June late afternoon sunlight. So many things had happened to him in the past year, but this was the best. He smiled at the thought of him and Betty together for a lifetime. Maybe his luck had returned after being absent for so long. He certainly hoped so.

***

Betty's parents were about as excited as Mata, but managed to disguise it better than she did. Mrs. Ross came over and kissed each of them on the cheek. Mr. Ross hugged Betty and shook Otto's hand. "I couldn't be more pleased," he said. "Welcome to the family, son. We're proud to have you."

"Thank you, sir. I promise to take good care of Betty."

"We know you will," said Mrs. Ross. "We think of you as part of the family already, Otto, and wish you both every happiness."

Mrs. Ross took Betty's arm and escorted her into the parlor. "We've got a lot of planning to do, so we might as well get started."

"Thanks, Mom, but I want Mata involved. I've asked her to be my maid of honor."

"How delightful! What a lovely girl she is. Well, we'll just have to wait until we can all be together. Why don't we do it over dinner, say this Friday about seven? Come early for drinks."

Mr. Ross asked Otto, "Who will be your best man?"

"I thought I'd ask Mata's beau, Pete Johanssen."

"Oh, yes, I know the family. Good solid people. Off the subject, I want to ask you something, Otto."

"Certainly."

"You know that vets have been going back to college on the G.I. bill. I think that's commendable. However, I heard a story that somewhat bothered me, and I wanted to get your perspective as a veteran on it."

"Go ahead, please." They had reached the parlor by this time and all took seats. Mrs. Ross took a small silver bell and rang it. Sarah appeared.

"Sarah, we'd like some tea, please. And we have great news—Betty and Otto are engaged."

Sarah clapped her hands and then quickly dropped them and curtsied. "Yes, ma'am," she murmured, and left the room.

"So," Mr. Ross continued, "I heard that a group of vets, students at the U. of W. at Madison, came into the cafeteria to find the tables covered with trays and dishes left by other students who weren't vets. The veterans swept everything off the table onto the floor. Can you explain why they would do such a thing? It doesn't make sense to me, as responsible as they are normally."

Otto thought for a second. "I don't know the people involved, so this is just a surmise, but in the military, you're taught to be responsible for yourself and for others with you. I think the vets saw the students who had left a mess for others as immature and irresponsible and reacted by clearing the tables. They probably also saw it as showing a lack of respect for those using the tables after them since I believe students are supposed to clear the table after they're done."

Mr. Ross looked thoughtful. "That makes sense. Thank you very much for your perspective."

Otto nodded. "Glad to share what I think."

Sarah appeared with a tea service and set it down on the table in front of Betty and her mother.

"Thank you, Sarah. That will be all for now," Mrs. Ross said.

Sarah curtsied. "Yes, ma'am. And may I convey my best wishes to Miss Betty and Captain Kerchner?"

"Thank you, Sarah. We want you to attend, of course, and James as well."

"Thank you, ma'am. I would be honored and I know James will be also." She turned and glided out of the room.

"Well, would you care to join us for dinner? We're having roast," Mrs. Ross offered.

"Thanks, Mom, but we have some other people we want to tell and Mata is expecting us for dinner. You're very kind to offer."

They all stood. "We're so happy and pleased," Mr. Ross told them, offering his hand to Otto and then kissing Betty on the cheek. Betty kissed her mother on the cheek and Otto gave her a hug. Saying their good-byes, they walked out the front door, which James held for them.

"May I say 'best wishes' to the happy couple," he smiled, leaning his head in their direction.

"Thank you, James," they said in unison and then laughed at themselves. James joined in.

Otto and Betty climbed in her Packard. "Well, where to?" Betty smiled.

"Anywhere you want," Otto told her. "The world is ours."

"I like the way you think, mister. What about your place for a meal?"

"Sounds good to me," Otto replied, thinking, I must be the luckiest guy in the world.

Chapter 48

On the Wings of Eagles—December 14, 1946

The wedding took place at the Presbyterian Church Betty's family attended. Holiday greens and wreaths decorated the long sanctuary, lending color to the white walls and dark trim. Mata and Betty and a couple of their friends worked for three days to put up wedding decorations. The reception was to be at her parents' house.

Betty stood in her mother's wedding gown, which fit her perfectly. Mata fussed with her train and veil. "Are you nervous, Betty?"

Betty laughed. "What do I have to be nervous about? I'm marrying the man of my dreams!"

"I haven't seen Otto as happy as he has been these past few months. I think he could fly without an airplane."

"We'll have plenty of time to fly with airplanes. Did I tell you that we've decided to build a house out by the airport?"

"No, there have been so many details I don't recall you telling me that. That sounds wonderful. When will the house be ready?"

"February, we hope. In the meantime we'll live at my house and sell it when the new house is ready. Daddy already has a buyer for it."

The door opened and Mrs. Ross came in. She embraced Betty and Mata. "You both look so lovely," she told them. "This is such a happy day."

The lady in charge of the ceremony stuck her head in the door. "Five minutes, ladies."

"I have something to say to you, Betty, Mrs. Ross," said Mata.

"Yes?"

"I have never said this before, so I want to now. I want to thank you both for accepting and loving Otto after he came back. Few people did, and you and Mr. Ross have made such a difference in his life. I can hardly wait to see what tomorrow brings."

The three women embraced briefly, and then the coordinator was back at the door. "It's time," she told them.

Mrs. Ross went out to be seated. Betty and Mata could hear the organ briefly grow louder as the door to the sanctuary opened and closed. "Well, here we go," Mata said. "Me first."

Betty laughed as she slipped through the door to meet her father, who stood waiting in the narthex. He kissed her on the cheek and offered his arm. She took it. "I hope I don't stumble," he told her.

"You'll do fine, Dad."

An usher opened the double doors to the sanctuary. Every pew was filled, and Betty saw Mata and the bridesmaids standing in a line to the left of the minister, while Pete and the groomsmen stood to the right. Otto, wearing a dark suit, stood with the minister in his robes on the elevated platform in front of the altar.

The organist played a fanfare and launched into Wagner's "Bridal Chorus" from *Loehengrin*. Betty and her father stepped carefully down the aisle, the heads of the congregants turning to follow their progress. They arrived at the front and stood there as the processional came to an end.

Otto smiled as Betty and Mr. Ross came up. The minister began, "Dearly beloved, we are gathered here in the sight of God and these witnesses…"

Otto could not help thinking of the long path that led him here. After the accident and Alice's rejection, he expected he would never be close to a woman again. And here was Betty, so kind, so true, so beautiful.

"And do you, Otto, take this woman to be your lawfully wedded wife?"

"I do," Otto said in a firm voice.

That wasn't so hard, he thought, and tried to remain focused on the ceremony. He had always been a daydreamer and it seemed that recently most of his dreams came true. He was not only flying: he was actually paid to fly.

The war was over and business was good. He looked to the future with great anticipation.

"I now pronounce you man and wife. Captain Kerchner, you may kiss the bride."

Otto kissed Betty with perhaps more fervor than the occasion called for. He didn't care. They then turned around and stood together facing the congregation.

"Ladies and gentlemen, I present to you Captain and Mrs. Otto Kerchner."

The organist started Mendelssohn's "Wedding March" from *A Midsummer Night's Dream*. Otto and Betty walked quickly down the aisle, kissing again in the narthex. "Well, how do you like being Mrs. Kerchner?"

"I love it!" she told him and wrapped him in a huge hug.

The rest of the afternoon passed as if in a rapid montage from a movie. James drove them from the church to the reception at Betty's parents. Otto had the impression that they greeted what seemed like everybody in town, followed by a meal with multiple toasts. They finally made their escape, with James driving them to Betty's house. There they changed clothes and drove themselves to the airport where they would fly to Minneapolis for their honeymoon. Jimmy had the J-5 ready for them.

They climbed into the Cub and ran through the preflight. "Are you ready, Mrs. Kerchner?" Otto said, smiling.

"I'm ready, Mr. Kerchner!"

"Let's go, then," and he advanced the throttle. The Cub bounced over the frozen grass and then reached for the sky.

Chapter 49

Flying—December, 1946

Otto and Betty were flying.

THE END

May 1, 2012—October 10, 2012

Dedication

This book is dedicated to the brave men and women and their families and friends who fought on the Allied side in World War II, for their courage and sacrifice, and for the lasting legacy they left all of us, and particularly to my father, Clyde D. Verner, US Army, China-Burma-India Theater, 1943-1946.

Acknowledgements

I have always wondered about acknowledgements, which sometimes run to dozens of names. Could that many people involved in the making of a book?

Writing this novel showed me that the answer is an emphatic "yes!" I couldn't possibly acknowledge all those who contributed individually without omitting someone, so I'll list them in groups. A sincere and heartfelt "thank you" to you all.

-The writers of Write by the Rails, the Prince William County-Manassas Chapter of the Virginia Writers Club. You provided encouragement, insight and expertise throughout the long process of creating Otto's story.

-My twenty or so "beta readers." Your attention to detail and honesty vastly improved what I had done.

-All those who told me about the experiences of their friends and relatives during World War II. Your stories touched me and affirmed the connection between fiction and reality.

-My family and friends, who listened to me talk about this work for over a year and kept smiling. In particular, I want to recognize my father Clyde, and my wife Becky. Our two daughters Alyssa and Amy, as always, kept me from taking myself too seriously. They thought the story would be improved by the addition of vampires and zombies. Sorry, guys: maybe next time.

Made in the USA
Charleston, SC
25 October 2013